BANKING ON FORM

Banking on Form is an amusing and irreverent record of a powerfully–built young athlete who became caught up in the world of Banking.

The problems confronting young Pook as he struggles to combine the art of Banking with sex, body–building and a football career – a feat which understandably threatens to overwhelm him until a clever Austrian gentleman steps in with a timely solution – are told in fast tempo and with dry humour.

In the process, to the lay reader's delight and edification at least, Pook reveals the mysteries of the British banking system; becomes entangled in the night–life of Paris; develops into the strong–man of the financial world; plays soccer on the blood–feud principle, and antagonises every person he comes in contact with – including himself.

During the resultant chaos the Banks, amongst others, undergo a gentle pulling of their pin–striped legs. Pook sums up his own feelings when he says "Reading *How to Win Friends and Influence People* doesn't seem to have done *me* much good. All I can do is to lose friends and injure people." But it is all good clean fun, and the laughter which will follow the earnest young man through his hectic career will win him plenty of friends among readers – at any rate outside the ranks of bankers.

Also by Peter Pook:

Pook in Boots
Pook in Business
Pook Sahib
Bwana Pook
Professor Pook
Banker Pook Confesses
Pook at College
Pook's Tender Years
Pook and Partners
Playboy Pook
Pook's Class War
Pook's Tale of Woo
Pook's Eastern Promise
Beau Pook Proposes
Pook's Tours
The Teacher's Hand-Pook
Gigolo Pook
Pook's Love Nest
Pook Omnibus
Pook's China Doll
Pook's Curiosity Shop
Marine Pook Esquire
Pook's Viking Virgins

PETER POOK

BANKING ON FORM

EMISSARY PUBLISHING
P.O. Box 33, Bicester, Oxfordshire, OX6 8BU,
England.

First published in Great Britain March 1962
by Robert Hale Ltd., London.
Reprinted March, 1962.

This edition published 1992 by
Emissary Publishing, P.O. Box 33, Bicester, Oxfordshire, OX6 8BU

British Library Cataloguing-in-Publication Data.
A catalogue record for this book is available from the British Library.

ISBN 1-874490-00-7

Printed in Great Britain by Manuscript ReSearch, Oxfordshire.

To all my friends on both sides of the counter, in the hope that they will smile once more at that bumptious character portrayed within, whom they treated with such good humour and long-suffering patience.

ONE

Only those who have been through teenage and survived the operation can appreciate why I have been forced to tell you about Maria first. If it is possible to have more than one prime-mover then I was lumbered with about half-a-dozen at the age of seventeen, all fighting each other for first place in my mind.

Frankly, what should have been at the top of the list was my new career in the bank where they were vaccinating me against other people's money so I could handle it without automatically putting it in my wallet, but under the circumstances banking had dropped so far down the table that it was in danger of relegation.

Then there were various brands of sport pressing me to distraction if I were to gain the neon-lights of fame before the years galloped by and left me a burnt-out old has-been of one score years. These and other activities were rushing round my subconscious as though Nature had endowed me with a spin-drier in place of a brain, but it was noticeable that the faster the drier turned so Maria came to the surface first with increasing regularity, until I thought of her as though I had never known about anything else.

I must apologize for associating sex with banking, but life is a mixture of strange bedfellows, and at the time my bed was packed to capacity with restless prime-movers, all kicking in the throes of adolescent nightmares. Matters were hardly improved by my best friend, Alec, who passed through teenage with only one enormous prime-mover – so strong that it pushed every other competitor clean out of bed on the cuckoo principle – a remorseless dedication for amassing girl-friends like other lads collected cigarette-cards.

Alec was to girls what the hazel–twig is to water, so naturally enough he discovered the two French girls while I was still wasting time with Hilda Longbotham. He possessed a sixth sense about female–location, being the type whom girls followed home simply to be near him, for his blond wavy hair and dimpled smile made them feel slightly pregnant just to look at him. I sometimes had the reverse effect on them.

Alec was so madly in love with the short French girl Mimi that he was compelled to give the tall job, Maria, to me on the grounds that he could not possibly afford to woo both of them at once.

They were the most glamorous, most sophisticated, and the most hungry girls I had ever met. They did everything to perfection in the courting line but only after a meal, and then the heavy labour of teenage kissing left them as famished as a couple of homeless refugees. Consequently we fattened them up every evening as a prelude to a night out and returned to a café last thing in order to replenish their wants before we said good night, lest they should expire during the small hours.

I had already given up wondering how I was going to cope with Maria on top of the total war which had broken out at Cudford since my recent arrival there as Probationary Junior to the Zenith Bank.

"Don't they ever eat anything during the day?" I asked Alec, as we drove home one early morning after a night spent mainly in Jim's Fish Bar.

"*Eat;* don't talk to me about eat. Never mention the word again in my presence. I took them to Brighton for a whole day on the beach, swimming and all. You never saw anything to equal it in your life. Ever been to the zoo? They were at it all day long. Ice–cream, chocolates, sandwiches, fish and chips, cockles – the lot. I wore a furrow through the shingle, fetching and carrying. About midday we moved up the beach to be nearer the café: in fact, we used it as a backrest. I was so cleaned out, I had to rope you in to take Maria off my hands. It doesn't seem natural in such beautiful birds."

"Don't they pay their share?" I inquired, wondering if

the thrill of their company warranted the dispersal of my life savings.

"Not a hope! They're students over here to learn the language, and apart from the odd penny for the toilet, they've got treacle fingers. I can just about keep Mimi above starvation level but I'll never cope with both of them together. As it is, I've given them the best years of my life in about a fortnight."

Next evening we tried the experiment of penning them in their own flat, away from restaurants, in an endeavour to spin out the time till payday. We had a cosy evening, with Maria playing selections from *Dinner at Eight* on the piano while Mimi sang the words in a haunting, hungry voice. By way of an encore I asked for something from the *Beggars' Opera.*

Being our first encounter with any form of sophistication, Alec and I listened like a pair of pointer dogs. Alec was completely overcome; even Hilda Longbotham had nothing to offer in this category. Mimi followed up her advantage by swaying over to the sofa to caress his hair and whisper in broken English, "I do so want to have a baby, darling."

Alec giggled inanely to express his passion, as though he were feeble-minded.

Maria sat on my lap and kissed me expertly. From such close quarters I could see the tracks of her natural eyebrows below her latest ones, and her eyelids were smeared with a kind of blue margarine. Her perfume was so heavy that I had great difficulty in breathing, a situation worsened by the fact she kissed so long that I was in danger of blacking out. I felt very inexperienced and hopelessly out of my depth.

"Let's put out ze light," cried Mimi, apparently driven to an ecstasy of love by Alec's maddening giggle.

"*Non, non,* Mimi, first we must 'ave ze supper," Maria answered, raising her head sufficiently to allow me to gulp in some air.

"Supper! Ah, that's the idea," shouted Alec, whose face was now disfigured with its nightly coating of Max Factor. "Bring in the feast, girls, I can't make love on an empty stomach."

"I say we go to *Eros,*" sighed Mimi.

"Mais non, better we try the *Africano,*" Maria suggested.

"What's wrong with eating here?" Alec whined, obviously under a false impression.

Mimi smiled and kissed him. "Silly pretty boy, what 'ave we 'ere to dine on – ze flowers? Come along to the café, you lazy one. There shall you buy me ze big steak and many little chippies; then later we shall return 'ere wiz a bottle of wine."

Alec gave me his horror face.

"We'd better run out to Fred's Caff, where we can get it on tick," I suggested in my practical way. You couldn't eat cheaper than at Fred's, especially if you had beans-on-toast and four plates of bread-and-butter. Very filling.

As we walked down the stairs, Alec whispered to me, "It's a funny thing but you can't be with these girls half an hour with out they're ravenous. Now with English girls, you never dream of giving them anything to eat, although you might splash out with a coffee on Saturday night."

This was strictly true, because all mention of refreshment was absolutely taboo among our circle, who courted each other under the most stringent régime of economy, achieved mainly by locking in a close embrace and staring out over the monotonous sea for hours at a time, in silent rapture. This good clean fun was known as going steady, and accomplished without the artificial aids of drink, food, cigarettes, or money. When the weather was too cruel for examining the ocean for long periods, we turned our relentless gaze on the shop-windows, especially on Snuff Bros., whose jewellery display was always good for at least an hour's penetrating dissection. Apart from always having a running cold, which was passed back and forth between the lovers all through the winter, we were as happy as millionaires.

Outside the flat stood Alec's chariot of Cupid, a primitive Baby Austin, entirely devoid of any protection from the elements, which had cost thirty shillings. The two girls hipped across to it and got in, like film-stars riding a pram at the féte, before Alec and I pushed it round the corner to the petrol–station.

"Put in half a gallon, my good man, and look sharp about it," said Alec to the attendant, one Cyril. Meanwhile he used the facilities of the garage to pump up the tyres, and I filled the radiator from the water can. This happened every night to keep the transport going.

"Would you like me to top up your battery?" Cyril inquired with biting sarcasm, "or perhaps I could tempt you with twopennorth of oil?"

"No thanks, Cyril, maybe tomorrow. Put the juice on the slate till Friday, there's a good chap."

"But it's only a bob, mate, so let's have it."

"Remember your motto, Cyril, *'Service before Self.' Au revoir* till Friday. Give us a push, Peter." Off we went.

As the jalopy rushed through the side–streets so the ancient battery charged up enough to bring on the lamps, whereupon we were able to venture into the main road where the coppers lurked, waiting for our class of motorist who drove without lights and very often without tax or even the means of stopping quickly if there was no convenient upgrade ahead. This embarrassing lack of brake–power nearly cost us our skins on the way to Fred's Caff, because of Alec's habit of driving flat out wherever he went, whereas the logical requirement was to coast along as slowly as possible to spin out the evening and cut down eating time. We went round a curve like the Wall of Death, with the result that the car turned on its side in a ditch. I had a fleeting glimpse of my beloved Maria sailing over my head like a bat in a hurry, as though she had suddenly mastered the art of natural flight. Alec, Mimi, and myself lay in the ditch, but Maria had apparently gone into orbit.

"For heaven's sake get the car upright before we lose all the petrol," yelled Alec, who was probably too dazed to notice we were one short. We easily righted the car and saved our precious Russian fuel, when a surprisingly unsophisticated Maria came crawling out of some blackberry bushes, to announce in a bitter mixture of English and French that her Maker had spared her life but broken her leg. I examined her leg where the knee protruded through a silk stocking like a large white moon. By a professional process of bending and prodding, I diagnosed nothing worse than a severe bruise, so I gallantly handed her a safety pin to effect a temporary repair to the stocking, and gave her knee the healing benefit of a kiss.

"I've found a dockleaf to tie round her knee," exclaimed Alec brightly, apparently under the impression we were treating her for warts or something.

"Ze raw steak would be better," suggested Mimi, whose mind seemed confined to the narrow field of Alec and food.

"Let's do it on the cheap with a bread-poultice," I cried, terrified by the mere mention of meat. Alec decided we had best call it a day and return home, or, if possible, to the flat.

"Non, non, chérie, I will not be ze spoiling-sport and fracture up ze party," declared Maria bravely. "Am I dead? Am I wounded? *Non,* it is but a bite of the flea. We will continue as if nothing is happening as usual. *Pah*!"

Alec often remarked that when Maria said *"Pah"* like that, she could have blown his tyres up without the aid of a pump, and it did not pay to argue further.

Arriving at Fred's, she limped in like a crippled footballer, in marked contrast to her former Parisian wiggle, and hid her knee under the table. By now it had swollen fit to burst the pin. Fred personally brought out four giant loads of beans-on-toast, in quantities which satisfied the starving lorry-drivers who frequented the place. Added to this were four plates of bread-and-butter, each plate being a meal in its own right, and tea which he served in small buckets with handles.

Experience had taught me that this fascinating combination possessed the most blow-out qualities of any bulk food, with the possible exception of gruel. The girls had previously refused Fred's gruel on aesthetic grounds. So filling, in fact, that normally I became bogged down midway through the bread course, and to save myself from dough-asphyxiation, I was in the habit of giving the residue to Maria in the hope that she would stop scanning the menu as though she were eating in one of those revolting competitions, and had found herself behind schedule.

Alec and I had an unwritten agreement that we never asked the girls if they wanted any more, and at the least sign of such a desire we would depart to the Gents like monks under a vow of silence.

Mimi and Alec always eat their supper holding hands, but whether this was love, or Mimi's Gallic way of preventing him floating out into the night under the levitational properties of the beans, I never really found out. All I know is, that try as I might, I could never master the knack myself, unless I was prepared to force the entire acre of toast into my mouth with one hand – a feat I attempted only once and which gave me my first appreciation of a dislocated jaw since the day I foolishly pushed a billiard–ball in my mouth for a wager. This dreadful situation had arisen when the school bully declared that, although nature had endowed me with the largest cake–hole in the college, he would lay a shilling that I could not perform the interesting trick of using it as a billiard–pocket. I fell for this old catch, and had to be assisted to Doctor Jeans for the removal of the obstruction without having my teeth extracted to do it, and *en route* I startled passers–by with my horrific imitation of the pig and the apple. Personally, I was convinced that if the ball did not soon come out, my eyeballs certainly would if only in sympathy.

Doctor Jeans did not seem surprised to see me, because not long before I had visited him with a rare ailment he diagnosed as vaulters' croup. This distressing affliction was occasioned by my practising the pole–vault with a mop–handle, whereby as I sailed over our garden clothes–line the handle entered my mouth and damn–near forced my tonsils from their moorings.

"Boy, never try to swallow a pole till you are bigger," boomed the old doctor. "Be content with small swords in the meantime."

Now here I was in his surgery again, with a face–full of ivory, and noisily sucking air through my nostrils which by now were unnaturally dilated like a runaway stallion's. To prevent my early demise, he made me lean forward across a table while he levered the ball out with callipers. In the process, I thought my lower jaw had parted from the rest of my head for ever.

"Boy, for God's sake push off home, and don't go near any cannon–balls on the way," he roared, when it was over, "and try keeping that fly–catcher shut as you drift through life in future."

Maria thought I was very unromantic, eating with both hands, but I had no option under the circumstances. At the moment, Alec and Mimi had disengaged their hands so that he could try persuading Fred to put our meal on the slate till Friday; "Friendly Credit" as we called it. Fred was strictly for nourishing his customers on a cash basis, but Alec's proposition that the food was gone and we were broke was unanswerable.

"You come gallivanting up here by car with a load of foreign tarts, and no money," moaned Fred. "How do you expect me to live?"

Alec showed no interest in Fred's living arrangements.

"Take the log–book as security, Fred," said Alec, trustingly.

"No fear, mate; I've got enough troubles as it is, without your wreck. You be in here smart on Friday with the dibs, or your beans–on–toast days are over. You should work a bit more, and a lot less of the necking lark," concluded Fred, whose own sex–life seemed at a low ebb just then, judging by the female who was eternally engaged in breaking up the kitchen, by the sound of it, and whose piercing screams for domestic aid sent the death–rattle round the customers.

On the way back Maria showed us her swollen knee, which we inspected with the morbid curiosity of youth.

"Honey, it seems to me your leg is in ze family way," jested Mimi, with her usual limited sphere of thought. "Perhaps it is best you 'ave 'im off."

As Maria was practically unable to walk at all, owing to the difficulty of getting her enlarged knee past the normal one, we parked on the sea–front to commence our ceaseless and economical vigil of the ocean, like coastguards on duty.

"Tomorrow you must see the doctor without fail," I advised Maria, who was straining her eyes out to sea as though searching for a glimpse of her family physician on the coast of France. "Tomorrow" was a magic word which freed me from all responsibility for Maria's physical condition.

"Let's go in for a moonlight swim," suggested Alec, secure in the knowledge that there was no risk of another meal so late at night. Not satisfied with just looking at the water, he now wanted to hare down the beach and jump in it. Leaving the invalid without a word, we undressed and plunged into the warm ink. Not wishing to play gooseberry, I tactfully struck out for the Isle of Wight, leaving Alec and Mimi to drown each other near the shore in hilarious love–play.

Meanwhile Maria dragged herself to the water's edge like a cripple to the sacred pool, to bathe her injured limb with salt water. Returning to the car after dressing, I was horrified to note the lateness of the hour and I implored Alec to rush me home without delay.

Leaving Alec and the girls parked far down the road, I crept indoor to see if my parents were good for another hour of reckless living on my part. Far from it. Instead, all hell broke loose on my belated arrival, and I was sent to bed branded as a ne'er–do–well, and temporarily excluded from my father's will on the grounds that the family fortune, such as it was, had not been amassed for the purpose of being squandered by a playboy heir.

I lay in bed half an hour with my ears at radar stations, well aware that if I did not soon get a message down the road, Alec would start knocking to ask if I could come out to play. This dreadful thought brought me out in a hot sweat. Realizing that my father would not look kindly on any application for the return of my clothes from his room before daybreak, I climbed down the well–worn spout from my bedroom window in pyjamas, and ran along the High Street to the car in sheer desperation.

Maria presented a picture of dejection in the back–seat, while Alec and Mimi wrestled in the front. I often thought the pair of them had successfully over come the normal standards of human fatigue.

"Ah, so, you naughty boy, you 'ave come prepared,"

cried Mimi, eyeing my technicolor pyjamas with approval. Alec, whose face was never free from lipstick these days, said, "I was just going to call for you."

"'Ave you come to invite us in for ze supper?" inquired Maria, whose life did not include any reference to time.

"Big trouble. Beat it, Alec!" I hissed, melodramatically, and fled like an arrow – right into the prominent stomach of our local constable, who was able to materialize anywhere, haunted-house fashion.

"Ho, ho, what have we here? This looks a queer kettle of fish, my lad," the Law intoned, in that maddeningly slow dialogue of those who have eight lonely hours to kill. I heard the car scream off down the road to safety. Alec and Constable Bull had come to know each other intimately over the years.

"Where do you think you're going to, this time of night, in your nightshirt?" inquired the Law, evidently intent on making a night of it with facetious questions.

"I was just going back to bed, sir," I answered truthfully, and praying that my father was in his.

"So I suppose you thought you'd pop down the High Street to see if all's well with the world? Thought you'd help me do my job. If you ask me, you've been to a pyjama-party, though I can't smell any alcohol."

While he continued his speculations, heads began to appear at windows.

"Please, sir, I'm cold. May I go home now?" I begged, putting on a snivelling Oliver Twist voice in an attempt to end the interview safely. "Sometimes I walk in my sleep, but usually I only wander about the house. This is the first time I've been outside."

"That's what they all say. No, my lad, that won't do. You can't walk up to a car full of your mates and get away with it. I was not born yesterdee, you know," said the all-seeing eye. "I think you had better sleep-walk round to the station, with me to guide you." Surely the doddering old fool wasn't going to lock me up? A surging wave of confession overtook me.

"What really happened, Officer, was just that I nipped

out to say good night to my pals. No trouble or anything like that. You know I've got a good character."

"That's better. Now you run on back to bed, and don't do it again. Perhaps I'll have a word with your dad tomorrow."

"Please, sir, don't do anything dreadful like that, if you have any pity in your heart. You know how it is," I pleaded, stretching forth my hands as though they held the empty porridge-bowl.

"Well, we'll see, you crafty little devil. Now buzz off. Oh, you might tell our mutual friend to fit oil-lamps if he can't afford a battery on that heap of his." He allowed himself a slight smile.

I pythoned into bed and listened. A powerful snore issued from the next room, causing the windows to rattle a trifle in unison. This was father's signal to the outside world that he was engaged in slumber, and it reminded me of our last summer holiday when the hotel guests of floor three had sat up all night listening to it, and wishing to God they were home. Heavenly bliss, the family slept peacefully, unaware of the latest exploit of their wastrel son, now turned night-prowler.

I dropped off into the sleep of innocence, and dreamed of cuddling Maria despite the distracting presence of a bald head between us, which gradually revealed itself as her swollen knee.

TWO

Yesterday, I was looking through the photo–album to recapture the romantic thrill of those exciting days, but the result was a little disappointing in some respects. One thing the French girls were lavish with was the camera, because I well remember that we were everlastingly snapping each other like beach–photographers on a bank holiday. Judging by the results, we had a habit of taking ourselves in every possible combination, rather like the three draws on the Pools.

For example, there is Mimi and Alec; Maria and me; Mimi and Maria; Alec, Mimi and me; Maria, Alec and Mimi, and so on, through every conceivable permutation. Lastly comes a photo miraculously containing all four of us, as though the camera were now capable of working on its own initiative.

In nearly every photo Alec and I employ one hand to keep our hair down, for in those days the slightest stern breeze tumbled our fashionable locks forward, causing them to black–out our faces like hanging ferns. We repeated these permutations in front of every well–known edifice in the district, and the various backgrounds provide interesting information concerning pre–war Britain. For instance, we are informed that Heaven's Light is our Guide; Charles Dickens was born here; and Left for Public Conveniences.

Another recurring announcement provides the joyous news that Lobby Lud is Here At Last, which figures so regularly over our heads that at the time it must have had some vital significance in our lives. Alec, the debonair man–about–town, loses some of his polish, pictorially, by appearing as a young angel on loan from above, and his snappy shorts reveal that he relies for support on one extremely thick leg. In actual fact, his soul was about as pure as the driven slush. We are portrayed in every state of dress, from the near–nudity of the beach, to formal best. In the former, I am the bronzed Adonis of the sands, pointing in the general direction of the meridian, and blissfully unaware of the embarrassing anatomical details disclosed by my tight Hawaiian–trunks below.

Our efforts to record Maria's beautiful long legs for posterity as she reclines by the water's–edge, make them appear like railway lines running out to sea. In this particular photo, my head has accidentally come in at the side, at an angle indicative of my intention to soar into the picture horizontally.

Perhaps the worst compositions are the formal ones wherein we have dressed up for effect, because nothing dates so badly as clothes. There stands Maria, apparently balancing a briefcase on her head, while Mimi is surely wearing the Lutine Bell, in lieu of a hat. I fare even worse because my new Burtons Special with the wide Oxford–bags is a nightmare. A gusty squall has caught them like yacht sails, giving the impression that I am a wasp–waisted Edwardian lady with full skirts, who wears her hair over her face.

Mimi's captivating air of sophisticated hauteur has not survived the years to the best advantage. Her *retroussé* nose is pawing the air as though there is a bad smell about, while her body leans so far backwards in langourous pose that one wonders what on earth prevents her toppling over on Lobby Lud.

There is also a monotonous series of four, in which everyone of us is driving Alec's motorized pram in turn; and an intriguing sequel wherein all four of us have squeezed into the driving–seat by some unique method of physical contraction. Getting more ambitious, we see the alarming phenomenon of Mimi driving the rear wheel over Alec's throat, while the severed head laughs hysterically at death.

Alec's appearance in the majority of the photos was necessitated by his lack of skill with the camera. His efforts either endowed us with double bodies and no heads, or enormous feet and no heads. Furthermore, he had a weakness for photographing his own index finger, a feat beyond the capabili–

ties of Mimi's box–camera which reproduced it as a partial eclipse of the sun. Consequently, Alec's function was to supply us with situations for trick photography when he had run out of suitable backgrounds for the three draws.

Hence we are not surprised to see Alec holding out his hand, on which stands a dwarf Mimi eating a microscopic choc–ice; but we observe with horror that Maria has emulated the lion–tamer by thrusting her head inside my capacious mouth. In yet another, against the essential backcloth of Lobby Lud's long awaited arrival at the public convenience, we have an ensemble of Alec in loin–cloth holdingMimi above him like a human umbrella, while at his feet reposes Maria's bodiless head smoking a stick of rock, on the sands. Mimi's convex posture conveys the impression that her brassière cannot cope with nature's generosity much longer, in such an agonizing position.

The album is a complete record of that glorious summer, and provides permanent proof that we enjoyed it with the minimum of expense. You cannot find us in speedboats, roundabouts, Big Dippers, or any comparable luxuries. Even the traditional weighing snapshot discloses us on the scales *en bloc,* while the attendant searches bad–temperedly for more weights.

Only two of the photos bring back somewhat unhappy memories. The first is of a powerfully–built gentleman, which caused Alec to exclaim, "It's George Carpentier with pince–nez," before Mimi told us it was her father. We had the pleasure of meeting him later on, when he suddenly arrived in Britain to rush his daughters back to France prematurely, and we gathered from his demeanour, as he spoke no English, that they were destined for reform–school.

The second one is the largest photograph in the album, on the back of which Maria has modestly written, "Saying *au revoir* to a few of our good English friends." When I showed this panoramic view of Britain's youth to my Uncle Paul, he asked, "I suppose it's the day–shift leaving Ford's, at Dagenham?"

"No, of course not. Only some of the French girls' friends," I replied, secretly peeved by the sea of faces. He laughed.

"Well, all I can say is I'm glad it's only a few of the good ones, because it would be an experience to see some of the bad 'uns. Anyway, there's only two girls among the lot of 'em. That don't seem right to me, but then, I'm old–fashioned."

"That's Maria and Mimi," I explained miserably.

Our brief flight into Paradise ended when the gentleman in the pince–nez arrived from France in answer to a disturbing letter from the girls' landlady, who hinted, among other things, that learning the English language might be better accomplished from more erudite sources than Alec and me. When the fatal news reached us, and we heard the word "father," we abandoned the girls like deserters from the Western Front, except for our final farewell. This last meeting was achieved at a dance held by the college the girls were supposed to attend, and to which we were invited clandestinely.

Alec and I hired claw–hammer suits, and purchased new boiled–shirts for the occasion. I took the whole afternoon to dress, most of it being taken up with boring my sundry studs and links into the shirt – a feat which I accomplished in the end with a pair of pliers. Alec and I did not get off to a very auspicious start, because first of all his car broke down – or broke up, to be exact. I walked to the hall and Alec came on his brother's bicycle. Waiting for him on the foyer steps, I noticed that the commissionaires took over the cars of the arriving guests and parked them at the rear. When Alec arrived he handed a key to a commissionaire, and said, "Here you are, my good man. Take my machine and chain it to the railings."

The good man glared at Alec, and remarked loudly to the bystanders, with reference to our nineteenth–century dandy's outfits, that he was unaware of any fancy–dress arrangements for that night.

Maria and Mimi drew up with a heavy escort of matrons and fathers, having been sworn to saintly behaviour under pain of flogging. As it was the first dance Alec and I had ever attended, we were under many disadvantages, especially the hired tails and strangulation collars, but none so heavy as not being able to dance.

In fact, I had long noticed that when Alec walked, his left arm swung in time with his left leg, and this basic handicap, coupled with a complete lack of rhythm, ruled him out as a soldier, let alone as a dancer. Early on that evening I scotched his eager suggestion that we two should dance together, in an effort "to get the hang of the blasted business," as something just not done. Consequently we stood on the sidelines and stared at the couples with that concentration we had previously bestowed on the ocean.

Father was treating our two saints at the buffet, but when they were allowed to dance with the aged, they floated round the floor like young Pavlovas, exuding an air of party hilarity which did not seem much like the grief of parting.

"By the look of things, we shall have to say good-bye anywhere you fancy, but not on the dance-floor," I advised Alec. "We don't want to undo a summer's good work in one waltz."

"I don't see how this waltz business goes," complained Alec, who was itching to glide round with Mimi.

"It's simple really; you walk forwards and the girl walks backwards like moving furniture, but the secret is to do it in time with the music."

"Well then, if it's so easy why don't you ask someone to try it with you," said Alec, adjusting the rivet-like fastenings of his enormous cuffs, which covered his hands as completely as if he had had them amputated.

"Sure I will. Just you watch me." The band struck up a Paul Jones and I joined the circle of men who shuffled self-consciously around the inner ring of ladies. Despite a lot of cheating, I ended up opposite a blank space, and returned to Alec. When I had returned to Alec five times he accused me of cowardice, and I secretly despaired of ever obtaining a partner.

"You're not really trying," he jeered. "You might do better if you went round with the inner circle."

On the sixth perambulation I got a partner by the process of fixing on one lady and following her until the music stopped. She clasped me to her ample bosom, and we began a quickstep as though we were dedicated to saving each other on the deck of a sinking liner – and a sloping one at that. I felt certain that either one or the other of us had eight feet, because wherever I put down some of mine, the lady had plenty of hers there before me.

This unfortunate situation led us into a stampede round the ballroom, like a couple of drunkards in a three–legged race. I eventually solved the problem by walking slowly forward with my legs so wide apart, coat–hanger fashion, that I was in danger of performing the splits. Meantime my partner did what steps she pleased in the middle. As she was extremely short I held her round the head, so that her face was pressed against my stomach. We never turned, but concentrated upon moving solely in one direction, as though we were wrestling on a conveyor belt.

I could feel the sweat running down my shirt, which was boiled to the hardness of aluminium and went "blop" at every movement. All the other couples swept past us in the gay abandon of the dance, including Maria, who greeted my exhibition with a shrill society titter. My unfortunate partner raised her perspiring face and said, "Do you enjoy dancing?"

"Yes, rather. I love it," I replied, gaining confidence.

"Then why for good luck's sake don't you take it up?" she snarled.

Just when I thought we had been on the march for at least two hours, the music changed to an old–fashioned waltz, and the lilting melody compelled me to change into the peculiar up–and–down progression of a bull–frog. This new motion was sheer hell.

"I think my husband is calling me," lied my partner, who was also bobbing up and down but in a faster tempo than mine, thus creating stifling bodily friction.

"Who is he?" I asked breathlessly.

"Over there with that party of gentlemen – Doctor Oswald Stilton, the skin specialist."

"The tall man with the pimples?" I asked, tactlessly.

"Os––wald," she shrieked, "here I am. Come quickly."

Oswald ran over and lifted his wife off my stomach.

"My stockings are laddered, and my shoes are a write–

off, but I don't think I'm physically injured," she gasped. "Oswald, bring me a gin this instant. Go away young man, and find another victim. I'm too old to fight back."

I returned to the statue of Alec, whose Victorian mashers' uniform forced him to stand rigid, like wearing armour.

"Don't dance any more, Peter, or we shall be thrown out. You were mowing down everybody within range," he pleaded, unable to turn his head which was embedded in his chimney–pot collar.

"Worst of all, those fools at that table keep shouting to me to bring the wine–list over, and I don't like it."

"We're better off here. It's positive murder on the dance–floor. Tell me, Alec, what happened to the old Austin?"

"A rotten bit of luck, Peter, believe me. Three cars pulled up at the traffic–lights, and I had to be the centre one. There is a tidy slope there, and I rolled back and touched the car behind me. I didn't know it at the time, but my luggage–grid had caught over his bumper, so when I tried to pull away, nothing happened. I revved up a tidy bit until suddenly his bumper sheared off and I shot up the road right into the car in front, bang, just like that."

"Was anyone hurt?"

"Well, the poor bloke in front didn't realize what was coming his way, and at first we thought he had broken his neck. He was sitting in the back–seat as though he was a passenger, and the front–seat was torn clean off the floor. I've got to go round tomorrow and see how he is."

"What sort of state is your bus in? "

"Nothing serious, except that the radiator is wrapped round the engine. Cyril will fix it for me all right."

"I don't reckon this is one of your best days, Alec."

About eleven o'clock Maria came over and ordered me to dance with her. She was a good instructress. She bent me in a bear–hug, and pushed me round the floor by brute force, and our knees thudded into each other at every step.

"Darling *chérie,* this is the end," she whispered ambigu–ously. "Tomorrow we sail for home, and I am dying for love of you. Perhaps it is better that I go because I do not believe in hasty marriages and I consider we should wait a few weeks. When shall we again meet?''

"I am dying for love of you, too," I replied, unable to think of anything original to say under the stress of dance-warfare. The jerky progress of two expiring lovers is not conducive to much Noel Coward dialogue.

"Alec and I want to come over to France later this year to visit you both. My summer holiday is due soon, and the bank has promised me the first fortnight in November."

"But *chérie,* surely this is a winter vacation?"

"No, Maria; we have to take our holidays according to seniority, and one can't have August until one is very near pension. Fortunately one is not allowed to go in December because it would clash with Christmas and the half-yearly balance."

I worked in the Zenith Bank, where they were teaching me how to juggle with the numerals nought to nine for the remainder of my life.

"Then I am 'appy, for now I am living for November only. Warning; 'ere is coming Papa. *Adieu,* my own."

"Good-bye Maria. See you in Paris very soon."

Alec, whose plaster-cast shirt and frayed nerves would not permit of dancing with Mimi, or anyone else, had been exchanging ardent vows with her in the privacy of the ballroom's broom cupboard, whence he had emerged with his customary display of jammy lipstick. In an effort to delay the sweet sorrow of parting he finally shook hands with both girls by offering his tubular cuff all round, like Captain Hook.

Maria and Mimi were marched off in the centre of a solid phalanx of matrons who looked capable of preserving the chastity of Jezebel. I was near to tears, but Alec was even more upset, and he turned inwards in a kind of spiritual hibernation to shorten the time till November.

Late that night I returned to my lonely room, full of nostalgia for my first-love but my mind was quickly diverted from romance by the furious battle to remove the rivets which bound my aluminium shirt to my body like a straight–jacket. By 2 a.m. I had arrived at the notion of cutting it off with scissors, but was so tired that I crawled into bed and slept in it – collar and all.

Next morning, my father laid me across the bed and prised the thing off as though he were opening a tin of sardines with his bare hands.

THREE

Maria's removal enabled me gradually to throw off the guise of an absent–minded professor in his dotage and remember my employers. This distressing symptom of first–love nearly drove Mr. Putty, the bank manager, out of his mind, especially when I returned to his office once after an interview to ask him not only what I had said, but if I had even visited him to say it. His face turned red–hot.

"When we were in the Navy together, Mr. Pants," he confided to the chief clerk in his Force 8 gale voice, "the birch soon cured amnesia – it made 'em forget they ever had it."

The extraordinary thing is how I even came to be in a bank at all, because, mainly through my own fault, my school education had been directed primarily at pushing me out on Life's highway as a professional footballer.

The college had a history master who kept a secret from me for eight years that he was also the careers' adviser, or even that such an occupation existed. He must have been under the impression that I would leave school and go straight on the dole.

Practically as we were saying good–bye he offered me the choice of the Church, the Law, the Army, Insurance, or his own personal suggestion for me – itinerant lavender–pedlar. He presented these vocations for my inspection like a plate of assorted biscuits. The professions were listed on a form, and against each one I wrote, "Not Keen." At the bottom was a space for the scholar's own choice, if not listed above, so I put, "I would like to sign on for Portsmouth Football Club. If they are all full up, Arsenal."

After that he washed his hands of me, with a short lecture on the improbability of the educational authorities teaching me

Latin for eight years in order to produce a hired gladiator, as he put it. He then wrote a note to my father, which I read on the way home. It said, "See if you can use your influence to get him in a bank, or anywhere else.

Today it is difficult to realize how hard it was to obtain employment during the pre–war period unless you were titled, or a boy–Einstein, so my father was not exactly thrilled by the note. He took me round to his bank–manager, who went very sad at the sight of me.

"Mr. Pook, I know you are a good customer of ours, but to tell you in confidence, I can't even get my own sons into this bank as things are at present. The staff position is very distressing. They tell me at head office the situation may brighten up about 1940! "

This forecast was of little consolation then. That evening my father sat down and wrote a letter to the only baronet we knew, advising him of the position, and by return of post came a reply from the Zenith Bank requesting me to produce my body, *Habeus Corpus* fashion, in Lombard Street the following day, by order of one Thos. Renault, Asst. Staff Cont. (South. Reg.).

Rather than risk being late, I travelled up on the milk train and arrived at Lombard Street just after daybreak, under the threat of transportation if I failed to qualify. Having first mistaken it for St. Pauls, I located the enormous structure of the Zenith Bank, and entered along with the charwomen, under the impression they were early customers, only to be informed that the staff itself did not arrive for another two hours. The night security officer put me outside in case I was part of an organized raid on the vaults.

Fearful lest the bank should disappear if I wandered away, I stood on the steps and asked everyone who approached if he were the Asst. Staff Cont. One character replied, "No, mate, I ain't. I'm only the bloody postman."

Around nine o'clock several thousands of the staff arrived like they were fleeing before the Flood, and they swept me bodily through the building and right into the cloak–rooms.

"Are you the Asst. Staff Cont., sir?" I inquired of an

elderly man who was washing himself as though his journey to work took him through the London sewers.

"Bless my soul, laddie, of course not, and never shall be. I'm a messenger." I revered him as the oldest messenger-boy in the business. "His lordship won't be in till ten, but follow me and I'll take you to his secretary, Miss Littlewig."

He put on a coachman's hat and led me along corridors and up lifts until I imagined Miss Littlewig worked in the vicinity of Ramsgate.

"So you're Pook," she said, when I produced the introductory letter. She flicked through an index file. "Pogie, Polly, Povie, Pomfret, Potty, Potter, Porter, ah, here we are – Pook."

She yanked me out of the file of my competitors.

"Can you use a typewriter, Pook?"

"Yes, miss," I replied, proud to find one of my two accomplishments in demand. I had always typed all the school football reports, in which my name figured more often than all the others put together.

"Splendid. You have to pass at forty-five words a minute, so while we are waiting for Mr. Renault you can take the test."

She conducted me into an adjoining office, where the noise sounded like a shipyard as some thirty girls worked off that early morning feeling on typewriters. I sat down at a spare machine and Miss Littlewig produced a test-piece for me.

"This sounds jolly interesting stuff," she enthused, handing me *Principles of Banking,* page 2487. "Start here where it says, 'A cheque is an unconditional order in writing.' Are you ready?" I raised my hands high over the machine in vulture-like anticipation. "Go," she cried, checking her watch.

Down crashed my hands with a frenzy of fingerwork, like a neurotic pianist rushing the *Minute Waltz.* The warning bell at the end of each line went, *clang, clang, clang, clang, clang, clang,* as though summoning the staff to fire-stations.

"Stop – good heavens, you are fast," exclaimed Miss Littlewig, archly, when the sixty seconds were up. The girls giggled, while the secretary checked the test.

"Well, Pook, you've broken the bank's record," she announced. I smiled modestly, hoping I hadn't broken the bank's typewriter in the attempt.

"Yes, you've made thirty-one errors in sixty-three words, but I expect Mr. Renault will pass you nevertheless, if only on output." I never again had to touch a typewriter during my banking career.

"Now for some simple sums. I want you to add up these figures for me," said Miss Littlewig, producing a new horror in the shape of Britain's exports from 1815 to 1914. I had never realized the magnitude of our trade abroad. When I had got to 1823 by using my fingers as a computer, Mr. Renault saved me from nervous hysteria by yelling, "Send in Pook – the type-writing prodigy."

He wasted no time with formalities, but said, "Now, Pook, tell me in your own words why you want to join this bank?"

"Because I want a good job, with security, sir," I replied, without adding anything about transportation for life.

"Right. Now tell me in your own words what attainments you achieved at college?"

"I was captain of house football, and captain of school football, sir," I answered, racking my brains to think of any lesser glories I ever earned, not connected with goal-posts. Nothing presented itself. "I also wrote up the football reports," I added modestly.

"I see. Anything else, apart from your prowess on the field?"

"Oh, yes, sir; I was captain of school boxing," I exclaimed, with a burst of new information, "and I played soccer for the county."

"Let us pass on to general knowledge," said Mr. Renault hastily. "Now tell me in your own words all you know about plumbago?"

"Sir, plumbago is a very painful disease of the back in cold weather," I enlightened him, remembering Uncle Paul's dreadful language when last he was seized with it. It seemed that all I knew about plumbago was disastrous, in my own words or anybody else's. Mr. Renault stared at me as though he were interviewing the village idiot, and then glanced inquiringly at the letter from our sole friend in the aristocracy.

"Did you never hear of *'plumbum'* during your Latin studies?"

"I'm afraid not, sir. You see, we did *Caesar,* not *Plumbum.*"

Mr. Renault leaned far back in his chair and closed his eyes. I thought he was taking a short nap. Suddenly he said, "Can you start work on Monday, Pook?"

"Yes, sir, any time you say."

"Good. At least you sound willing. In the meanwhile get a barber to shorten your golden tresses, or do them up in a bun, and then report to Cudford branch, Monday morning sharp. Take this letter to Doctor Crippen in Harley Street for a medical examination now, and return to this office with his report. Good-day, Pook."

Half an hour later, I reported back to Miss Littlewig.

"My, how quickly you do everything," she cried; "surely you haven't been to the doctor already?"

"No, miss, but your bank is so big I can't get out of it," I confessed, looking most unlike the man of the world who had recently swept Maria off her feet. How anybody could rob the Zenith Bank was beyond me, because once I had left Miss Littlewig's office, I walked around without once seeing a sign of a way out, and I began to feel frightened that I might be locked in when the placed closed. My perambulations took me past her office twice, and on the third occasion the good soul phoned for a messenger who guided me through the maze and out to the pavement.

For some unaccountable reason I walked right across London to Harley Street, as though the Underground had not yet been dug, with the result that I arrived there rather late.

"Please sir, are you Doctor Crippen?" I inquired of the thug who opened the door.

"No, I ain't. I'm the butler. Wait 'ere." Everybody in

London seemed to live behind an outworks of flunkeys. I sat on the hide settee in the hall. Eventually the butler pushed me into the consulting-room, where a very small man sat hidden behind an organ of a desk.

"Please sir, are you Doctor Crippen?" I asked relentlessly, determined not to let my bank letter fall into alien hands.

"Yes, young man, that is my unfortunate name, and I shall take it as uncommonly civil of you not to make light of it, after enduring a lifetime of other peoples' cheap wit." I had no idea what he was talking about. "Perhaps you would care to verify it by inspecting my credentials? Where is your letter, lad?"

Mr. Renault had warned me not to fold the envelope, on the Christmas calendar principle, so I had carried it under my arm like a small plank. Inside was a form about the size of *The Times,* for Dr. Crippen's personal observations on my bodily condition.

"Go behind that screen, boy; undress, and use this," he said, handing me a sherry-glass.

Afraid to ask questions, I went behind the screen, removed all my clothes, and endeavoured to spit in the glass. I returned naked to the desk with my offering of saliva. He had to laugh at my ignorance, and kindly explained what he required. I retired modestly to the screen and waited for nature to fulfil the doctor's strange wish. After a long fruitless interval, he gave me a glass of water to drink, in the hope of better results.

"I can't wait all day, boy, so meanwhile let's have a look at you." I proudly inflated the muscle-bound body which football had given me.

"Good grief, lad, what are you – a stevedore? You don't appear at all the bank type," he gasped, echoing Mr. Renault's opinion, but for a different reason.

"I play a lot of football, sir," I explained, glancing down at the two mighty columns which once had been my normal legs.

"I see. So it's not elephantiasis. But how do you account for your torso?"

"My what, sir?"

"Your shoulders, and that superstructure of triceps, deltoids, and biceps cluttering up your arms."

"Oh, well sir, I do weight-lifting, rowing, boxing, and bodybuilding."

"Why do you favour those particular sports?"

"Because *Brute Strength* magazine says they will help my football."

"Don't you ever think about anything else except this ubiquitous football of yours?"

"No, sir, not very often," I replied, deeming it unwise to bring Maria into a medical discussion.

"Bless my soul. Nevertheless we must run through the formalities of your bodily condition," he said, as he fingered my bas-relief dorsals with professional fascination.

I coughed, ahed, and ninety-nined to his satisfaction; detected a watch ticking from the far end of the room; and when he told me to read the bottom line of the sight chart I said, in good faith, "Printed by Adams and Sons Ltd., Cheapside, London." In fact, I could do everything except fill the sherry-glass.

Later in life, when I was taking the medical examination to join the Forces I had a slightly similar experience during the lung-capacity test. I was blowing up the rubber container as though it was a barrage-balloon, when the M.O. begged me to desist.

"That will do, Pook," he said testily, "we've got another five hundred recruits to come yet, but only one of those machines."

"Am I fit enough for the bank, sir?" I asked Dr. Crippen at the end.

"Yes, my boy, I think you will last the day out. If you don't join the bank, you might make your name by being the first man to boot a ball clean through the ionisphere."

He sealed up Mr. Renault's plank and bade me farewell. I then walked across London again, and gave the messenger threepence to guide me to Miss Littlewig's office. Mr. Renault read the doctor's report with noticeable interest, before giving me another introductory plank for Monday morning, and a booklet of the bank's regulations.

"Do you smoke or drink, Pook? " he asked.

"It's very kind of you, sir, but I'm afraid I don't, especially during the football season," I replied, with the economical fervour of a man who is having a day in Town on coppers.

"May I presume that at least you are allowed to eat?"

"Oh, yes indeed, thank you, sir. Quite a lot, believe me."

"Especially during the football season, of course? Well, that's a weight off my mind. You've finished here today, so you had better go out and get some lunch," he concluded, looking up at the office clock which registered half past five.

My belated lunch consisted of seven doughnuts for sixpence, known to us as "angels' food," and long considered the ideal meal by Alec and me. This monotonous diet was washed down with a glass of cold water. I walked across London to Waterloo Station, feeling very pleased with the day's work, and whiled away the train journey by perusing the bank regulations.

Rule 163 decreed that I must not, on pain of instant dismissal, take part in any political activities, "but this is not to be taken as a prohibition of exercising the vote at a General Election." I couldn't care less at my age. Rule 209 prophesied the likelihood of a pension at some incredible age, providing one had survived Rules 1 to 208 in the interim. Again, I could not care less at my age. Sixty-odd years was a vast span of time, as incomprehensible to the human mind as the Eolithic Period.

But Rule 7 struck me to the heart. "No. 7: No officer shall enter into matrimony until on or after his twenty-fifth birthday." By comparing Rule 7 with Rule 342, which gave the yearly salary scales, it was clear to see that, Rule 7 apart, nobody under twenty-five could hope to keep a wife unless the couple were prepared to take up residence in the parish workhouse. Rule 7 seemed to be directly written in for Maria's benefit, and Rule 342 also affected her indirectly because sub-section (a) Probationers, recorded in black and white the horrifying news that I was to receive only £60 per annum, less superannuation contributions, less Health Stamps, less Life Insurance, less Guild Subscriptions, less examination tuition fees, and so on.

I spent the rest of the journey working out that £60 a year

is about twenty–four shillings a week, and then I began to wonder what my father's reaction would be if I returned home with the hot news that I had decided to resign.

In actual fact, he was so delighted at my success in storming the financial world that he presented me with five pounds on the strength of it. I invested a shilling of this fortune to have the barber shear half an inch off my hair as a sop to Mr. Renault, before depositing five shillings in the Post Office in order to keep the account open. The balance went into our fund for the two refugees from France.

The Zenith Bank at Cudford was a magnificent edifice in stone, and I could never gaze upon it without a strong feeling that in some indirect way my low wages had helped to build it. The bank was often confused by tourists with the cathedral across the road, for they were indeed very similar, except that the cathedral had music.

I arrived by bicycle, having ridden the long journey from home against a head–wind, and unaware that the route lay over a local version of the Himalayan foothills. I crawled half dead into the bank, with the feeling that my feet would go on revolving of their own accord for the rest of my natural life. After a lightning introduction to the manager, the chief clerk, Mr. Pants, handed me over to an elderly minion of twenty–four by the name of Fork, who was detailed to initiate me into the art of slavery.

"Books up first, Pook," he ordered, disappearing down a shaft in the floor. I saw six huge ledgers rise slowly from below, not, as I assumed, on a lift but on Fork, whose thin body staggered up the stairs under this colossal burden. I piled up six more ledgers and tottered up top with them, under the handicap of being unable to see where I was going because the highest ledger was altering the shape of my nose.

"You'll soon get the hang of it," said Fork, guiding me to a bench for the ledgers. "I used to carry seven, but the typists are not allowed to lift even one."

Between us, we carried up enough books for a small public library, until Fork called, "Cash up next." This was our cue to lug up sufficient loot for the five cashiers – banknotes first, then silver and copper. At every trip I carried up four hundred pounds' worth of silver or twenty pounds' worth of copper, at a pace which slowed down considerably by the time I served Cashier No. 5.

"Gubbins up next," cried Fork, dashing down into the vaults.

"Who's he?" I inquired, wondering if it were part of our duties to carry up some night–watchman.

"Gubbins are odds and ends," he explained, loading me with trays of assorted cheques and vouchers, as though I was to be a street–pedlar after all.

"That's the lot, Pook, thank goodness," said my sweating tutor.

"I suppose we have to do that every Monday?"

"Yes, and every other day as well. Then at night we take it all down again."

"What on earth for? Why not leave it up here?"

"Too valuable. Besides, there's the risk of fire."

"Have we finished till tonight then?"

"Finished what?"

"Work."

"Good gracious no. Everything has to be on deck by nine o'clock, and now we can start banking proper."

Banking proper consisted of changing blotting–paper, nibs and ink, rolling the calendars forward, winding the clocks, and a hundred similar chores. While this was in progress, Fork occasionally ran off to answer bells.

"One ring for the manager, two for Mr. Pants," he explained.

"You have to fetch and carry for them, but I'll do it for today."

Finally, Fork led me down into the bowels of the earth, where a furnace blazed as though we were in Hell's kitchen.

"You've got to keep this going to heat the bank," he gasped, shovelling coke like a naval stoker.

"By the sound of it, I should think the bank is on the boil," I remarked, aghast to discover I was to work on top of a foundry.

In the office I was assigned to a desk squeezed in between the top of the strong–room stairs and the door to the cloak–rooms – a region of eternal night and wintry draughts.

"Now this is your real job," said Fork, as though up till then we had been playing the fool. "You've got two ledgers, *'a to as,'* and *'at to bo,'* so you go through them and enter up the entries in the customers' passbooks. Cheques on the right, credits on the left, and you agree your figures with the ledgers. Got it?"

I had not so much got it, as had it.

"I'll show you how it's done," he offered, heaving up *"a to as"* like a trunk with pages, and opening it at "Aaron, Gabriel Frank."

"Now, to find Mr. Aaron's passbook." Here he visited our public library – "and the relevant vouchers" – here he plunged into a gubbins' tray – "and enter them neatly in the correct columns, so. Lastly you agree your figures with those in the ledger, so. Buckets of blood, here's a wrong–post for a start! That idiot of a ledger–keeper, Mr. Balls, has debited a cheque here instead of Aaron, Montague Clive. This must be corrected before Mr. Pants calls over the ledgers."

Up to now, Fork might have been addressing me in *Tamil,* for all I understood him, but the correction ritual completely floored me. Various bald men made drastic alterations to the brothers Aaron, and to numerous lesser journals dependent on *"a to as."* Finally, a Laurel and Hardy couple came over, like witnesses to a will, and initialled every alteration. They all joined in branding Mr. Balls a menace. Mr. Balls was nearly the downfall of me later in the week, because when the manager inquired who was responsible for all the errors in *"a to as,"* I said in all innocence, "Mr. Balls, sir."

"Who?" he snorted.

"Mr. Balls, sir."

"There's no such person on the staff. Are you being impudent, Pook? "

"Of course not, sir. There he is, over there."

"That happens to be Mr. Pills, you stupid young ass."

Later on, I asked Fork to explain my error to me. He laughed till his tears ran down the gubbins. "That's old Pills's nickname, you fool, because he says it every time he makes a wrong–post, and you can hear him all day long."

"It's a good thing he doesn't swear, anyway," I replied, unable to see why Fork should be so hysterical about the matter.

"For heaven's sake go and die in a corner," he pleaded, burying his face in *"br to ca."*

At stated times during the day, Fork sang out strange cries for my benefit, as though calling the faithful to prayer.

"Doors," he hollered at ten o'clock. This was my signal to open up and let the public thunder in. Having been parted from their money all night, they knocked me over in their rush to get it back in the morning. Shopkeepers staggered in with the gold of yesterday's takings, and staggered out again, bearing our sacks of small change like coalheavers.

By three o'clock, Fork fairly screamed, "Doors," in a frantic desire for me to lay my tremendous shoulders against the portals in an effort to shut them against the fury of latecomers, and at the same time eject the milling throng still raving in the banking–hall, on the principle of a one–way valve. Only then were the cashiers able to emerge from the mass of gubbins which threatened to bury them alive all day. In fact, the first time I left the office on a Saturday morning, I was unable to get back in again through the crowd of customers, who always behaved on Saturdays as though we were never going to open again.

Another interesting cry of Fork's was "Wallets," at nine–thirty. This entailed Fork and I descending under the floor of the bank, until we came to a concrete chimney–breast with an oven–door in it. This task was so important that it required the presence of two men, each with a different key. We opened the oven and I had to reach inside and throw out numerous handbags to Fork, who tossed them in a clothes–basket. Every morning we carried the bulging basket upstairs, and gave it to harassed Cashier No. 3, who always acknowledged its safe receipt with the codeword, "Soddit." Not until I had been there a whole month did I discover that the mysterious morning offering in the oven was the night–

safe, where our prosperous tradesmen, afraid to wait for the ten o'clock stampede, pushed their wealth down a hole in the wall overnight. I never solved the code–word.

From my point of view, the most exhilarating cry of Fork's was, "Locals." On this call, I grabbed a leather hat–box and belted out of the bank like a bag–snatcher, to run full tilt in to Barclays Bank down the road. In there gathered five pimply–faced slaves of my own age, one from each bank, who performed a kind of Christmas morning scene by giving each other parcels of cheques from their hat–boxes. If I received small packets, I cried "Hooray," but if I was given big ones, I swore horribly. Anybody who gave me an outsize packet got hit.

My role as probationary junior was a post involving normal office work, but what with answering the bells and Fork's everlasting cries, it was practically impossible to get on with it until the rest of the staff had gone home. Answering the telephone was also on my plate, but after the first two days of my manipulating the switchboard, the typist took it over for the time being. This lightening of my load was brought about by Mr. Pants, in a belated attempt to prevent the Zenith Bank being cut off from the outside world, and to calm the tempers of distant customers who were driven to distraction by my inability to say anything else except "What, sir?" and my tendency to connect them, finally, with other customers whom they had never met, and had nothing in common, barring their hatred of me.

Worst of all, the manager, Mr. Putty, nearly went off his head one day by my repeatedly putting him through to the R.S.P.C.A. in Cudford, which he considered to be no substitute for his solicitors. He came running into the office, and ordered Mr. Pants to forbid my touching the telephone, even if the bank were burning down – a calamity which was quite on the cards owing to my lavish work down below in the foundry with the firm's coke.

Fork's last cry of the day was usually "Post," whereupon the two of us walked down to the G.P.O. to inundate them with two sacks of mail from our letter–writing factory on the first floor. For this journey I was chained to another leather hat–box contain–

ing the High Value Packages, on the theory that bandits would be discouraged by the thought of having me in their home along with the hat–box.

My first day was a nightmare all round, and also the longest day I had ever known, because at the close of business the bank's check–sheets, which had to agree to a penny, differed by nearly twenty–four thousand pounds. Fork helped me to narrow the gap to twenty pounds, after which the senior men gathered round to assist in the search, anxious to be away. By seven o'clock everybody was phoning up wives, friends, and clubs, to postpone appointments, and by ten o'clock they were cancelling them altogether. I seemed to have upset the whole social life of Cudford. The entire staff stood round my desk to check and recheck the day's work, while I looked on from the back, helpless and hopeless.

By midnight Mr. Pants announced that we had better call it a day, because the London Letter must go off – whatever that meant, unless it was a firework. Fork escorted me to the railway station to put the London Letter on the train in person.

It appeared that the effect of the mysterious twenty pounds did not confine itself just to Cudford, but caused up–heaval right through the banking system, into the London Clearing House itself. Head Office took the unusual step of sending down a mathematical wizard to us, who checked my work for three days before he gave in. He told Mr. Pants it was his first defeat in twenty years, and that we had better straighten out the banking calculations of the British Isles by crediting the superfluous twenty pounds to a new account, to be designated, *"Fairies' Money,"* and so balance the books. Mr. Pants asked me, "If ever you remember how you did it, for goodness sake let us into the secret, Pook."

After watching the train depart for London, I slouched home to my new lodgings too tired to worry any more, and wondering if my early–morning cycle ride was just a childhood memory.

FOUR

I resided at Mrs. Ruck's Commercial Hotel, near the station, where, for economy reasons, I had chosen the cheapest room. This room did not differ from the others except that it had no window. I was able to distinguish night from day by means of a glass panel in the ceiling, which also informed me if it was raining by letting some of it in for my personal inspection. I saved the water in a tin chamber, apparently as a safeguard against drought.

Mrs. Ruck had a buxom daughter who would have been quite pretty had not nature begrudged her a nose, and given her a cobnut instead. As my own nose had been broken into a novel shape when I had tried to knock down a goal–post with it, I hated Ivy's cobnut as much as I did my own, and I could never love it, as much as I might admire the rest of her. Consequently, I always locked my door at night, in case Ivy tried to force her way in and seduce me. I believe I derived this unlikely idea from the cinema, and probably Ivy bolted her own door for the same reason. Both of us were pretty safe.

The rest of Mrs. Ruck's boarders consisted of older bank–clerks, who ate their breakfasts behind *Daily Telegraphs.* I did not read at meals, because I needed all my seeing–power at the office, and *Brute Strength* had hinted that such a practice might lessen one's chances of playing for England. Instead, I ate everything in range with astonishing rapidity, so that when the hands of the readers came groping round the newspapers for more toast, they felt about in vain.

Mrs. Ruck's terms were two guineas a week, excluding weekends, which I generally spent at home, where my family generously supplemented the bank's twenty–four bob. My father estimated that these weekends set him back about a fiver a time.

The only incident of note at the hotel was a fight I had there with the junior of Barclays Bank.

"You're gutty, that's what you are," he accused me one morning at breakfast. "You've had the blinkin' lot while I was doing the crossword. I'll knock your big head off after tea."

I told him I would be most interested to see him do it. "Ivy's more your cup of tea," I teased him.

The scene of the contest was Mrs. Ruck's parlour, where we squared up in borrowed gloves. At the time, Mrs. Ruck was sweating it out at the hairdresser's, under the drier, and blissfully unaware of the slaughter about to take place in her precious parlour. Owing to the accumulation of arm-chairs and Victoriana in the room, there was little space for any footwork, so we contented ourselves with murderous feints and elbow-work, laced with long discussions about each other's characters. When we had softened one another up for several minutes without striking a blow, I stepped over to my opponent and lifted him off his feet with a left-hook. He lay dazed on the floor, with his head clean through Mrs. Ruck's cabinet of stuffed birds. Hearing the crash, Ivy came running in and lifted up my victim's head. His dentures tumbled onto her lap in two halves.

"You've killed my Francis, you cruel beast," she screamed. "I'm all right, I think," murmured the corpse, removing a partridge from his face. Ivy pressed his head to her bosom and kissed his brow. Francis responded with a gummy smile. We shook hands in true British style and became firm friends. My reputation was made at the hotel, for I was the hero of the bank-clerks, and the ruthless killer to Ivy. Our fight had a happy ending because she and Francis became engaged shortly afterwards, despite his extreme youth, so at least I did a bit of good. Mrs. Ruck even forgave me for the birds, in an unparalleled orgy of gratitude.

On my third day at the office, Fork surprised me with an unfamiliar call of "Bucket and Cloth." I presumed this was another example of the new language one had to learn in order to survive in banks.

"What in hell do you want now?" I hissed, fed up with

his eternal Cries of Old London.

"Go outside and fetch the bucket and cloth. Lady Erge has just arrived with her dog, and you'll soon need them. Glad *you* are here."

Fork returned to his writing, which he did faster than I have ever seen before or since, as though he were copying out the Bible in an hour flat.

"Forward with the bucket, Pook," yelled Fork, five minutes later.

From his desk he had a clear view of the banking–hall. I shuffled round with the necessary equipment.

"Over here, please, Mr. Pook. Lady Erge's dear little dachshund has been caught short, poor wee soul," drooled Mr. Putty, the manager, tittering delightedly at having his marble floor fouled up.

"Aren't I simply a frightful nuisance," giggled Lady Erge. I nodded respectfully.

"Our Mr. Pook here will soon put that right," laughed Mr. Putty.

It was the first time anyone, let alone the manager, had called me Mister. I looked round to see if he meant me.

"Come in to my office, and we'll talk things over, dear lady," continued the manager, in his nobility voice, and whispering to me in his Pook voice, "Don't just stare at it, remove it. And kick the little wretch in the fire if he does it again."

I commenced Operation Plonk on my hands and knees, looking very different from the Dixie Dean of youth–football.

"Get out of it, you elongated marrow," I snarled savagely at Boodles when he started pulling my floor–cloth away. He showed me his white fangs, and I startled him by showing him mine. Mr. Putty appeared at his door, wreathed in uncle smiles.

"Please bring in Boodles to her ladyship, Mr. Pook."

I gave Boodles a vicious swipe directly the door closed, and, picking him up in a full nelson, bent him in halves for carrying inside.

"Ah, you dear boy, thank you for your kindness," cooed

the unsuspecting Lady Erge, "how fond you must be of animals."

"Yes, your grace, I am indeed."

"I don't think I look *quite* like a bishop, you know. Tell me all about your pets, dear boy."

"We have four Alsatians at home, your grace," I said, thinking to myself I must be a born liar.

"Four indeed. How sweet; and what are their names?"

I rattled off the first names which entered my head. "Maria, Mimi, Ivy, and Hilda, your grace."

"Oh, four bitches?" replied her Grace.

"No, ma'am, they're quite nice dogs really," I replied, seriously.

'Well, well. It is most fortunate they are not here now, for naughty little Boodles is a perfect terror with big dogs."

"My dogs wouldn't hurt him for the world," I grinned, getting a mental flash of Boodles lying in our garden – disembowelled.

Mr. Putty chipped in with, "That will be be all, Mr. Pook. Go and fetch me *'erf to ev,'* please. '

"Fetch who?" cried Lady Erge.

"Oh, I beg your pardon, your grace, I mean your ladyship. That is just our funny banking parlance for the ledger in which we have the honour of keeping your valued account. Hurry up, Pook."

"Hew, hew, I thought you were going to introduce me to some nice Russian gentleman," she jested, hopefully.

I brought in *"erf to ev,"* opened at Erge, Gertrude Violet; balance £9 18s. 3d. See Flag.

"See Flag" was a warning to read the list of customers' eccentricities typed on a small version of the Red Flag which flew from an elastic pole down the centre of the ledger. Typical Flags were, "Print passbook entries in large capitals"; "Under no circumstances disclose balance to wife"; "No overdraft"; "Customer deaf, but do not shout"; and so on. It was through not Seeing Flag that later on I was to send Mr. Putty's mother-in-law's passbook by sea-mail to the Fiji Isles, whereas in actual fact she was waiting for it in Kensington. It was the only time I ever saw him break down and sob.

Not satisfied with *"erf to ev,"* Mr. Putty rang for Lady Erge's box. To obtain this, the office chant was, "Keys," whereupon Mr. Pants and Mr. Lecher hurled their rings of safe–opening equipment over to Fork and me, because the strong–room had to be opened by a quorum of two. We located *Erge, G.V. 1572.*, and lugged out a metal coffin from the catacomb, which we hauled upstairs by sliding it.

"Go easy, Peter; the last junior got hernia with this one," Fork moaned. "They say it's full of gold bullion."

"Judging by the weight of it I should think it's full of her late husbands," I gasped, dragging it with all my might towards Mr. Putty's office, like a barge. At that precise moment came a cry of "Bucket and cloth quickly, Pook." I abandoned the barge and rushed in with the plonk kit, to discover Mr. Putty joyfully pointing to the centre of his new Wilton carpet. Apparently I had not improved Boodles's self–control by folding him up. Mr. Putty was still laughing, but I could see his heart was not really in it. Boodles gave me a triumphant grin. When mopping up was over, I returned to the barge and commenced dragging, when I heard a new sound.

"*Phit. . . . Plack . . . tinkle, tinkle, tinkle* – Dustpan and Brush." Mr. Putty appeared at his door. "Hurry, Pook," he roared.

I went in and swept up Mr. Putty's disintegrated chandelier, which, up till now, had hung from the ceiling. The manager, looking extremely red in the eyes, was holding a golf–club, and I hoped he had run amuck with it on Boodles.

"Poor Mr. Putty was demonstrating his new swing to me, and tragedy came and spoilt it on the follow–through. Such a shame," explained Lady Erge, whose Flag recorded she was Vice–Pres. Cudford Golf Association. Tel. 2222. Care with Box.

I thought the manager was going to have a stroke, but he said, "Bring in Lady Erge's box, Pook, and then get someone to phone the electrician; don't *you* do it."

Later experience taught me that the swishing noise which issued regularly from the managerial office was caused by Mr. Putty's burning ambition to be chosen for the Cudford Golf Team before he was forced to take up bowls, and this remote goal involved the provision of a new chandelier about once a month, on average. Many a time the calling over of ledgers between Mr. Pants and myself was interrupted by the *"Phit.... Plack . . . tinkle, tinkle, tinkle.* Dustpan and brush, Pook." Mr. Pants would shake his head sadly and say, "He's done it again. I'd like to see the old man make the team, but I don't think he's got a hope."

This checking of ledgers was accomplished by Mr. Pants singing out the customers' names in turn, and at each name I chanted back the entry figures to him in the toneless dirge of utter disinterest, like choir–boys' responses. As everything had to be double–checked, there was not a moment of the day when at least two of the staff were not engaged in this odd droning, giving the place the sound of an Eastern shrine at sunset. (During the war, when I visited the Temple of the Tooth in Ceylon, the priests were in full chant and my mind automatically assumed they were calling over the Zenith Bank's ledgers in *Pali*.) Every Wednesday evening, all the ledgers had to be balanced, and for this purpose the entire staff split into pairs as if about to dance. The combined efforts of some forty bored men mechanically baying together in a tuneless groan cannot be described in words. All we lacked was the Great Bell of Sebastopol tolling overhead.

It was almost lunch–time when I finally dragged in Lady Erge's box, which I opened in order to find her will. This necessitated taking out dozens of brown–paper parcels.

"It looks as though you have been doing your Christmas shopping early this year," chuckled Mr. Putty, waggishly, as I turned his office into a G.P.O. sorting department. Lady Erge hew hewed.

"Oh, you dear man, how can you? They are all my bits and pieces, my papers, and the letters from my late husbands."

I thought, they could not have spent much time with her if they had corresponded on this scale. When the will came to light, Lady Erge, overcome with nostalgia, decided to take the box home in order to indulge in a flood of sentiment by rereading the epistles of the departed.

"Get a taxi quickly, Pook," ordered the manager, mentally smelling his burnt dinner in the oven. I left him tearing the will from Boodles's very jaws, while I hailed a taxi. Fork and I inched the coffin outside, where the taxi-driver pronounced it to be an impossible size.

"I'm a taxi, mate, not a ruddy train," he wailed.

"Really now? Then you're the first taxi I've ever spoken to," said Fork, who could be very awkward when Beryl was in one of her moods. (Fork was courting Beryl, our typist, as though she were the last girl left on earth.) The three of us lifted the box onto the luggage-grid, where the man lashed it secure with ropes.

"Mind your car don't tip up," sneered Fork.

Mr. Putty personally shoved Lady Erge through the taxi door, which I held open, with my hand out as though anticipating rain. Nothing fell on my palm.

"I'm late for lunch now, but later on you must tell me *more* about your four Alsatians, Pook," said Mr. Putty, drilling his eyes into my very soul. He hurried off to his burnt offering.

Fork and I repaired to the transport-café by the bridge, where Fork ate every day in order to get married next year to Beryl. He was collecting a home together by existing on a threepenny pork-pie and a penny apple, while I kept faith with Maria on my staple diet of seven doughnuts for sixpence and a glass of water. This continuous orgy of doughnuts and water so nauseated Fork that he rudely ate with his back to me, while he read the *Daily Telegraph*. When he perused the sports page I did likewise over his shoulder, which deepened his dislike for doughnuts and their scenty smell even more.

The café was run by Stanley, who was also goalkeeper for Cudford United which I had already joined.

"What's on the menu today, Stanley?" Fork inquired, as

though he ate something different every day.

"Well, we've got some noice hoys," honked Stanley, who had a slight impediment of speech he seemed very proud of. "Noice fresh heat hoys, they are."

"What kind of meat pies?"

"Hork of course, hork hoys like you 'ad yesdee and all last year."

"One hork hoy then, please, Stanley."

"Don't you make hun of me, you hilly hool, or you'll get a hunch on your hig honk."

Fork's lavish helpings of tomato–sauce served him in place of vegetables. He always poured on the sauce until the pie submerged from view.

"Don't hake all our huddy hauce," moaned Stanley. "You huy a hrippenny hoy and hen use a hilling's–worth of hauce. it's the hame with your hup of hea. You have a huppenny hup of hea and then hut all our heeding hugar in it."

"Shut up, Stanley, for Pete's sake " said Fork, "What with you gassing all the time, and Pook breathing jam all over me, I wonder why I still come here."

"I'll hell you why you hum here," continued Stanley, who talked all the eighteen hours a day his café was open. "You hum here because you're too huddy mean to huy a hecent heal."

"Pook, for heaven's sake shut your mouth while you're grinding those sickly balls to powder," snarled Fork irritably. Fork always got huffy at any reference to his habit of drinking tea in treacle form.

"Hext time you hink your hea, I'll give you a heeding knife and hork," persisted Stanley, whose tongue had long achieved perpetual motion.

"No luck with Beryl last night?" I inquired tactlessly. Fork bit savagely into the pie, up to his ears.

Through Stanley's introduction, I was already playing for Cudford United, as centre–forward. On Saturdays we finished work at two o'clock if all went smoothly, so I changed in the bank's cloak–room and fortified myself with doughnuts at the same time. The *Cudford Echo* had given me the nickname of

Powerhouse Pook, after my fabulous feat of barging the entire Wotton defence into their own goal. Unfortunately, none of us had the ball at the time.

When I scored my first goal, the Echo reporter wrote, "Pook crashed the leather sphere into the rigging." Whatever this meant, he failed to add that in my follow-through I too crashed into the rigging, which parted from the posts, and play was held up for five minutes while both teams unwound me from the nets like a spider's breakfast. As a result of this accident I limped badly for the remaining minutes of the game, and a Wotton wag yelled out in slow deliberate words, "Pook is now bravely carrying on in great pain, but it is nothing to the torture we've been through this afternoon watching him." This taunt aroused my dander and when next I received the ball, I hit it with such force that I folded forward on to the top of my head in agony. Thirty yards away, the Wotton goalkeeper was also lying on the ground, having been unable to get out of the way in time. He was motionless and still clasping the ball to his stomach, both of which were over the goal-line.

"Well done, Peter," cried Kite, our captain, "you've scored again. Now we're only 9–2 down."

"Practically a draw!" roared the Wotton wag. "Send the dirty fouler off."

Having no further interest in the match, I was carried back to my digs, with a suspected seizure of the pelvis – at least that is what I suspected myself. In those days of under-staffing in the banks, staying away from work was regarded as second only to high treason, and nothing short of the plague was sufficient excuse for a whole day off. So on Monday, Francis and Beryl kindly assisted me to the office, where I scuffed about by keeping my thighs rigid and moving only those parts below the knees.

"Why in hell is Pook mincing around and saying 'Oo' all the time?" demanded the manager of Mr. Pants.

"I believe he has done himself a mischief playing soccer, sir, and I heard he has just received a message to say some goalkeeper is off the danger-list."

"Then send him home to bed, and if he can't walk like a normal human-being tomorrow, tell him to call Dr. Mernst in. This office has been like a circus since he joined us."

I spent the rest of the day bedridden, with the feeling that I was in labour. The following day I returned to duty, not so much because I was better but because I could not face another day of eating the plates of cold glue which Ivy brought up for me, in her unfamiliar role of nurse.

When I joined Cudford United they were well down the league table, but after I had been with them six weeks they were bottom. This was mainly due to their woodwormy defence, which had conceded eighty-one goals in ten matches. Stanley, our goalkeeper, who lived only for the weekly fixtures, spent his Saturday afternoons in a sea of mud, retrieving the ball from the back of the net, and always claiming a foul as he did it. I never knew Stanley beaten by a clean, uncontroversial shot. He performed acrobatic marvels between the posts, but they were usually split-seconds behind the flight of the ball.

"The hilthy hine hicked me in the hace. It ought to he a hee-hick," Stanley would honk, as he tramped his well-worn path to the rear of the net. Anything that went past him fairly was denounced as, "*Off-hide,* ref, *off-hide.* Use your huddy eyes."

All through the match, Stanley kept the crowd informed on the state of play by a running commentary, and he also advised our players on tactics, and the opposing side on football etiquette, with bitter emphasis on their unsporting determination to win at any price.

At the final whistle, as a substitute for leaving the field covered with glory, he departed covered with mud and grass. In fact, after some of our more violent defeats he looked like a portion of the pitch with legs.

Stanley did not consider he had had his money's worth unless he bled profusely, and sustained some enormous pancake bruises to show his adoring girl-friend, who passed her half-days in blizzards and monsoons behind his frail citadel. From this suicidal vantage-point she urged Stanley on with piercing screams to feats of reckless flight which defied the very laws of gravity, as though there would be no hot kisses for him that night unless he were reduced to pulp beforehand.

When Stanley did get his hands on the ball, opposing forwards who resorted to barging and kicking him into the net were subjected to a frightening display of female invective from the snarling tigress in the background, who thought nothing of running on to the field and pulling at the attackers' shirts. Stanley himself conducted a post–mortem after every goal by holding his earthy fist under the scorer's nose and requesting him to repeat the vile tactics which had resulted in his scoring.

Nobody who witnessed it will ever forget the day Stanley scored himself. He took a goal–kick by his customary drill of completely disappearing among the crowd behind the posts as a prelude to streaking suddenly from their midst towards the ball, as though his friends there had a plane–launcher concealed somewhere. When Stanley really got into his stride he could hit a ball with the best of them, as the spectators in the stands knew to their cost, but this time his cannon–ball only went as far as the halfway line, where the wind boomeranged it back towards Stanley in a beautiful ellipse. Stanley's follow–through usually carried him within speaking distance of his opposite number, where he halted his momentum by falling prostrate, as though a sniper had picked him off in full flight.

Aware of the danger by his girl–friend's frantic calls to "Get back in goal, Stanley love," he did a Jessie Owens down the field, and at the critical moment, soared aloft and snatched the ball like a striking falcon, to bring off a miraculous save. Unhappily, no one could have travelled so far from the ground without coming back to earth inside the net, and although the stadium rang with applause for his unique exhibition, even his girl–friend had to admit it was a legitimate goal. Not so Stanley. When we had prised his head out of the mud, javelin–wise, he told the crowd that "the hoddin hun hot in my eyes and blinded me."

Cudford United were united only in the sense that we wore the same shirts, because, as we descended the league table, we abandoned the W–plan for the frying–pan formation.

This demanded one forward and nine defenders. Stanley was not included among the defenders, being more in the nature of a ball–boy. As centre–forward, I was only called back to help in defence as a last resort; that is to say, about every five minutes. My chief task was to shout, "Send it down the middle," and if the ball ever did emerge from our gyrating swarm of defenders, I thundered down the centre as a one–man forward line. In the match against Sayling Shipyard Rovers, our opponents had a boy–Carnera at centre–half, who clung to me as though we were handcuffed, and crudely checked my breakaway thrusts by colliding with me like a train. When I could not risk another collision for fear of having my chest staved in, I tried to zoom around him, but he stopped that move by bringing me down with one banana leg and driving my face into the mud with the other. Under the dirt my face was livid, and I spluttered, "Just you try and do that again, you gingeredded closet." Whereupon he began to do it, until we flew at each other like Sayers versus Heenan.

When the other players had dragged us apart, I was amazed to see that Stanley was being ordered off the field by a linesman, while the second linesman was reviving the referee with a sponge. Before I could get to the bottom of the situation, the Rovers decided to take up Stanley's challenge that they would have to drag him off if they wanted to be rid of him. Of course, we went to his rescue, along with several hundred spectators, and I seemed to be involved with the Rovers' captain. Then everything went black.

They tell me that P.C. Tharge summoned police reinforcements in the shape of cyclist P.C. Barrington, and through some regrettable misunderstandings, Stanley, myself, and the red–headed fouler were taken into protective custody – "Case to come up Chewsdee week."

We were released later in the evening, one hour after Ginger, and as usual following a match, we went with the rest of the team to the *George and Vulture,* to celebrate our latest debacle.

"Well, we were jolly lucky to have the game abandoned,

after being 7–1 down," said our skipper. "At least we didn't lose, and the match won't count for points." This made everything all right.

Punctually at nine–thirty, Stanley rose to inform the company in weird song that there is no place like home. When he had confirmed this truism for eight choruses, the landlord shouted, "Then for heaven's sake go 'ome, and 'ave done with it there," being alarmed at the number of paying customers who were rapidly taking Stanley's advice.

On Monday morning, Mr. Putty belled me. I saw the *Echo* on his desk, headlined, "Powerhouse in Ugly Scene. Ref. Hurt."

"Come in, Powerhouse – I mean Pook, and shut the door. I hear you have been charged with making an affray."

"Oh, goodness, nothing like that, sir. It was a fight. I tried to protect some of my friends from ruffians, sir."

"The *Echo* seems to put it in a different light, and this is a very serious matter from the bank's point of view. Also, Pook, while we are on the subject, Dr. Mernst tells me he is treating young Francis of Barclays Bank for glass splinters embedded in his scalp, and your name cropped up in the conversation."

"Oh, goodness gracious, sir, that is awful. Anybody could get badly hurt like that," I replied, making a mental note of it for Ginger.

"Did you have anything to do with it, Pook?

"Only insofar as I live in the same hotel, sir. I wouldn't hurt a fly, sir." Mr. Putty searched my swollen face for flies.

"Who was it who set upon you so unjustly, Pook? "

"I don't know his name, sir, except Ginger. He is a big young man, and I would know him again if I saw him." In fact, I had been toying with the idea of spending a day at Sayling, to refresh my memory. "It's bad enough him being ginger, but he's Welsh as well."

"Then I happen to be his fellow–countryman, Pook, so have a care."

"Oh, lor'."

"Now, would he be the Ginger Jones the Echo jargon

refers to as 'The giant pivot of a sterling half–back row'?''

''Oh, that's him, sir. Centre–half. Big as a house.''

''And you agree your name is Pook, alias Powerhouse?''

''Yes, sir, but that's just football ballyhoo.''

''Never mind that. Allow me to read out an extract. 'Powerhouse picked himself up with a ribald ejaculation, and suddenly assailed Jones with both fists flying. The stalwart pivot was not loath to join battle, there being little love lost between the pair all through the match, and he gave as good as he received. When the skipper intervened, Powerhouse turned his rain of blows on that innocent bystander until Jones had the presence of mind to fell the attacker from behind'.''

I was carried away by the description.

''So, it *was* Ginger who did for me,'' I shouted bitterly.

''Now, Pook, don't you ever defend your friends again in this dreadful manner, or I shall have to report you to Head Office, under Rule 413, *Brawling*. You understand? And meanwhile, try to do something about your face – several of our elderly customers have been scared by it.''

Later, at lunch, Stanley's girl–friend pronounced it to be the best match of the season, and the highwater–mark of Stanley's career. She said, ''Stanley's ever so delighted, because we play them away, next month, and he says to tell you he'll help you give Jones the chop.''

When I went to bed that night I was awake half the time, beating Ginger Jones senseless, over and over again.

FIVE

In midsummer the Premises Department decided to have the bank re-decorated throughout, and to brighten up the outside paintwork with two coats of black. This was conveniently scheduled to coincide with Mr. Putty's holiday. As I did everything else around the place, I fully expected Fork to holler one day, "Ladders and Brush" for my benefit, so it came as a pleasant surprise to learn that Messrs. Lovejoy and Crittal were going to do it for me. Mr. Pants briefed me. "Pook, you will arrive each morning at 5 a.m., to let in Messrs. Lovejoy and Crittal, and stay on duty, supervising them, until you are relieved at nine o'clock. The decorating cannot be done during banking hours, for reasons which will be obvious even to you."

"Five a.m., sir?" Words failed me. "Who will do my job during the day, then?"

"*You* will, Pook, immediately you have had your breakfast at nine."

This was disturbing news, because, in direct defiance of *Brute Strength's* ban on anything remotely connected with sex, I was secretly taking out Lily, our second typist, during the short interval between "Books Away" and bedtime, in the hope that the editor would not find out. If everyone acted strictly in accordance with the editor's policy, our population would be wiped out in one generation. The editor was not the only person on my secret list. There were also my father, Maria, Mr. Pants, Ivy, Hilda Longbotham, and Lily's boy-friend serving in Hong Kong. Courting Lily was not going to be made any easier by my rising before dawn.

Lily was a very nice girl who helped me a lot with the bank work when she could spare any time. She was a trifle short, but quite pretty except that she had a tiny mouth and no lips. This made kissing rather a matter of guesswork, like pecking the hole of a luggage–label, but nature had compensated her with a very full figure. In fact, Cashier No. 4 used to remark that he always checked his silver–bags, in case a couple were missing, until I hinted to him as bluntly as I dare without ending my career on probation, that such jests might result in him finding his two front teeth missing instead.

Once, when Lily took me to the pictures to see her favourite actress, I was surprised to find the film–star had huge sensual lips like inner–tubes, and Lily confessed to me how she would love to be like her. That particular winter's night we had been exchanging icy kisses as we sat on a tomb, round the south side of the Cathedral where the sleet was less troublesome. The beautiful moonlit night revealed the trees like black icicles against the snow. After an hour and a half, I completely lost the use of my limbs, and I began to tremble as though I were dying in the Arctic.

"Oh, my goodness me, you *are* cold tonight, Peter," Lily moaned, whose hot blood and ample proportions immunized her against cold.

"Get me to a fire, Lily, please – quickly, before I'm ill."

"Oh, my goodness me, don't talk like that, Peter. You do worry me. Take my hand and follow me as best you can. Mind the graves, dear."

Lily led me to the Troxy, where she put me in the foyer while she bought the tickets. Then she got hold of my marble hand and pulled me to our usual front–seats at the foot of the screen, as Lily was slightly short–sighted. From these seats I had watched a film every week, and I never got over the feeling that when the eighteen–foot lady opened her mouth to sing I was in danger of being sucked into it. I tried to keep Lily away from Spectaculars, ever since we saw *The Last Days of Pompeii,* which kept me awake for a week afterwards. First of all, we were attacked by the enemy chariots, and I was continually ducking under spears, arrows, and hooves. Then the flood–waters surged around us, full of screaming bodies, until I felt drowned in my seat. All through these scenes the augmented Hollywood Orchestras were belting all hell out of their instruments, about six feet in front of us.

The grand finale of the destruction of the city was too much for my nerves, and I fled before the advancing wall of lava and crashing palaces into the silence of the "Gents."

Tonight, as I sat there shaking with zero coldness, Lily put her glasses on, the better to devour every detail of Captain Scott sledging towards the South Pole. He had my deepest sympathy.

Even the hot, breathy atmosphere of the Troxy, notorious for sending old ladies off in faints, took an hour to thaw me out and produce some semblance of feeling in my numbed body.

"Intit lovely, Peter dear," Lily bellowed, above the explosions of ice-floes breaking up. Lily always enjoyed her three hours to the full – even the adverts, which she read aloud in case the rest of the audience was illiterate. During the interval, all our row had to stand up, so that the public could file in and out like shift-workers. Lily bought herself an ice-cream tub. From the side of my eyes I could not help noticing that the little wooden shovel exactly fitted her mouth. Conversation was impossible during the interval, because Raymond and his Mighty Wurlitzer rose from his subterranean pit before our very eyes, and if I were not careful my long legs went up with it. Lily always cried, "Take your feet off the organ, Peter. Everyone's looking at us."

Having waited hours for his moment of glory, Raymond impatiently began his music while still buried in the bowels of the earth, but when he ascended to the dizzy heights of the circle he really opened up full blast. In fact, his weekly rendering of *In a Monastery Garden* compelled me to remark to Lily, "Thank heavens I'm not a monk."

"I'm glad you're not, as well," she replied blushing.

Raymond made a great show of playing a sort of xylophone with his feet, while his hands worked frantically at the keys and stops, as though he were operating our switchboard at the bank.

"Intit lovely," exclaimed Lily, clapping in ecstasy as Raymond stood up and bowed to the applause. The spotlight showed us that Raymond went a bit heavy on mascara.

"Int he lovely," shrieked Lily, waving to Raymond as he passed by our knees into the cellar. Raymond had to time his last bow with great care if he were not to strike his head on the floor which came rushing up to meet and swallow him. Blissful silence.

"You feeling better now, sweetheart?"

"Yes thanks, Lily. I think I'm strong enough now to hold your hand."

"Oh, good. Jew like the picture, Peter?"

"Not madly keen. I'd rather see *Slaughter in the Jungle.*"

"Jew know my favourite? You will laugh at me. 'Scalled *Naked Love* – week after next. Then I'm going to take you to see *your* favourite. Jew know what it is?"

"The Invasion of the Worm-Men?"

"No. Try again."

"Death Strikes Wembley Stadium?"

"Yes, love. I know you'd like to see it again, wouldn't you? Lily should have said "see it for the ninth time," because by sitting through several continuous performances, Lily and I had thrilled to the fascinating drama of five international footballers being brutally murdered in the dressing-room at half-time, against a background of the Cup Final. We both knew the murderer to be handsome Lyle Ketchup, the trainer who gambled, but when he was on the scaffold Lily howled her eyes out at such waste of manpower, and when the camera gave a quick flash of the rope going "zoink" – for the ninth time – she screamed out in anguish. Her tears were only stemmed by the timely arrival of Raymond and his massed-bands.

After the interval, Lily and I locked in a lovers' embrace which threatened to dislocate the arm which went round her shoulder. Lily held my free hand like it was caught in a mangle, and permitted me to kiss her ear.

"You can come round and meet my mum if you like

Sundee.'' Lily always said that when I was making love to her, and I always ignored it. I could never see what attraction her mother could have, that Lily didn't.

''Git your big 'eds apart, and let others see the screen,'' grumbled the man behind. I always ignored that, too.

After we had stood for the King, we went out into the snow, to say good night in Lily's porch. We never left the cinema till the Anthem, no matter how early we went in. When *Death Strikes Wembley Stadium* was first shown, we arrived at two–thirty, and when we rose for the King, Lily said, ''Intit lovely. I could stay here all night like this with you.''

Perhaps Lily should have been an usherette.

The last thing I wanted, under the circumstances, was to get out of bed at 4 a.m., and then sit in the Zenith Bank, listening to the Dawn Chorus. But Mr. Pants was adamant. By borrowing Ivy's alarm–clock, I contrived to rise on time, and sleep–walk along the dark streets.

''Morning, Powerhouse,'' said Constable Barrington, sarcastically. That man never knew the joys of bed – he was always up and out.

''Going to get in some extra practice? Four points from twelve games! You need it.''

I arrived at the bank before five, but the money–grabbing Lovejoy and Crittal were already smoking their Woodbines in the early light, surrounded by apprentices leaning on a truck of ladders. I unlocked the doors and the men dragged in their gear. Within five minutes the hall rang with the songs and oaths peculiar to the building–trade, as the decorators stripped the walls like vandals on holiday.

I shut myself in Mr. Putty's office and went sound asleep on his bear–rug. At seven our old bearded charwoman with the cloth–cap came in to do the dusting, which she accomplished without waking me.

''Pook,'' shouted Mr. Pants, ''get up this instant. What ever do you think you're doing?''

''I must have dropped off, sir.''

''By the look of things, I should have thought you'd

dropped dead on the rug. A fine way to supervise the workmen, indeed. Just you run along home to breakfast, and mind you're back here within half an hour. I've got a surprise for you today which will keep you awake and on your toes.'' Who hadn't?

Mr. Pants's unimaginative idea of a surprise was the half-yearly passbook audit, whereby he made a list of all customers who had not seen their passbooks during the past six months. It was my job to post off the books he listed. Our customers ranged from those who had the bank on the brain and came in twice a day to have a look, to those who couldn't stand the sight of anything in account form and had Flags worded, ''Under no circumstances send client passbook.''

''It's quite simple,'' said Fork, who didn't have to do it. ''You just take the passbook, the envelope, the return envelope addressed to us, and the Manager's Comps slip. Don't forget the Manager's Comps slip, it adds the personal touch. You agree each book with the ledger, and Bob's your uncle. Be sure to make a note of the posting date against each account, and read all Flags.''

During the day I worked steadily through Mr. Pants's surprise for keeping me awake.

''Have you despatched the audit passpooks, Pook?'' he demanded, always terrified lest I should have enough spare time to go to the toilet.

''Yes, sir; the lot. All initialled and safely on their way,'' I replied, trying hard to make his eyes see my halo.

''Now remember, Pook, I want you here at 5 a.m. tomorrow, conscious, and on your feet, to supervise the work-men. Bed is the proper place for slumber, not Mr. Putty's rug.''

I thought to myself that I saw damn-all of mine.

''And recollect, Pook, the half-yearly balance is nearly upon us, and so is the end of your probationary period. Be warned.''

Mr. Pants and everyone I knew connected with banks were always harping on the horrors of past balance-nights, as though savouring the darkest hours of the Great War.

''We worked right round the clock,'' said Mr. Balls, ''and

still we couldn't get through it. But of course, that was in 1897, when Juniors slept under the counters.''

More recent memories evoked stories of Juniors being rushed to hospital with brainstorms and cerebral black-outs. Bygone managers were carried raving into mental institutions, by the dozen.

''I don't suppose I shall be able to go out balance-night, sir, by what they tell me?''

''No, Pook, you won't, nor any night that week. You will find it to be six days of unremitting toil, and you will be well advised to bring your meals to the office – this is a special concession for balance-week only.''

Now the old dotard had started talking about a week of it.

''No pictures balance-time,'' moaned Lily, sadly.

To be on the safe side, I now slept upright in Mr. Putty's swivel-chair, while the decorators demolished the remainder of the bank outside. It was not that I shirked my duty but just that it was physically impossible to keep awake. I figured the endless succession of steel doors below would look after the vaults. To get to the safe required the presence of all our senior men, who possessed the necessary keys to open one prison-grill after another, in a gradual progression of strong-rooms, terminating at the vault. At the rear of the vault stood the sacred safe, like a kitchen fridge. Only the manager and sub-manager could open this, with the possible exception of Messrs. Chubbs, which they accomplished with long skewer-like keys. Mr. Putty always inserted his skewer last of all, on the principle of an Admiral entering his barge, and then threw open the door with the air of a conjurer's climax finale.

The safe walls were so thick that there was very little space inside, but right in the centre was a tiny steel drawer. Only Mr. Putty possessed a key to this compartment, and I was never able to peer in it.

''Please Mr. Pants, what does the manager keep in his little drawer?''

''Pook, you ask too many questions for your own good.

If you must know, it's his blasted golf–balls.'' I thought this over a long time. Whenever Mr. Pants shouted, ''Coupons,'' I had to accompany him to the vault ''to see I don't steal anything,'' as he put it, with an arch smile to let me know he had a sense of humour.

''I think you could be trusted down here alone, sir,'' I replied, determined not to know, and anxious to get on with my work.

''Why do you do your Pools in the vault, sir?''

''Pook, for the last time, take in what I am saying. I am not doing the Pools, and never shall. I am clipping the coupons from the bearer–bonds.''

''Why can't you do it upstairs, sir?''

''For heaven's sake shut up.''

This was the only job in the bank, apart from answering the phone, which I was not allowed to participate in, presumably on account of the skill needed to tear out the coupons with a little set square. It aggravated Mr. Pants to see me idle.

''Pook, refrain from yawning all over me. If you require something to occupy your tiny mind, recite to me the Bills of Exchange Act.''

''Why do you always draw the pins through your hair, sir?'' I fell back on the pin routine whenever he mentioned Bills of Exchange. Anything but that. This flattered Mr. Pants.

''Ah, that's a little trick of the trade. My hair contains a small quantity of brilliantine which oils the pin.''

''Why do you want an oily pin, sir?''

''Ah, that's the clever part. The film of oil allows me to push the pin into the coupons when they have to be fastened together again. You will benefit from my experience later, in the unlikely event of your passing beyond probation.''

The Bills of Exchange Act was now safely shut out.

''Did you pass your probation, sir?''

''Don't tempt me, Pook. I'm too near pension to risk violence.''

''Did I tell you we're playing Salisbury Wanderers Saturday, sir?''

"You did not, and you are not going to. That will do, Pook."

"Can I go early this Saturday, sir?"

"Hold it, Pook. Let us lock up and shut up."

Early one morning, a workman shook me out of Mr. Putty's chair to apprise me of a visitor.

"It's the postman, mate."

"What do you want so early, postman?"

"I'm not the ruddy postman, I'm the painter. He's outside."

"Morning, Guvnor," said the postman.

"What do you want, Morning? "

"Lot of extra mail for you today. The van had to bring it in a sack."

"Ta. Throw it in the hall." I immediately returned to drug–state. When Mr. Pants arrived, I saw him in conference with his first lieutenant, Mr. Lecher.

"Box, Pook." I hurried to the small glass cage which Mr. Pants's rank warranted. The contents of the sack lay all over the floor.

"I thought I had experienced every phenomenon the banking world has to offer, but never have I seen the like of this," raved the sub–manager, as though he could have well done without this climax to his career. "Praise the Saints Mr. Putty is on holiday, or you would be out on your ear."

I failed to see anything unusual. "I didn't know the sack would break, sir."

"Break? *Break?* You flaming halfwit, can't you read?"

"Everything seems in order, sir. Every package is addressed to us."

"Don't you recognize the packages, boy?"

"They look like passbooks, sir."

"Then open one, and tell me what is inside."

"This one is Mr. Fleabody's passbook, an envelope, and a Manager's Comps – just like I sent it off, sir."

"Did you think it would be an improvement on the old system to post the entire passbook audit in the return envelopes, you stupid football–maniac? Did you suppose we post off all our mail, addressed to ourselves? *Did you,* Pook?"

Suddenly I got the message. It panicked me badly. I went to emergency stations with the Oliver Twist snivel.

"I haven't quite got the hang of it, please sir. Would it help if I paid for the postages? What can I do, sir? Oh, can I ever be forgiven?" I had not seen Mr. Pants so atavistically enraged since he caught me with Lily, down in the foundry.

"Well, boy, for a start, send out the passbooks again, but I will check them myself before they go off."

"That's very kind of you, sir. Anything else, sir?"

"In my day, a foolish error like that would have got you hanged, drawn, and quartered, Pook, but, of course, those were the days when we had brains and used them."

"Oh, lor'." Mr. Pants had been the perfect probationer, sinless and all–wise, as he never tired of telling me. As early as his second day in the bank he was competent to stand in for all staff up to chief–clerk, if called upon. His providential entry into banking enabled Head Office to release two senior officials for the Boer War, and the manager's report at the end of his probation was nothing less than a lyrical hymn of praise. During his everlasting autobiography about what he did then, as compared with what I didn't do now, I passed the time by mentally answering him at the end of each sentence, thus:

"*I* always shaved every morning Pook." – *"You lying toad, pity you didn't this morning."*

"*I* always had my hair cropped short, and *I* never wasted the bank's gas." – *"You can bet your life you didn't – you mean old custard."*

"*I* never pinched the typists, or used the bank phone for private calls." – *"Don't you ever run down, you old windbag."*

I am certain he never detected my contributions to his sermons, because he seemed incapable of understanding anything not in cheque form.

"And one thing more, Pook. Before he left, the manager said he would take it as a personal favour if you told your newsagent to deliver *Brute Strength* to your hotel and not to this office. It lowers the tone of the bank.''

This arrangement of mine had been due to my eagerness to get my weekly magazine as quickly as possible, even though there was only time to glance at the lurid cover before lunch. Every week the cover sported colour–photographs of at least four human gorillas in shorts, who posed in muscle–bound agony. Others, taken in profile, had chests like pouter–pigeons. Sometimes, one gorilla would be towing a London bus with his teeth, or straining at the four–hundred–pound barbell similar to a pair of train–wheels.

Inside, the editor exhorted us to stop being hospital rejects, and become like the cover men. His name was Bruce Bold, and he begged his readers to write (no callers, please) to the Mecca of Muscle in our great metropolis, Dept. 247d, for advice on all personal problems remotely connected with body–building. The address was off Clapton Common, London, E.5., and Bruce Bold's notepaper heading included a blurred print of the Parthenon, presumably to convey to his readers the type of edifice which housed Dept. 247d. I gathered from the Letters' Page of the magazine that many of my fellow–readers suffered from pimples, and chronic constipation, while most of the lady–readers *(Worried Dolly, Streatham.)* were in the family way. It always puzzled me what all this had to do with our Cult.

The magazine was intensely masculine, except for the Woman's Page, and even there the poseurs were strictly unprovocative, looking like smaller men in brassieres. I read each issue until I knew it off by heart, in my search for the secret of Power–Surge, which would eventually endear me to Portsmouth Football Club. Every number contained a fresh set of exercises to develop Power–Surge, which I carried out in the privacy of my bedroom. One week, it seemed that the elusive Power–Surge could never be attained without legs of steel. The following week, a neck like a tree–trunk was indispensable. The next issue demanded pectoral muscles barely distinguishable from wire–hawsers, and so on. Bruce Bold even had an exercise for improving the tiny muscles which control the eyelids, but why, I never knew.

As the exercises accumulated, so my bedroom struggles went on far into the night, until the miracle of it was that my tortured physique did not succumb to cardiac collapse. I refused to eliminate one single issue's instructions. One night a very strange thing happened. Not possessing an omnibus to pull along, I often dragged the brass bed across the room by fastening my teeth into the bedclothes, and this particular evening I had done this, and rounded off my performance of Power–Surge Control with two hundred press–ups. I staggered over to the bed, a sweating mass of twitching muscles, and, uttering a primeval roar, I involuntarily bent the bed rail in two with my bare hands.

This incident so scared me that for days afterwards I examined my skin, in the fear that a coat of black fur might make its appearance on my pale body.

During this period, the sensational American beefcake advertisements began to appear in *Brute Strength,* which depicted in vivid pictures the familiar "before and after" sequence of certain body–building courses. I sent away for particulars of all these, by filling in my address on the coupons, which were already printed, thus: "Say there, Mister Samson, I sure do need a noo body, fast. Rush full details to: Name (block letters, please.)............................. (Enclose sixpence in stamps.)."

Even I did not expect the postman to deliver my new body by return of post, but the price of these courses, when eventually disclosed, were far above my pocket. However, the promoters conducted long correspondences with me by sending their follow–up literature to the bank for months afterwards. One such effort bore the printed message: "Hi, you lazy fella, you admit you gotta no–good body, but we haven't heard from you to date. Maybe you're too weak to write to us. Our Mister Samson here sure is rarin' to go on that lousy figure you've just gotta do sumin' about. Simply mail twenty–nine dollars fifty – we do the rest. Money refunded if we fail to enlarge you as per diagram. Buddy–you jes' can't lose. *Flash:* Our Mister Samson says he'll knock ten dollars fifty off right now, if you enrol within thirty days."

Every December, *Brute Strength* held a competition in

London, to select the Biggest Brute of the Year. Although I could never watch the show myself, I saw the parade of cavemen on the newsreel, where the commentator remarked, "Every time these supermen walk round, you can hear their deltoids crashing into their triceps."

One day, Mr. Pants called me into his box, and said, "Pook, it has been brought to my notice that you are carrying up nine ledgers at a time. Now, I am all for speed, but this is a dangerous practice."

"Oh, that's O.K., sir. I am seeking for PSS, that's all."

"And may one inquire who PSS may be, when he's at home?"

"Oh, that means Power–Surge Strength, sir."

How ignorant can a man get?

"Indeed; very interesting, but have you seen anybody about it?"

"Of course not, sir. It is a form of husky manhood – every man's gift to his bride, as the papers put it."

"May I ask what form, Pook?"

"Certainly, sir," I replied, eager for a new recruit to the Cult.

"It is hard to explain really, but The Biggest Brute of 1934 defined it as a tank ploughing through the enemy fortifications. One exercise is to try and run up the stairs with a heavy weight, such as our ledgers."

"Good grief, lad."

This was Secret Exercise 23, which stated, "Locate a long flight of steps – St. Paul's Cathedral is an obvious example – and endeavour to run up and down them, carrying Barbell 7, twenty times, rest, and repeat till legs refuse further action. You have now arrived at Maximum Endurance."

My first choice had been Cudford Town Hall, which possessed thirty–two concrete steps leading up to the main entrance. When I had performed eighteen preliminary ascents and returns, the caretaker came out and shouted, "Make up your blasted mind whether you're comin' in or not, 'cos I'm waiting to lock up."

"That's how I gained this badge, sir," I continued, proudly indicating a brass lapel–button, inscribed, "B.S."

"I assumed that was a Boy Scout badge, Pook."

"Oh, no, sir, that stands for *Brute Strength.* You see, I used to wear the celluloid one, when I was only a Regular Brute, but when I passed the test I became a Perfect Brute."

Gaining my brass badge, which was awarded only to those paid–up members who satisfied the editor that they had lifted a certain tonnage clear of the ground, was the nearest approach to hernia I ever experienced.

"I can't go any higher, sir, except Biggest Brute of the Year, at Earls Court, and I'd never win that because I'm only six–foot–three."

"Practically a dwarf, I take it, Pook?

"Oh, yes, sir. Last year's champion was over seven foot. Why, even the winning Lady Brute was as tall as me."

"What a ghastly thought. Pook, I think it would be as well if you never mentioned these matters to the manager, and stop people sending that dreadful American literature to the office. Now, try and tear your strange mind away from the world of Hercules, and take in what I am about to tell you. The bank now optimistically expects you to pass its own old–fashioned test, in the shape of the Institute of Bankers' Examinations, and if you can pass within ten years, they award you the sum of forty–five pounds."

I whistled. This was quite a carrot, coming from my miserly employers.

"First of all, concentrate on passing Part I in five years. This is comprised of English, Geography, Economics, Book–keeping, and Banking." My face lit up.

"Well, sir, I know English, for a start."

"That's a matter of opinion, Pook, but one thing is certain you know damn–all about Banking."

"Do I have to leave the bank to study at college, sir?" I inquired hopefully.

"No, you most definitely do not. You study in your spare time."

Great Scott, what would Bruce Bold say about this?

"Who is going to teach me, sir? You?"

"Spare me that, please, Pook. You will find many suitable correspondence courses advertised in the *Bankers' Gazette.*"

"Who pays for the course, sir?"

"If you don't, no one else is going to."

I could picture just such an ad. "Say there, fella, you sure gotta lousy mind. Gen it up with our quick–fire brain–developer. Rush ten dollars fifty for complete mind–massifying course."

On inspection, I learned that the ads in the *Bankers' Gazette* were of a much more sober kind. The one I chose was, "The Bank–Clerks' Friendly School of Banking. Pass guaranteed or money refunded." This sounded a safe bet, but it was the picture story which really won my patronage. An elderly man was depicted as straining his tired old frame to carry up ledgers, and the bubble informed us that he was still a struggling junior, despite his bald head and white moustache. The manager stood by, saying, "Pity, but Todders will have to go." It might have been me!

Picture No. 2 showed Todders in the security of his home, gulping down reviving Oxo, surrounded by his starving children. Between draughts he says, "I am a *failure,* that's what I am." He certainly looks it – and a dirty one at that. Picture No. 3 portrays him asking a large, genial man the way to the Labour Exchange, but the jovial stranger is saying, "No, no, not that. It's not too late. Let me be your uncle. I will guide you to success, despite your total ignorance, as I have done for 79,287 others."

The last picture showed him sitting at an enormous desk, and we learn from the glass–door that Todders is *General Manager, Head Office, Knock and wait.* Standing by his side is his Uncle. The ex–junior bubbles, "I owe it all to Uncle Friendly and his staff of twenty–five qualified tutors." Outside in the passage, we observe his former manager, his face contorted with jealousy, carrying in the morning tea.

This irresistible ad swept me off my feet, and I persuaded my father to send Uncle Friendly fifteen pounds, which covered the whole of Part 1, and a letter begging him to let me be his nephew.

By return of post came numerous pamphlets, the guarantee, and a hundredweight tea–chest of text–books, which Ivy mistook for the do–it–yourself greenhouse she had sent away for. The guarantee gave me the reassuring news that, under the "no pass, money back" offer, Uncle Friendly engaged to teach me for eternity, until either one of us passed on to a better world above. I was rather disappointed to find that Uncle Friendly would not be my personal tutor, but that he was putting me into the capable hands of Uncle Fingelbaum, B.Sc. (failed). Nevertheless, Uncle Friendly would be ever hovering in the background, checking my day to day progress, and the monthly instalments, if any.

I immediately wrote a personal letter to the editor of *Brute Strength,* acquainting him of my new commitments, and requesting him not to take it as any disloyalty to the Cult on my part. I also told him that as proof of my sincerity, I was prepared to continue with his abridged course of Power–Surge, specially prepared at considerable expense for slaves like myself, who were short of time, entitled, "Compressed Power–Surge for busy Brutes." This enabled me, without seriously impairing my chances with Portsmouth F.C., to cut down my nightly stint to a mere two and a half hours.

Bruce Bold sent me a signed photograph of himself dressed in a leopard–skin, in the pose of Rodin's *Thinker,* and a letter saying this might give me the idea of studying and Power–Surging simultaneously. I tried out this ingenious suggestion, but I found that studying in a pair of briefs was mighty cold work.

SIX

Please don't run way with the idea that all this time I had been out of touch with Maria. Far from it. Maria sent me a letter every week from Paris, in a large custardy envelope covered with flags-of-all-nations stamps. My name and address were scrawled right across it, green ink, in a kind of signwriting. Ivy, who examined all mail arriving at the hotel for every possible scrap of gossip, like a private eye, made cutting comments on these scented letters. In the end I was forced to invent a French Aunt Fifi, to clear my good name.

"A funny sort of Aunty she must be, sending you pages and pages of smelly news every week," Ivy leered each Friday.

She didn't possess a mind, only a receptacle for keeping suspicion in. "If it's really your Aunty, you won't be afraid of letting me read a page, will you?"

Not wanting to commit social suicide, I kissed her cobnut and ran off to the privacy of the bathroom, to devour the latest welter of foreign romance.

Our letters practically killed our love stone-dead, because the combination of Maria's English and my French could have easily landed either of us in court. Maria naturally took all my slang and idioms at their face value, with disastrous results. After the preliminary exchange of letters, our correspondence degenerated into dreary explanations of previous letters, and even to detailed analysis of the explanations themselves. In an effort to break the deadlock, I tried writing to Maria in the basic French of the guide books. My sole source of supply were sentences culled from the work, *On making the Grand Tour of Europe* – a volume full of requests to fetch the coach and four grey horses, and orders to the innkeeper to set up tankards of his finest porter.

By taking such phrases as, "The ladies would be obliged if Monsieur would engage to escort them to view the Bastille," I was able to work up passable sentences by substituting words more appropriate to my purpose direct from Collins' English–French Dictionary. I could discover no loophole in such a mathematically exact translation, but by return of post, and airmail at that, Maria fired back, "What in the name of the *bon Dieu* do you speaking about? Is it that you wish to love me or to insult me? Perhaps it is better for you, and it is better for me that we never should again make no more correspondences, that we should never again have no more meetings. Am I to be degraded in my own doorstep, on such monstrous fashions. Never allow me to hear of you more."…. and so on, for page after page, until the tears blurred my vision.

To make matters worse, and to be quite honest, I was seldom ever able to understand what Maria was driving at, whether she wrote in French or in English. Her most aggravating habit was that of telling me what my own words meant. My early letters had been abridged versions of *Boswell's Life of Johnson,* recording not only the hour by hour progress of my days, but also the most intimate details of my private life, such as cutting my nails, and espying a wasp on Mr. Pants bald patch. Now, in desperation, I tried a short letter written in French, thus: "Dear Maria, How goes it with you? It goes well with me. Yours faithfully, Peter."

We were three weeks wrangling over my sinister use of the term, "Yours faithfully," and in the end I not only didn't know what I had meant in that particular note, but I didn't even know what the words meant in any context. Finally, Maria sank me with all hands, by declaring that no man who wrote such a disgustingly brief letter could possibly love any girl.

By now my nerves refused to allow me to be drawn any further into controversy, so as a last resort, and no matter what Maria wrote, I always replied, "Dear Maria, Till November, Peter." This short repetition nearly drove her insane, but there was nothing more I dare do.

"Box, Pook," cried Mr. Pants. Mr. Pants and I were so

often in conclave inside his confounded box that we might have been a couple of buskers working a Punch–and–Judy show.

"I have a pleasant surprise for you today, Pook."

I tried to look excited, but failed. Mr. Pants's last pleasant surprise had resulted in Cashiers No. 4 and No. 5 suspending me by my legs, upside down, into the very bowels of the bank's hot–air heating system, in search of a penny which had rolled through the floor–grating. As I could only stay down there in the stifling currents as long as I could hold my breath, I was hauled up filthy and semi–conscious, but clutching the coin by instinct.

"What do you want now?"

"Remember to sir me, Pook. Today I have arranged for you to superintend the burning of the rubbish bags."

Surely he didn't mean Lily and Beryl?

"What time does sir want me to go?" I asked sourly, still feeling the effects of the coin hunt in my lungs.

"Sir has decided on 3 p.m.," replied Mr. Pants, narrowing his eyes to slits. The bank had a mania for preserving all the contents of our waste–paper baskets in sacks which were stored in the cellar, rather like a housewife dumping the kitchen refuse in the front room to await the annual visit of the dustmen. The bank's excuse for this tremendous accumulation was that discarded envelopes, cigarette packets, and the paper Mr. Pants's bloater sandwiches were wrapped in, were too confidential to be exposed to the publicity of the normal garbage collection. Furthermore, there was the remote risk of the bank's losing a shilling postal–order or a tuppenny stamp beyond retrieve on the local tip. It was my job every evening to empty the waste–paper baskets into log–sacks, and store them against the annual sacrificial holocaust.

Consequently, whenever Mr. Pants shouted, "Rubbish! Pook, go down and search the rubbish bags for a missing cheque–stub," I would descend into the cellar where they were stacked, and sit down to read *Brute Strength* for half an hour. Even I wasn't that daft.

When Messrs. Lovejoy and Crittal's ancient lorry arrived, we loaded it up with the sacks, as though we had succeeded in growing an acre of potatoes in the bank's cellars.

"Now remember, Pook. See every scrap is burned. Don't fall in the fire, and if you value your life, *do not try to sell it* to a salvage firm. I can't think of anything else at the moment that even you can do wrong." Mr. Pants wasn't thinking hard enough.

He made me climb up to the summit of the pile and sit there, lest one precious sack should fall off *en route,* and bring ruin on the Zenith Bank by coming into the hands of some unscrupulous rubbish reader.

All went well until we came to the outskirts of the town, where the road to the paper–crematorium followed the River Cud. Mr. Lovejoy's antiquated lorry swayed ominously for a hundred yards or so, and then the whole caboodle fell into the river, including me. Mr. Lovejoy climbed out of his cab as though he were emerging from a bathosphere.

"The blasted steering–wheel come off," he shouted. I believed him if only because he was still clasping it, in about four feet of water.

"Just look at them sacks," he remarked. That was exactly what I had been doing, while it was still possible, because they were racing down the Cud, like Henley Regatta.

"You men got a permit to fish here?" The familiar tones of sleepless Constable Barrington, now cyclist, floated down to us. "I know your lorry's unroadworthy, Lovejoy, but don't dump it in the river." Constable Barrington never let up, anywhere, any time.

I left the two of them arguing, to report the loss to the bank. When I walked in the office, Cashiers No. 1 to No. 4 broke down and wept. Cashier No. 5 spluttered his cup of tea all over the counter. Mr. Pants's voice broke half–way through, into a hoarse soprano.

"What on earth has happened to you now, boy?" he hissed, eyeing my drooping Burton's Special with amazement.

"I got thrown into the River Cud, sir."

"Who in heaven's name had the good sense to throw you in there?"

"Nobody, sir. Mr. Lovejoy's lorry turned over, and the lot went in the drink."

"Goodness gracious. What happened to the bank's rubbish sacks? Were they safely burned?"

"Never mind the damned sacks; what about my suit?"

"What did you say, Pook? I trust I didn't hear you aright, you wretched boy."

"I said the sacks disappeared down the river, sir."

"Oh, my sainted aunt. Where to?"

"I dunno, sir. Wherever the Cud goes to, I suppose."

"Run home to change, Pook, and return immediately. We shall have to organize a search–party without delay."

Mr. Pants opened Head Office Instructions, which was his favourite reading material, but even that monumental work did not give a ruling on "Sacks, waste–paper, loss in rivers," despite the four pages it devoted to the subject in general. I took the precaution of staying so long to change that when I returned, it was too dark to go ahunting. All Mr. Pants could do was to inform the police – who knew anyway.

Some days later, I read in the *Echo* that the keeper of the Needies' Lighthouse had reported a mass of free–floating mines drifting south–west off the Isle of Wight.

Urgent postcards now began to arrive at the hotel, on which were printed messages from Uncle Fingelbaum inquiring if I had used the official stickers to post him my homework in, because he hadn't received any, and he presumed they had gone astray in the post. Apparently Uncle Fingelbaum was kicking his heels and chain–smoking up there in Hackney, for want of my exercises to correct, but truth to tell, if he depended on me for his employment he would soon be following the footsteps of Todders, before he asked Uncle Friendly the way to the Labour Exchange. It took me a whole evening to open the chest of books, because Uncle Friendly had nailed up the crate and then welded steel straps round it, as if he were sending me bullion. Ivy went round to the local garage and borrowed a pair of metal–shears for me to sever these bands. Under the lid was sufficient straw to cover Mrs. Ruck's carpet all over, as we proved by experiment. By way of compensation, I presented the crate to her to keep the coal in.

It took me another evening to sort out the books, the questionnaires, the instructions, and the complicated procedure for sending up my homework. Lastly, Uncle Friendly had enclosed a brochure like a telephone directory, in which he listed all the examinations he wanted me to take, after I had passed the Institute of Bankers'. It seemed that in his view, every bank–clerk worth his salt should also be a qualified surveyor, accountant, architect, and, if time permitted, a dispensing chemist. Also highly recommended were Almoner, and H.M. Prison Warder.

For those who, like Todders, were not quite ready to prepare for these examinations, Uncle Friendly offered Course No. 2, at only five shillings a week, which taught you to read and write.

The second half of the volume contained a collection of fascinating letters from grateful students, many of whom had found time to pen a few lines whilst controlling the destinies of the British Empire. The most remarkable testimonial (No. 26365. The original may be inspected in our files) was from a successful barrister, thanking Uncle Friendly for guiding him along the road to a career which he found a lot more congenial than his former occupation as itinerant kettle–mender.

Although I read the books as thoroughly as utter boredom would permit, nothing of the mass of facts which entered my head ever seemed to re–present itself when the homework sheets had to be filled up. Having struggled right through *The Economics of Private Enterprise* I was disappointed to see that my answer to a question on the purpose of the treatise said, "Prof. Jones sets out the economics of private enterprise at great length. He definitely states that inflation will put the price of everything up." Uncle Fingelbaum wrote back to say that, while he could find no error of principle in my answer, he begged me not to allow modesty to prevent me putting down greater elaboration of detail, if I could manage it, during a two–hour paper.

Another book was entitled, *What is Monetary Convertibility?* by Professor Kragy. If he didn't know, what chance had I?

When I joined the Uncle Friendly Society, my probationary period was just about up, so Mr. Putty belled me inside. I stood to attention, waiting to be fired.

"Now Pook, what have we here?" he began, thumbing through Mr. Pants's Gestapo *dossier* on me. I glimpsed phrases about sacks in rivers, and not saying "sir" on every other word.

"Has my mother-in-law's passbook returned from the farthest outpost of the Empire yet, Pook? The Fiji Islands, I believe." This was a cruel blow at such a moment. The old battle-axe had given Mr. Putty hell, through my not seeing Flag, "Foreign address cancelled. Send passbook to Kensington. *Great Care.*" Apparently, the sea journey to Fiji and back took several years.

"No, sir, not quite back yet, sir."

"Your record reads something like the *Police Gazette,* Pook. What have you to say for yourself? "

"I've done my best, sir, and no man can do more." This was my standard text to Mr. Pants, when he came trembling to my desk, totally incapable of speech, to throw some new catastrophe on to it.

I was very anxious to pass out of probation so I could relax my strict behaviour, because once one was "confirmed" on the permanent staff, nothing short of going on holiday with the bearer-bonds could get one the push.

"Mr. Balls says when he was a junior he used to sleep under the counter, sir."

"What the devil has that got to do with our discussion, Pook? "

I had found it good tactics when in trouble with seniors, to introduce some absorbing item of general knowledge, in an effort to stem the flood of abuse.

"Only that I'm glad I wasn't in the bank in those days, sir."

This was a carrot for Mr. Putty to start his own endless

reminiscences of a bygone age, during which I always dreamed about Portsmouth. Mr. Putty gave me an odd look.

"There is one thing in your favour, Pook. You appear to have a very influential friend at Court."

I prayed I had. Preferably the Prince of Wales.

"So by some inexplicable intervention of Providence, Head Office has decided to confirm you, and you may consider yourself extremely fortunate." I considered myself as requested.

"Thank you most sincerely, sir. I owe it all to you, sir," I crooned, bowing double. If circumstances required it, I could crawl with the best of them.

"Stand up straight, lad, and get your hair off your face. Now go and offer up the celebration pint at the *George.*"

"Would you do me the honour of joining me, sir?"

"Very kind of you, but I must ask to be excused on this occasion. Have you any more questions to put, before you leave?"

"Is it true you keep your golf–balls in the safe, sir?"

"Don't press your luck, boy. Be off with you."

Mr. Pants received the news that I was now irremovable, as though the doctor had told him he was changing sex. He said, "I don't know how you did it, Pook, but whatever the guilty secret is, let it die with you."

"Can I go on holiday now, sir?"

"No, you can't. Hop it."

Lily and I spent a celibate week preparing for the half–yearly balance. Each night I finished about ten o'clock, which forced me to slash my Power–Surge to two hours, and completely eliminated the tiny trickle of homework I sent to idle Uncle Fingelbaum. Actually, on balance day we squeezed in three days' work. First came the normal daily routine, then the extra graft of dividends, overdraft interest, bank charges, pensions, and a hundred other chores which swamped us every half–year. Next came the standing–orders for our customers' subscriptions, payable to every known society in the land. These bankers' payments were recorded on cards, and they came in solid blocks, a foot high. I gathered from them that our entire clientele belonged to the A.A. and the Prudential. Lastly, we had to balance the ledgers and rule them off.

At eight o'clock, Fork invited me to join him for a pint at the *George,* along with Mr. Balls and Cashiers No.1 to No.5, "to break up the long night," as he put it. Everybody bought a round except me, and then my colleagues kindly helped me back to the office, where I fell prostrate on the marble floor.

Total abstainer Mr. Pants shot up above his glass box like a Polaris missile, to see what the noise was.

"It's only Pook, sir. He tripped over the mat," Fork explained.

"Then why doesn't he get up? Has he gone to sleep again?"

"He's just getting up, sir," said Fork, trying to lift me up bodily, with the aid of the cashiers.

"Is he ill or something, Fork?"

"Oh, no, sir. I think he must be overtired."

Mr. Pants strode round the counter to examine me.

"Good grief, the lad's drunk," he exclaimed, his mind automatically searching Head Office Instructions, under the heading, "Insobriety of Staff."

Mr. Balls laughed beerily. "He'll be all right, sir. He had a pint or two, and the night air finished him off. Let him sit on his stool a minute and he'll soon get on with his work." Cashiers No. 4 and No. 5 put me on my stool, where I got on with my work by burying my face in an open ledger and groaning eerily.

Lily ran along with her little bottle of sal volatile. "Don't let the manager see him in this disgraceful condition, whatever happens," Mr. Pants commanded. "It's nearly time for supper, so try and sober him up by then."

It was the bank tradition for the manager to gild the pill of Balance Nights by having the staff upstairs for a blow-out supper, which was presided over by Mrs. Putty and her daughter. In preparation for the feast, Lily asphyxiated me with smelling salts while Fork held my head under the tap in the cloakroom with unnatural relish.

"Where is our Mr. Pook?" asked Miss Putty, when the

staff had penguined upstairs and assembled in dejected ranks, awaiting the signal to charge over to the buffet table and gollop everything in sight, like ducklings. Miss Putty was very beautiful, but unfortunately too short for me to add to my list. It had often puzzled me how a fiery man like the manager could have sired such a fascinating daughter, and I had resolved to ask him when next I needed a red-herring to divert his lashing tongue.

"Our Mr. Pook is just sprucing himself up for you, and he'll be here in a second, Miss Putty," drooled Mr. Pants, in his promotion voice. Actually I was still drying my long hair over the hot-air grill on the bank floor. Eventually I made a dramatic solo entrance, like Hamlet pondering the ghost.

"Oh, dear me, how terribly pale you are tonight, Peter. I'll get you a small brandy. You have been working too hard," cried Miss Putty. Mr. Pants burst out laughing. "I rather think it's his Power-Surge exercises, dear. He seems to look a very seedy Brute tonight – in fact it's driving him to drink."

I smiled sadly across to our chief clerk, and made a mental X on the side of his chin, exactly where my left-hook would embed itself.

Mr. Putty arose for the toast of the evening. "Are all your glasses charged, ladies and gentlemen?" I raised my small brandy at the ready. "I give you the Zenith Bank, and all who serve in her. I wish you a happy and prosperous voyage."

"Rhubarb, rhubarb," mumbled the crew, mutinously, and draining their grog ration. If Mr. Putty thought he was launching a ship, perhaps I should have told him that I was ready to go over the side.

"And now, I give you the Directors of the Zenith Bank," he said.

"Now, ladies and gentlemen, perhaps you will be so good as to partake of a little refreshment," announced Mrs. Putty, extending a refined hand in the direction of the festive-board, as though it had escaped our notice so far. The ranks shuffled forward in a solid phalanx of appetites, and as a latecomer I had to use my Cudford United tactics of shouldering through to goal. The entire staff were shovelling sandwiches into themselves with racing jaws, as if the Siege of Paris had just been lifted. All except Lily, whose tap–washer mouth was a serious handicap on such occasions. She was inserting asparagus into it.

"Are you feeling better now, Peter?" Miss Putty called out from the safety of the fireplace. I nodded my head vigorously. Speech was impossible if one was to compete with my fellow vultures. I had already taken the precaution of holding a plate of sausage–rolls immediately below my mouth, which I kept pushing in two at a time, and swallowing them whole. Even then predatory claws snatched some away, like seagulls round a kind old lady with biscuits. Talk about feeding the five thousand!

When the dishes had been cleared beyond the need of washing up, Mr. Pants proposed the toast of the combined Putty family in his potential manager's voice. This was drunk with considerable enthusiasm by the red–nosed assembly. Then we filed back to the night–shift, a burping mob of dyspeptics. Miss Putty laid a detaining hand on my bulging bicep, and said, "Are you sure you're well enough to go down, Peter? I've never seen you looking so ill, and usually you're bursting with energy." I was now bursting with hiccups. Lily thundered by with the whooping–cough.

"I'll pull through, thanks awfully, Miss Putty. In fact, I was wondering if you would care to. . . ." We never knew if she would care to, because Mr. Pants crept up. "Allow me to assist our pale young friend back to his work, which is all behind schedule, dear Miss Putty." He assisted me with a vicious grip round the back of my neck. "Good night, and many thanks, Miss Putty," I smiled. "Good night, Peter. Let me know how you are tomorrow."

"Come along, Peter; lean on me, poor boy," chuckled Mr. Pants. As we descended the stairs, his grip tightened. "I want no more nonsense out of you, you gutty little Casanova. Get stuck into that work of yours – you're delaying the whole office," he gritted.

Antony and Cleopatra themselves would have given up, if Mr. Pants had been around at the time.

Downstairs, the great hall rang with the chanting monks in search of innumerable differences in the ledgers.

"Has the post gone off yet, Pook?" yelled Mr. Pants above the dirge.

"Not quite, sir," I replied, staring in horror at the Mount Pleasant sorting office which had accumulated round my desk.

"Great Scott, man, the last post goes at midnight." This news failed to flood my soul with ecstasy. I should be lucky to catch tomorrow's.

"Everybody drop everything and help with the post," bellowed Mr. Pants, rolling his eyeballs in anguish when he saw my chain of Alps all over the floor. The chanting wound down to just a piping solo from Lily to Beryl, as the staff shuffled round to do the post.

The open envelopes were laid out in thirty–feet columns along the desks, while I ran along them with a wet distemper brush to moisten the gum. A similar process enabled us to affix the stamps, mass–production fashion. This was repeated with the passbook envelopes, after each one had been weighed on my brass scales. Finally, Fork and I entered up every one in the Post Book, as though we were writing shorthand.

"Hurry, hurry, men. You needn't put sealing–wax on them, just for this once," cried Mr. Pants, whose life was moulded by Head Office Instructions and the office clock. Fork and I ran all the way to the station, in time to see the last train leaving. The Head Office Letter had to catch it, or else we did.

"That's torn it," wailed Fork, whose life was rapidly shaping like our chief clerk's.

"Shove everything in the G.P.O. and chance it," I ordered.

"But what about the H.O. Letter? Pants will want to see the receipt."

"Say you lost it in the dark, or you swallowed it acciden–tally. If we take the Letter back, the old fool is just as likely to make me cycle up to Lombard Street with it."

When we returned, Mr. Pants was so bogged down in toil that he forgot about the receipt for once.

"How are you enjoying Balance Night? Looks as if you'll have to sleep under the counter after all, Pook," leered Mr. Balls, who loved working late on account of his wife. I once met her, and that was the only time I ever did voluntary overtime.

"Put your silly head in the ink, Balls," I hissed, safely out of probation.

"You cheeky young monkey, I'll report you to the chief clerk."

"And I'll tell him how you cooked the overdraft decimals," I grinned. Mr. Balls retired hastily, and buried himself in *"ha to hum."* His decimal calculations, which governed the interest payable on overdrafts, were notorious for two things. Firstly, nobody else could decipher them, and secondly, they were wrong anyway – as a constant flow of customers willingly testified.

Tucked away at the end of the counter was a glass partition, known to us as "Lunatics' Corner," where the cashiers gratefully escorted dissatisfied clients to be pacified by Mr. Lecher, and hidden from the manager. When a customer had a complaint, he was led to Lunatics' Corner to cool off and regain the normal use of his faculties, while I went in search of Mr. Lecher. Very often these clients had already wasted half a day failing to penetrate the maze of obstacles set up by our telephone system, so in final desperation they rushed gibbering into the bank, demanding to see the manager. Of all our vast staff, this was the one man they had no chance of meeting. My drill was to say, "I'll bring the manager at once, sir." This lulled them into a feeling of new hope. In practice, I had to leave them as long as possible to simmer down, before I asked Mr. Lecher, who detested grumblers, to visit Bedlam and handle them as diplomatically as possible. The whole object was four-fold. To mollify them with servile flattery; to stop them taking their account away from us; to prevent, at all cost, their seeing the manager; and, most important of all, to get rid of them.

The entire staff listened gleefully when Mr. Lecher disappeared into the Asylum. First would come the shouting and hammering, as the frantic customer threw a fit. This was the cue for all of us to call out loudly and drop ledgers, to drown the noise for the manager's benefit. Then Mr. Lecher would commence laying on his oily diplomacy to quell the uproar. After ten minutes he would have the customer talking coherently and calmly, and at the end of the half-hour the client would emerge from Lunatics' Corner a complete cure, with Mr. Lecher's arm around his shoulder and Mr. Lecher's Woodbine in his mouth, all chuckles and goodwill.

Mr. Lecher got so much practice in this soothing art that some customers actually wrote us letters of apology, later, for being so bad-tempered over, say, temporarily losing a mere hundred pounds to another client's account. Once again, these letters had to be screened from Mr. Putty by every trick in the book, until I began to wonder if the manager was just our social figurehead, far above the carnage of our daily banking routine. Probably I was wrong. I usually was.

At one in the morning Mr. Pants mercifully allowed the girls to go home, and cruelly snatched me out from between them, at the very front door. "You don't sneak away yet, Pook. I'm up to all your dodges, you know," he gloated. We struggled on with the bewildering mass of journals and forms.

With its modern outlook, the bank had installed one Borroughs' adding-machine in the office, to save me wearing out my fingers with counting. Set in the back was a toilet-roll, which unwound as we imprinted figures on it from the ledgers, often extending to a length of several yards. When you arrived at the end of the ledger, you pressed a button and the machine said *"Grrr-clunk,"* and registered the sum total on the end of the unwound toilet-roll. Except on my first use of the machine, when it said *"Grrr-Jink,"* and registered zero.

On Balance-Night, everybody wanted to use *The Privy,* as we had christened the computer, so we formed a queue beside it, as though we were waiting for the one-and-nines at the *Troxy.* Appalled by this waste of man-hours, Mr. Pants came striding round to organize the superior system of a written waiting-list. Mr. Pants was a born organizer, and he pinned the roster on the notice-board. I observed his name was first, and mine was last.

"How can you be first, sir, when you weren't even in the queue?" I demanded indignantly.

"Hold your insolent tongue, Pook. That list is in order of seniority, and it is time you learned that sub-managers do not queue for anything. Of course, you will never have read it, but the good book says, 'The first shall be last,' and that includes you."

"Well, that's an undemocratic rule to put in Head Office Instructions, I must say", I grumbled. Mr. Pants always made me feel frustrated and ignorant. Worst of all, the floor kept swaying.

"Are all the ledgers proved wrong, Mr. Lecher?" inquired the chief clerk, through his porthole, later on.

"I'm afraid so, sir – all except *'wiz to zut'.*"

"*'Wiz to zut?'* That's Pook's ledger, isn't it? Did he get it right himself?"

"No, sir. He hasn't started it yet."

"At this time of night? Why not, Mr. Lecher?"

"He's lost it!"

"Lost it? Damnation take the boy; no one could mislay a thing that size."

"I agree, sir, but he has managed to find a way."

"Bless my soul. Perhaps he's eaten it. *Staff!* everybody search for *'wiz to zut,'* immediately." The staff went into search pantomime. Lily looked for it in her handbag. All she found was her lipstick, which she put on by inserting the stick in her mouth and revolving it, pencil-sharpener fashion. Loyal Lily had crept back into the office to help me get away before daybreak.

"I can't see Pook joining in the hunt, Mr. Lecher," said Mr. Pants.

"No, sir; he can't very well, at the moment."

"Why on earth not?"

"He's being ill in the toilet, sir."

Later still, Mr. Lecher reported, "I think they've found Pook's ledger, sir."

"Where was it located?"

"I believe Mr. Balls was sitting on it, sir," replied Mr. Lecher, trying to hide a grin. "Also, they've found Pook, sir, and he asked them to find out if there is anything in Head Office Instructions about dying in the bank's toilet. He says that if it's in order, he'll do it; otherwise would the staff carry him outside to the nearest gutter. I am to tell you personally that he does not want to infringe any more regulations, as his time is short."

Even Mr. Pants had to join in the laughter with his colleagues.

So it went on, all through the night of terror. Mr. Pants finally hauled down his flag just before 3 a.m. "We'll have to square off tomorrow night," he announced. "Clear up now, and let's call it a day." He would have been shocked to hear what the men were calling it. I stood in the banking-hall, with a head like a treacle-pudding. "Good-night, Pook. I want to see you here at 8.30 sharp, tomorrow morning," he blared.

"Then I don't have to come in today that's already started?" I asked in good faith.

"Soon you'll come the clever-cuts with me once too often. Watch your step, lad. *Cave canem.*"

I arrived home far too exhausted to be evenly remotely interested in Power-Surge, but during that week I managed to write a letter to Bruce Bold, confessing my alcoholic orgy and inquiring if it would retard my Surging beyond repair, with particular reference to Portsmouth F.C. He sent me a stern rebuke, which, while not actually excommunicating me from the Cult, warned me never again to fall into outer darkness. For good measure, he explained to me that the body requires fifteen days to recover from such debauchery, as against twenty days in the case of sexual indulgence, and even these calculations were based on the assumption that one repented with double Surging during the cleansing period. In a *P.S.,* he reminded me that my subscription was overdue.

SEVEN

Mr. Lecher was captain of the bank cricket team, for which I played as demon bowler. It seemed our matches were more an excuse for a real beer up afterwards, than for a display of the finer arts. It's a funny thing, but you can't disguise bank-clerks, even in white flannels, because we still looked like bank-clerks, but wearing decorators' overalls.

When we played Westminster Bank, we faced the notorious fast bowling of David Goldberg. He based his whole cricket career on Harold Larwood, whom he referred to as "that medium-fast fellow." I was secretly jealous of Goldberg, because not only could he bowl much faster than I could, but he waltzed through his Bankers' Institute Examinations like a boy Newton counting change for peasants. When we were in the examination hall, I was delighted to notice him dozing off about half an hour after the commencement. I chivvied him about it afterwards, but he said, "I was not asleep. Having finished the paper, I was just passing the time by working out some chess problems in my head."

This annoyed me because I had fought every second of the three hours, and could have done with another three.

"I bet you owe it all to Uncle Friendly," I replied.

"Oh, dear, no. I just borrowed the set books from Francis, and glanced through them. The *Practice and Law of Banking* one I flipped through twice, just to be on the safe side, because I found myself a bit rusty on the Mercantile Law aspect."

I thought, we've got another bighead here. When the results were published, he was top entrant in all England, and took the Sutton Award for Accountancy.

I was very doubtful whether Portsmouth would approve of my playing any game with a crowd of weedy clerks, who might ruin my style by bad example. Or Goldberg might cripple me for life. However, I sportingly joined in the fun of village cricket, and a good time was had by all until I went in to bat.

Mr. Lecher received the batting order from that born organizer, Mr. Pants, whose infirm body would only allow of acting as scorer. Consequently we batted in strict order of seniority. Not that it made much difference, because Goldberg's terrorizing assault kept our men going in an unbroken relay trek from the wicket to the pavilion, like sentries walking their post. All except Cashier No. 5, whom we were obliged to carry off stunned.

Eventually I took guard, and Goldberg leered at me with a look of sadistic pleasure. "I'll teach you to punch me on the Local Exchanges," he called out. Then he proceeded to walk off the field. When he arrived at the boundary, he turned round slowly to start his run. I watched his minute figure leave the sight-screen in a long loping stride. As he grew bigger, so his run worked up to a thrilling gallop. In the stillness of the hot afternoon I could clearly hear his boots thrumming over the turf *derrom, derrom, derrom, derrom, derrom* – just like the finish of the Derby. The field crouched in anticipation of my wicket. I drew my head into my body, tortoise fashion. At last he reached firing point, where he appeared momentarily as a flashing X, before hurling the ball down to me, closely followed by his airborne body following through. I got a micro-second blur of the projectile approaching my direction, and then it was gone with a "phit" – just as I ducked instinctively.

"All right, Pook, you can get up now. It missed you. Four runs though," Fork called from the other end.

"Did I hit it?"

"Of course not. No blighter touched it. Went straight through to the boundary." This was the peculiar thing about Goldberg's specials. You were either out, or four runs to the good, even though the deputy wicket-keeper and a longstop stood practically together among the spectators. Francis was standing in for the regular wicket–keeper, who had been working left–handed since the last match Goldberg played in, owing to a broken arm.

"That will be enough of the showing–off, Goldie. Play fair. Remember, I'm bowling when you go in," I yelled furiously. Portsmouth would never sign me on with a cricket–ball lodged in my body, beyond extraction.

"Ah, Peter, it's my turn now to call the tune. I don't forget last month," he jeered. This feat of memory concerned a little personal bodyline play on my part, when, having given up all hope of getting Goldberg out, I made no bones about the matter, but simply threw the ball straight at his head.

"Eye on the ball, and glance it to leg," Fork advised, from the safety of the other end.

"Shut up, you damned fool," I snarled.

A faint call of "Play" wafted across the ground from the midget figure of Goldberg, down by the River Cud. Then he was sprinting noiselessly in the distance. Soon I heard *derrom, derrom, derrom, derrom, derrom,* as he galloped towards the field of play, gathering momentum with every hoof. I tucked my face behind a shoulder, crouched low, and swung the bat with all my Power–Surge strength. *"Clack!"* My hands stung, as a shock–wave ran up the arms and all over my frame.

"You rotter, Goldie, you've busted my bat," I cried holding up the handle, from which the blade dangled by a binding–cord as though I had caught a large fish with a very small rod.

"What's more, you're out. Clean bowled," said Goldberg, grinning triumphantly. My leg–stump was being brought back to its mates by the longstop.

"Oh, no, he's not. It was a no–ball," decreed umpire Lecher belatedly. Mr. Lecher was not going to let his side collapse without a struggle. Goldberg gave Mr. Lecher a friendly smile, without a word of protest. He did not seem to mind going on with the game in the least. As he passed me he whispered, "Just as well; I've not got you yet. I can wait." He began his long hike to the river, and I could see he was working himself up to a new pitch of revenge by massaging his bowling arm and polishing the ball on his trousers till it shone.

"We'll never finish the match if you keep taking such a stupid long run," I called after him.

"I will. You'll see," he answered casually.

This time I really was scared, because when Goldberg came pounding the earth towards me, I glimpsed his face. For a fleeting second I was back in the *Troxy,* petrified with watching *Trampled to Death!* (Lily had forced me to see this blood-freezing drama from our usual seats at the base of the screen, right in front of the flailing hooves of three thousand head of buffalo, whose frothy nostrils syphoned steam all over me in glorious technicolor. To add to the suspense, I knew that Molly, the heroine, lay unconscious, bound, and gagged, only a few feet behind me, while her simple-minded lover was playing poker in a saloon back in Arizona. At the climax of the stampede, Lily screamed with joyful terror as the herd fixed their blood-shot eyes on us, and finally engulfed us. I shut my eyes just as I was going down under a raging sea of beef and horns, and was compelled to rush past poor doomed Molly to the refuge of the Gents).

Goldberg's face had supreme effort written all over it. His mouth was wide open, teeth bared, and his head was flung far back. That's all I remember. When I came to, I was lying in the pavilion beside Cashier No. 5, who told me Doctor Mernst had been in and sewed my left ear on for me.

"He was ever so quick, and very few stitches," he said, enjoying the details. "Reminded me of sail-making."

"Where is he now?"

"Outside, watching us field."

"I was out then?"

"Oh, yes. Even Lecher couldn't cover that up. You were draped over the top of your stumps like a towel. Mr. Pants put you down as 'Retired hurt.' Sounds better."

The final score-board read, Zenith Bank 16. Westminster Bank I27. Goldberg, not out, 119. That boy would have played for England, had he not been handicapped with brains.

After the match, he came inside to say, "Sorry about your ear, Peter. I wouldn't have had it happen for the world, you know that."

"That's O.K., Goldie. It's just the luck of the draw. I would have done the same for you." I was British, if nothing.

"I'm afraid I'm losing the old touch, Peter. I was aiming for your nose."

I invited Goldberg to play centre–half next time the Zenith Bank played Westminster Bank at soccer, where I could really carve him up. He declined, on the grounds that he did not hold with blood sports. Afterwards we became firm friends, and he often helped me with my exam work. So much so, in fact, that I obtained my first success after only three years. It was a pass in English.

The ending of my probation entitled me to a bank–account, wherein my monthly fiver was credited before the bank proceeded to take most of it away again. Much to Mr. Balls's annoyance, I inspected this account in the staff ledger every few hours.

"Shove off, Pook," he remonstrated. "The blasted page won't run away."

"I don't suppose it will, but I don't want you mucking it up like you do the customers. Hey, what's all these amounts debited to it?" I screamed, alighting on two items specified as *Pen.* and *Ins.*

"That's your contributory pension deductions, and your life insurance premiums. They go in every pay–day. Now buzz off."

"Well, that beats the band, I must say. I'll see Pants about it. Nobody can snaffle my money without my signature. And what's all these decimal figures you've put down and crossed out and blotted all over the auction? I haven't got an overdraft."

"That's the five per cent interest you get on your balance, you ignorant perisher. Now push off." I pushed off to Mr. Pants's box.

"How is it that I'm paying pension money, sir?" I demanded, when Mr. Pants had come back to earth from reading

Head Office Instructions.

"You want a pension at sixty, don't you? Well, this is how you get one. Every month the bank, in its wisdom, takes some of your salary to go towards it. Not that you will ever live to see it, the way you're carrying on, but at least it will support your penniless widow."

"But I don't care about when I'm senile, sir. I need every cent I can lay my hands on, right now, and that's little enough, lor' knows."

"Head Office think otherwise, Pook, so don't argue. The bank is only guarding itself against having you on its hands later on, destitute. Besides, you should overcome poverty by quelling your lurid desires."

"I thought the Compulsory Contributory Pension Scheme was voluntary, sir."

"Please don't be more ludicrous than usual, Pook. It irks me."

"Why am I insured for £250, sir? I'm not a film star, am I?"

"You certainly are not. A very true observation, although sometimes I think you are more cut out for the stage."

"I would like to have gone on the stage, sir, but acting and football don't mix. It's like banking and happiness."

"Your life is insured for £250, not because you personally are worth a light, but because Head Office Instruction 857 orders you to be. Now go and do some work. No, wait a moment, I have a pleasant surprise for you."

"You are going to send me on holiday, sir?"

"No, I am not, and if you dare mention that word again, I'll run you straight in to the manager. You have been warned for the last time. However, I am going to send you to Aston, on temporary relief."

"That will be a relief, sir."

"You don't realize how true that is. Now, the manager of our Aston branch has had a stroke."

"How did he have that, sir? "

"I don't know, Pook, unless you have been anywhere

near him. What matters is that you have been selected by Mr. Putty to go there."

"But surely I couldn't do the manager's job, sir?"

"Couldn't you really? How surprising. Then perhaps you would be content to do the junior's duties instead?"

My selection for the posting had come about this way. Staff Department advised us that Aston branch required a relief man immediately, whilst their manager was in a nursing-home. This was a blow to Mr. Pants, because we were under-staffed at the best of times. Mr. Putty said to him, "I don't care what kind of clerk they want, they're going to get Pook. I'd send him even if they were calling for a midwife."

"Now, Pook, listen to what I have to say," continued Mr. Pants. "This special posting is an honour for you, and so, if you queer anyone's pitch at Aston I shall not hold myself responsible for what happens to you afterwards. Be warned, lad."

"You can rely on me to do my best, sir, and no man can do more," I replied, flushed with unaccustomed honour.

"That's exactly what I'm afraid of. I can't quite make out what causes you to be so repulsive to other people. An interesting psychological question, I should say."

"I suppose it's just a gift, sir. Either you've got it or you haven't," I philosophized cheerily. "But what about the match with Sayling Shipyard Rovers, on Saturday?"

"I don't doubt but that you will find a way to be there in good time, my boy. Now beat it."

That afternoon, I wrote to Bruce Bold advising him of my temporary address, and bade a sad farewell to my colleagues. Nobody answered.

Arriving at Aston by miniature railway, I sauntered through the village to locate the bank. It proved to be a small building which had obviously been a sweetshop before our Premises Department snapped it up. Inside, it was not much bigger than Lunatics' Corner back at Cudford. I was rather surprised to knock on the door and see it opened by a pretty maid, as though it were early-closing day at *Lyons.* I put her on my short list, and walked in.

"Mr. Hut says you're to go straight up," said Tilly, the maid, raising her eyes to the ceiling. Up I went. I let Tilly go first, so I could have a look at her legs.

"You would be Mr. Pook, hey?" said Mr. Hut. I handed him the introductory plank, without which nothing was possible in the Zenith. He introduced me to Mrs. Hut, and numerous children. "I call these my little sheds," explained Mr. Hut, wittily.

"And very often, his little watersheds," added his wife. "You must be absolutely starving after the journey, so I've put up a little something for you."

"Very kind, I'm sure," I responded, in my best Hamp–shire.

When I had eaten the family's breakfast, Mr. Hut invited me to join him in a chair by the fire. The nude lady on the mantlepiece struck ten o'clock.

"Hadn't I better pop down and open up?" I asked, alarmed at not hearing Fork yell, "Doors."

"That's extremely nice of you to offer, but I expect our Mr. Rutter will look after things for a bit, Peter." Mr. Hut lit his pipe.

"Now, old chap, tell me all about yourself, and what's happening down at Cudford these days."

"This *is* the Zenith Bank, Aston, isn't it?" I inquired, wondering if I had got lost, and ended up at Butlins Holiday Camp.

"Of course, Peter. Why do you ask?"

"Oh, nothing, sir." After we had had a heart–to–heart chat, Mr. Hut suggested I might care to come down with him and meet the staff, while we were waiting for our elevenses.

"Naturally, we're a bit pushed, now Mr. Ronuk is away sick, but we manage to cope somehow. Your help will make all the difference to us from now on, Peter." I thought there must be a difference already, especially in the larder.

"This is our Mr. Rutter, Peter. Fred, meet Peter." Fred put down a magazine and shook hands. Directly our palms touched, I looked him in the eye and he nodded. He gave me his other hand, so that we shook hands as if we were doing a square–dance. Then our grips tightened, till Fred said, "Maximum Endurance Reached." I replied, "Relax from Maximum Endurance."

Mr. Hut scratched his head in astonishment at this performance. He little knew I had learned that Fred was a Regular Brute, and Fred had discovered I was a Perfect Brute. In PowerSurge, even a greeting was utilized to further the Cult, thus introducing practice into everyday life.

"I simply can't believe it. A 'P.B.' right here in the office. These things just don't happen to a fellow," cried Fred, with a glow of radiant joy on his face.

"Are you two Freemasons or something?" Mr. Hut inquired.

"Oh, Jim, it goes much deeper than that. You'd hardly credit it, but we're fellow–Surgers. How lucky can a man be?"

"Well, whatever that is, I hope you'll both be very happy together," replied Mr. Hut, trying to look impressed. "Anyway, I'm taking the dogs for a walk, but I'll be back for coffee. Take good care of Peter, and don't overwork him – he tells me he's been up since eight."

"O.K., Jim. Bring me back a granary loaf if you pass Mrs. Flits." Mr. Hut departed with four small horses on leads.

"It's just too good to be true, meeting you like this, Peter. I hope you won't mind working with an R.B."

"Of course not, Fred. In fact, you might do me the favour of not letting it affect our conventional bank seniority. After all, you're a fair bit older than me."

"Well, now you come to mention it, it's going to be difficult, but anyway, there's none of that old–fashioned bull here, thank goodness. I hardly like to ask, but I was wondering if you would help me pass my P.B. I've been working it up for months."

"You bet I would. How far have you got?"

"Only to Barbell 15, I'm sorry to say, Peter."

"Hm. Not too dusty though. I'll tell you what we'll do, Fred. Now we've got the chance, we'll work you up with an hour of Double–Surging every day. How does that strike you?" Fred pretended to swoon with bliss.

"Wonderful, Peter, absolutely wonderful. I've got Barbells 14, 15, 16, and 17, here in the strong–room. But will it work, with P.B. to R.B.?"

"Of course, Bruce Bold told me how to Surge down to R.B. for just such a case."

"What a pal you are, Peter, to be sure."

My favourite exercise in Double Power–Surge was No. 44, which operated like this: Both Brutes stood face to face, legs apart, and slowly isolated their neck muscles. Next, each Brute gripped the throat of the other with both hands, and on the command, "Surge Start," began to strangle him. As this particular exercise rendered it impossible to utter the second command, "Maximum Endurance Reached," the order was given by banging the feet on the floor, or sometimes, by sinking to one's knees, semi–conscious.

Having fixed up our new training programme, Fred asked me what I would like to do in the office, as a sop to the directors of the Zenith Bank.

"I always fancied myself on the counter," I said, modestly.

"Lovely idea. There it is – it's all yours. You'll find plenty of money in the till. We'll call you Chief Cashier."

"What will the rest of the staff say?"

"Who? Do you mean Mr. Ronuk? There's no one else."

"No one else? Only the three of us?" Apparently I had been wasting my time, down at Cudford. I began to practise sweeping up coins with the copper shovel.

"What happens if someone comes in, Fred?"

"Why worry. Wait till it happens. They either want to draw out, or pay in. In the unlikely event of a stranger barging in, I'll give you the nod. Just make a lot of noise with the shovel, and you can't go wrong."

At eleven o'clock, I said to Fred, "Doesn't anybody ever come in this place?"

"Of course they do, Peter. Just have patience, that's all."

I sat there, looking out across the High Street. At length I said, "Is it always like this, Fred?"

"Oh, no. This is market day, and the whole village is abustle. Ordinary days are rather slow.

At 11.15, I thought I had a customer, but it was a false alarm. Only Mr. Hut and his domesticated lions. Soon afterwards, Mrs. Hut and Tilly came down with a large tray, full of coffee, buns, cakes, and biscuits. We consumed the lot, around the fire. No wonder Mr. Ronuk had a stroke.

At noon, my first customer entered, dressed like a stage yokel. He began to laugh and talk dialect at the same time. I had no idea what he was saying, but it must have been extraordinarily humorous, because the tears ran down his brown, weatherbeaten face. Towards the end of his monologue, he put a naked duck on the counter scales, and pointed to the ceiling. Then he bowlegged out.

"Fred, was he an old Ukranian peasant, or something?" I asked in astonishment.

"No, of course not, Peter. That was Farmer Makin from Diddeldit. One of the richest men round these parts."

"Diddeldit? Where on earth is that?"

"Seven miles from here, right in the heart of the country."

"Well, what do I do with the poultry? Pay it in or put it in the safe?"

"That's his weekly present to Mrs. Hut. You'll get one soon."

At half past twelve, Fred suggested I go for lunch. "Don't hurry back, Peter. Have a look round the village. Lovely old church near the centre. The best pub is right next–door to us."

At three o'clock, we closed the bank doors, and Tilly brought down tea for the staff. I thought to myself, this is where I can eliminate the midday doughnuts and save money. By half past three Mr. Hut was worrying about my train home, and told me not to miss it. This really flabbergasted me. At Cudford, I would still be fighting the latecomers at the front door.

"That's very nice of you, Mr. Hut, but I can hardly leave

you two on your own like this,'' I protested.

"Please, Peter, don't worry about us. We'll be away in ten minutes. You see, we always have to stay late on market days."

I arrived back at Cudford by four–thirty, and, despite my fear of meeting Pants, I peeped through the bank windows. There they were, well and truly snowed under as usual. All the cashiers had their heads raised in chant, as they implored Providence to reveal the secrets of Mr. Balls's faulty ledger–keeping. Fork espied me from afar, so I gave him the old victory sign and scuttled off home.

"You got the sack?" said Ivy, who had never seen me in daylight before.

"Go jump in the lake, kid; I'm busy," I replied, in the romantic idiom of the time.

My short taste of Paradise at Aston rushed by far too quickly. It could not last. Even though I prayed every night for Mr. Ronuk's complete recovery by next year at the earliest, the day was rapidly approaching when I must leave and descend again to the grim reality of life at Cudford. We did not have customers at Aston; only life–long friends, relations, and sweet–hearts. Every day a little raven–haired gipsy of a girl paid in from the Co–op at eleven o'clock. As this happened to be coffee time, she learned to sit on my knee by the fire, and slowly sip her cup of *Red, White, and Blue* beverage while I ate the buns. Mr. Hut and Fred arranged for us to be married from the bank on Boxing Day, in order that we might consider ourselves as engaged and thus less likely to infringe Rule 642 of Head Office Instructions. Rule 642 gave one the impression that, though there might have been such a thing as sex during the Stone Age, the propagation of the species was now accomplished by Form 1497(f), do *not* fold.

The dreaded week of my departure arrived at last, and with it came torrential rains which kept our faithful circle of social callers away. To pass the time, Fred, who was the pride of the Aston Philharmonic Orchestra, played his mouth organ while Mr. Hut and I sang to it in our pub voices. We were loudly accompanied by the four wolves upstairs, who seemed to be under the impression that the pack had returned from the forest in search of them.

I bought a bottle of light ale from the *Travellers' Joy* next door to celebrate my departure, and borrowed three glasses. I was not risking an alcoholic orgy after the Balance Night catastrophe. Meantime the rain simply fell down, and it was rumoured that the River Cud was bursting its banks.

"There's a mighty lot of water in the Cud," I remarked to the landlord of the *Travellers' Joy,* as he handed me the three tumblers.

"Arr. Twouldn't be so bad if it stayed in it; trouble is, most of the durned stuff is out of it, lookee." Having learned some of the dialect, I was fast getting on equal terms with the local inhabitants and this is a free translation of what he said. As I left, I noticed him screwing a storm-board to the door.

"Expecting trouble?" I inquired, in fairly fluent Aston.

"Arr. Sure be, lookee. See that man-hole cover middle of the road, yonder? When 'e blows offen, watch out a tidy bit, yourn lookee."

Five minutes later, I heard *"bomf"* outside, and the cover shot up like a ping-pong ball on a gusher. Fred rushed out with our own storm-board, as the High Street rapidly became a tributary of the Cud. "Flood Drill," he shouted. We piled all the books and everything movable upon the desks.

Mr. Hut came down in waders, and said, "I'm afraid this is going to be a bad one, Peter; we're very low-lying down here in the valley. Lloyds Bank have already got their punt handy, just in case. I can't phone either the Midland or the National Provincial, and that's a bad sign. See if you can catch your train, Peter. Better phone them first. I've got some spare waders for you."

The station-master reported that his railway-lines had last been seen an hour ago, and now they were well and truly submerged. He advised me to take a canoe if my journey was essential. Next I rang the bus depot, but all I got was a continuous gurgling noise. "Sounds like the bus depot has sunk," I told Mr.

Hut.

All we could do was to watch the water rise over the pavement and up the storm–board. The rain lashed down in straight lines, like silver rods. Meanwhile, Fred showed me the previous high–water mark pencilled on the office wall. I stared at it, and felt glad I could swim. Fred placed a second storm–board on top of the first, and still the water rose. By five o'clock the level ran over the top of our defences, just like a weir, and slowly the office water–level equalized with that in the High Street. Fred put on waders and paddled off home. "Thank goodness I live on a hill," he chuckled.

Mr. Hut and I retreated upstairs and looked out of the bay window at the scene below. It was Venice with trees. That night I slept in the spare–room, next to Tilly, the maid. Through the thin partition I could distinctly hear her undressing. I knocked on the wall, and asked her if she was frightened. "Not now I've bolted my door," she replied. This riposte led to a lot of small–talk between us.

Next morning I phoned Mr. Pants, to break the good tidings to him. The water–logged cable, combined with the Zenith Bank's system of telephonic defences, did not help matters very much.

"You're *what*, Pook? *Where?* How deep? The trains can't *what?* I ought to *which?* Midland Bank gone *where?* Speak up, boy. . . ."

No wonder our customers rushed into Lunatics' Corner.

"The Cud has done *what? Who's* all wet? What the devil are you whispering about? *Which* burst? *Who's* floating in the strong–room? Shall you *swim?* Send a *boat?* What does it say in Head Office *what? ...*" By now our customers had my deepest sympathy.

"Belt up a second, you deaf old codger," I shrieked, furiously. Of course, that was the bit he did hear.

"I'll write a letter and tell you then," I shouted, banging down the phone in disgust.

"My word, you do go at it hammer and tongs, down at Cudford," said Mr. Hut, admiringly. He had listened in with rapture, to Mr. Pants's "Return at once, mother worried," appeal.

"Yes, I'm afraid we do, Jim, but the trouble is, we're like it all day and half the night." Mr. Pants was exhausting in any form.

Next day, Mr. Pants rang me from a phone–box. "Can you hear me, Pook? I can hear you very clearly, so perhaps I'm not such a deaf old codger after all. When do you intend to stop playing the fool and return to duty?"

"As soon as the water subsides, sir."

"Well, it's a funny thing we're not flooded at Cudford."

"I'm not surprised, sir. I reckon we've got all your water up this end."

"Is the bank open?"

"Yes, sir. Ten till three every day."

"I am well aware of the opening hours, wretched boy. I mean, has anyone been in."

"Only a swan, sir. Just looked in, and swam off."

"I can see that you and I are due for a long chat when you do return, Pook. What are you doing now?"

"Playing cards, sir."

"Who with? Not with Mr. Hut, no doubt?"

"No, sir. With Tilly, the maid. I play with her very often."

"I wouldn't put it past you, Pook. I suppose it did not occur to your muscle–bound brain to take advantage of this time, and swot up your studies?"

"It did, sir, but they're down at Cudford."

"But I expect you did not forget to take your muscle manuals? "

"Well, sir, I did happen to find a couple in my suitcase."

"And Tit–Bits' Football Annual?"

"Yes, Jim."

"My name happens to be Claude, but I'll thank you to call me plain sir."

"O.K., plain sir."

"Watch it, Pook. Remember what happened to Abraham Lincoln."

Just then we got the three pips, and Mr. Pants couldn't get the receiver down quick enough.

"I expect you back the moment the first train gets through, Pook. Mark it well, and act accordingly." Crash, went the receiver.

We were marooned four days before the trains got back to normal, and I waited an extra day so that the carriages would be well aired. I bade a sad farewell to Fred and the Hut family.

"I can never thank you enough for working me up to Barbell 18," cried Fred as we did the double-handshake.

"Keep at it, Fred, and you'll have your P.B. within weeks."

I kissed Tilly a long adieu in the privacy of the scullery, and she cried a little.

"I'm not looking forward to them long lonely nights," she whispered as we parted.

EIGHT

When I had returned to Cudford and survived Mr. Pants's welcome–home celebrations, I tried to get myself posted perm–anently to a small rest–home such as I had located at Aston. Unfortunately, Mr. Putty pointed out that men of my calibre were needed where the fighting was thickest, and that Cudford would probably be my residence for the rest of my working life.

"It's not as though I don't love it here, sir," I explained to him, in my career voice, "but in a small branch I can get so much more varied experience."

"I've heard all about the kind of experience you gained at Aston, Pook, and I can only pray there will be no disastrous consequences following your confinement in Mr. Hut's flat. We sent you there to help out while Mr. Ronuk was ill, not for stud services. In future I shall sleep better if I send Mr. Fork."

During the lunch–hour I saw Goldberg walking along the street hand–in–hand with a young Greta Garbo. I passed by, shaking Goldie's hand enthusiastically, but he did not seem to know me. I simply stared at the beautiful young lady until I walked into a pillar–box, which rammed my chest like Ginger Jones. Suddenly I felt a wave of friendship for Goldberg, which I displayed that afternoon, when we met in Barclays Bank to exchange the local cheques.

"Don't you dare hit me today, Peter. I've had enough of it," said Goldberg, whose memory had now returned to him.

"Aw, where's the old sense of humour, Goldie boy, complaining just because I gave you a friendly dig? "

"I don't call a full–blooded punch in the navel a friendly dig, so pack it up. You're getting too big for your boots, lately, Peter."

"Have a pear–drop, Goldie; any colour you like." I offered him Lily's latest bag of dyed sugar.

"Thanks, Peter. You don't seem your old self today, somehow."

"I'm really nice underneath. People just misunderstand me, that's all. By the way, that was a smashing Jane I saw you with lunch–time. Wouldn't mind one like that myself, Goldie."

"I thought I saw your face go green. Yes, she's up from Mendithorpe for a few days."

"Can't figure out what she sees in you, though. Is she your sister? "

"No, chum; far from it. And what she sees in me is brains and culture. Not every girl is looking for a poor man's Tarzan, as you'll discover when it's too late."

"Has she got a girl–friend for me, Goldie boy?"

"You're lucky, as usual. It so happens she has – a lovely girl who'd just suit you. I'll fix it up if you like. Shall we make up an awesome foursome, or would you prefer a gruesome twosome?"

"It would suit me if we all went together, Goldie. Where shall we take them?" (Goldberg possessed the added attraction of a car.)

"We'll have a night out in Mendithorpe when they go back. You can pay for the petrol, to ease your conscience, Peter."

"It's a date, Goldie, you old devil."

Goldberg had a merchant–prince father who provided his son with a Bentley to help out with the income–tax, wherein Goldie figured as window–cleaner and van.

Flushed with victory, I returned to the bank and Lily's rotund charms. Suddenly the office went very dark.

"Looks like a storm is blowing up," I remarked to her.

"Don't be silly, Peter; it's only a lorry drawn up outside."

"Stationery and money–bags," yelled Fork, who had eyes by Zeiss. Fork and I went outside, where a man was pulling a green tarpaulin off a six–wheeled transporter, which was piled high with boxes and money–bags.

''That's the annual gift from the Stationery Department,'' Fork explained, ''and the silver and copper comes from our branches where the Gas Company pays in the meter collections. All we have to do is to unload it. Cash off first.''

The bank seemed to have an inexhaustible fund of the most unlikely tasks which it revealed to you gradually, in case you were feeling overcheerful. We relayed the cash–sacks down to the vault, where Cashier No. 5 checked every one on his spring balance. Mr. Pants stood guard, armed to the teeth with the regulation police whistle, to repel bandits.

The work made me sweat so much that I took my coat off. Mr. Pants cried, ''Pook, put your jacket on this instant. Whatever will the customers say, seeing you in a state of undress?''

'''You need a clean shirt,' I expect, sir,'' I quipped.

''Wretched youth, do you always laugh at your own feeble jokes? ''

''Usually, sir; they're the best ones I hear, around this place.''

''Grrr.''

Then we carried in the tea chests of stationery, like a couple of Mincing Lane porters.

''Why doesn't the bank give us a trolley for this sort of thing, Fork?''

''Shush, not so loud. Don't be stupid, Peter,'' whispered Fork, as though I had suggested going over to the Communists.

It was the duty of Cashier No. 4 to check and dispose of the stationery, which he did by reading the *Racing Outlook* while I forced the lids off the chests with hammer and chisel, and threw the contents into our forms larder. He acknowledged the completion of the work with the passwords, ''I'll get it all back tomorrow at Kempton Park.''

The next morning, at exactly half past nine, I saw a tall, thin man wearing a bowler–hat glide silently into the banking–hall. Halfway down his body was another bowler–hat, presumably a spare. By peering over the counter, I discovered that the spare was, in actual fact, on the head of a short ball of a man. This meant trouble, because it was my responsibility to ensure that the doors were bolted against the lunatic fringe until the ten o'clock starting gun. The entire office went quieter than the Cathedral opposite.

"Your till–keys, please, gentlemen," cried the tall job. My mind flashed back to the *Troxy and The Dying Teller,* which depicted the most gory bank robbery ever perpetrated. We saw two hold–up gangsters wipe out almost the entire staff with tommy–guns. The gallant manager, or bank president as his office door indicated, had been sawn in half by a spray of bullets just as he was raising the whistle to his lips, and it was clearly inferred that the typist had been ravaged. Lily enjoyed every moment of it, and this part in particular. The blood–bath in the banking–hall put me in mind of our Aston branch during the floods. Surely this was not going to happen to me in real life? Suddenly I felt too young to die, especially defending the bank.

I had always thought that if my time was up, I should end it on the football field, and probably at the hands of Ginger Jones.

Fork tiptoed up to me and hissed, "Panic Stations. Inspectors. Slip three bob in the stamp–box quick."

All the cashiers locked their tills, handed over the keys, and stood to attention, while the two inspectors checked to see if they had been secretly augmenting their salaries from the bank's stock–in–trade. I slid three shillings into the stamp–box for Fork, and ten shillings for myself.

Mr. Pants frightened me out of my wits by creeping up behind me and whispering, "Best behaviour, Pook. Go and wash your face; it may be your last chance."

During the two weeks we had the inspectors on our plate, the staff tiptoed about, and if they had to speak they whispered very low, as though the manager had passed on and nobody would take him away. We no longer threw the ledgers about like coal, but gently slid them on to our desks in case they cracked. This had a strange effect on customers who came in bawling and cursing as usual, to compete with the staff bedlam, only to discover with marked embarrassment that they were roaring in a silent retreat for the dumb.

"What on earth's the matter?" they whispered to the cashiers. "Inspectors," signalled the tellers, by forming the word with their lips and raising a warning finger. In order not to make the slightest noise, they shovelled up the silver in slow motion, and tenderly placed it in the paper bags coin by coin.

Mr. Putty even complained about my pen scratching.

I now had two more men to fetch and carry for, but they were very nice to me, particularly the round senior inspector, who seemed very interested in my physique – now threatening to burst through my Burton's Special. He kept muttering, "Fancy, all that muscle – just to hold a little pen."

His name was Mr. Groke, and he asked me if I were happy in my work. I nodded violently, and made conventional gestures of supreme bliss.

"Have you got laryngitis, lad? Can't you ever speak to me?" he demanded, with a puzzled frown.

"Please sit, I am not to make a noise,' I whispered, wetting his ear with my lips.

"Quite right, Pook, but you don't have to act as if you're working in a chapel. Tell me, have you any complaints?"

I made pantomime of utter content, and the facial expressions of those souls enjoying the Mohammedan Paradise. Then I fell into the deep reverie of one who is trying his best to find fault, once he has safely got there.

Mr. Pants glared at me from the fighting–top of his box. Nobody ever complained to inspectors, unless they were tired of life. I bent down to Mr. Groke's ear and hissed in fairy–speech, "My desk is a weeny bit drafty, sir."

This was an understatement. The desk was squeezed in between the doors to the cloak–rooms and the top of the strong–room stairs. I had a clear view of the rear wall of the office, but in winter it was like working on the Russian Steppes. I waited to be handed my cards.

"Draughty? Did you say your desk is draughty, lad?" boomed the inspector. My guilty secret rang round the block.

"I should damn–well think it was draughty," Mr. Groke continued, smoothing down his thin hair which the wind was blowing up. "It's a blasted tornado, that's what it is."

Mr. Pants was obviously about to burst a blood–vessel. I could visualize Mr. Putty and him in the background, jumping up and down like the Keystone Cops.

"It makes me feel a pain in the neck sometimes," I blurted out. Mr. Pants agreed wholeheartedly. He looked as though he could gladly break it.

"Now, Mr. Pants, can't you find a more civilized position for young Pook, than this bleak raft of a landing?"

"I'm afraid not, sir; you see, we've expanded so till there's not another spare inch." He turned to me, "Oh, Mr. Pook, why didn't you tell me you were suffering from a draught? That's what I'm here for, to look after your welfare. Poor boy, draughts are nasty, dangerous things, especially in the winter. Fancy you just putting up with it and never saying a word to me."

I thought it wisest to skate over that one.

"What wall is that, Mr. Pants?" the Inspector asked.

"That's the Co–op, sir. The other wall is the Home and Colonial."

"Then the only way we can expand is this way, back–wards. This lot will have to come down," said Mr. Groke, indicating the rear half of the bank with his hand.

Good grief, surely he wasn't going to demolish the building just for my neck?

"Yes, that's obviously the only solution, Mr. Pants. Ah, there you are Mr. Putty; I know you will agree with these vital structural alterations in the interests of your staff. Remember, a happy staff is an efficient staff. I'll put the whole thing in my report, and I'll get on to Premises Department about it when I return to London."

"Splendid, splendid. Capital idea, Mr. Groke. Abso–lutely first class," laughed the manager, tickled pink at the thought of having his bank knocked down about his ears. "High time we moved outwards, with business soaring up and up ever since the day I took over here on April 3rd, 1933."

"Just think, if it hadn't been for Mr. Pook's poor old neck, we shouldn't have had this piece of sheer good fortune. It's an ill wind ... etcetera," Mr. Pants chimed in, with his new inspec–

tors' chuckle. Mr. Groke looked at me. "I want to see a contented staff, so while we're at it, Pook, have you any further suggestions to make things more congenial for you here?"

Mr. Putty looked sabres at me. "Nothing else, sir, thank you very much," I replied, suppressing a dozen good ones for next year, including a posting back to Aston branch. I avoided my seniors for the rest of the day by every trick in the book.

Mr. Tarrow, the tall inspector, spent the two weeks checking every item in the bank, from the Cash Reserve to the J–nibs. I was so impressed by his thoroughness that I brought him the piece of pumice–stone from the washroom. "I think you overlooked this item, sir," I said. He gave me a long, queer look. Eventually, he remarked, "You *may* go a long way in the bank, Pook. Now I'll check your postage–stamps if you please."

They balanced, all but a halfpenny. Mr. Tarrow remarked, "Well, we won't bother to put that discrepancy in the Report, will we? Some juniors have been known to misuse the stamp money to buy buns and cigarettes, but I know you wouldn't be so dishonest, eh Pook? They start on the stamp–box and end up by emigrating with the High Value Package. I remember young Drode when they gave him seven years. He should have gone a long way in the bank, too."

I gave him the choir–boy face and said nothing.

"So far so good, Mr. Pook," he continued cheerily. "Now all that remains to be done is to check my little notebook. Ah, yes; the only query outstanding there is the passbook of Messrs. Cod, Lumpit and Sofa, No. 1 Account. May I see it, please?"

"I must apologize for not bringing it this morning, sir, but you shall have it directly after lunch," I told him.

Messrs. Cod, Lumpit and Sofa, all long deceased, was the name of our biggest account – a firm of estate–agents and auctioneers who conducted the weekly cattle–sales at Cudford Market, and ran the County generally. On average, the firm drew about fifty cheques a day on No. 1 Account, besides numerous cheques on Accounts No. 2 to 7. Being a large firm, they had special cheques printed for them, as big as a child's slate, and a passbook to match, similar to a family–Bible.

"You haven't brought it from where?" demanded Mr. Tarrow, who checked every statement back to one's childhood.

"From my lodgings, sir."

"And what, may I ask, is a bank passbook doing at your lodgings?"

"It's being got wrote up, sir."

"'Written up' please, please. Don't you yet know that it is a serious offence to take home the bank's property?"

"No, sir. All I know is that I can't possibly get it wrote up here, so I take it home every night, and Ivy calls out the cheques while I get it wrote up." I could smell trouble in Mr. Tarrow's voice.

"Who may Ivy be, pray?"

"My landlady's daughter, sir."

"Oh, save us! Mr. Pants, would you kindly spare me a moment?"

Mr. Pants was already sparing a moment by literally gargling with fury, close by. For some time now he had got into the habit of dropping everything and just listening in an anguish of suspense, every time anyone opened their mouth to me.

"Mr. Tarrow, how can I make amends for this inexcusable lapse on the part of this dreadful boy? Pook, haven't I told you a hundred times that everything in the bank is highly confidential? Haven't I told you a thousand times that nothing in the bank must ever go outside of it; not so much as a paperclip?"

Mr. Pants always seemed to be clearing his own yard–arm, and abandoning me to sink in flames.

"Yes, sir, you have, of course, but I got up such a stick that I couldn't very well do anything else."

"Couldn't you have had the sense, just this once, to come and tell me you were behind with your work, so I could have put another member of the staff to assist you?"

I usually acquainted him with this fact about once every hour.

"I know I should have done so, sir, but I didn't want the

burden to fall on others, sir.'' The boy-martyr was speaking.

Mr. Tarrow interposed with, ''Very well, Pook; at least you have been truthful, but never do such a dangerous thing again. With Mr. Pants's permission, I will ask you to run home and fetch the passbook at once.''

I disappeared as if by magic, and ran all the way back to the hotel, where I grabbed Ivy and between us we wrote up Messrs. Cod, Lumpit and Sofa's confidential transactions covering the past three days. When I returned to the office, Mr. Tarrow seemed satisfied, except for an inquiry to know if I wrote with a fork. However, I could not help noticing how carefully he checked my entries against the ledger figures.

There was no time to keep my date with Goldberg and his twin film-stars until the inspectors had departed, and the office had returned to its last fling of Cup Final atmosphere before the breakers moved in to demolish it, in order to accommodate my sore neck. At the first opportunity, Goldie and I drove down in the Bentley to Mendithorpe, where we called for Margaret and Dawn.

Before we rang the bell, Goldie said, ''You wait in the car; we don't want to scare the girls off before we start. And keep your eyes off Margaret, she's mine, chum. Not that I wouldn't just as soon have Dawn, but Margaret is the one with the dough, and our love has strong bonds binding us – Government Bonds.''

I told him that love was too sacred to be influenced by such mercenary considerations, but, nevertheless, I could see his point.

Margaret sat in front, all beauty and eyelashes, while Dawn got in the back with me. ''Don't be shy, Peter; kiss Dawn hallo,'' laughed Goldie, who was welcoming his wealthy Margaret on the same principle. I could not see much in the dark, but I could see enough to know that Goldie was a treacherous sort of friend, and due for the chop, because when Dawn turned her face for the introductory kiss I did not know exactly where to get in, amid such a lot of hat, teeth, and spectacles. I pecked her coldly on the nose, to be on the safe side, which protruded like a weather-vane. Surely it must be Margaret's spinster aunt,

I thought bitterly.

"Let's drive down to the New Forest," suggested the romantic Goldie, little suspecting his days were numbered.

"I've got a better idea, Goldberg. We'll all go home, I mean, we'll all go ice-skating," I replied, desperate not to spend the evening trapped in the Bentley with Dawn. The girls were thrilled by the idea, but not so Goldie.

"I suppose you're a marvellous skater and you want to show off as usual," he gritted. "Peter is Oilcan Harry and can do everything."

"Well, I must admit I'm pretty hot on ice, but there, I suppose it's just talent, and if you've got it there's nothing you can do about it."

"Tell us all about the cups you've won," said Goldie coldly; "We've got an hour to spare, and I could do with a good yawn."

"Please teach us to skate, Peter," the girls pleaded. That clinched the matter.

At the ice-rink, Goldie and I went into the changing rooms to lash on our hired skates.

"I shan't forget this dirty trick in a hurry," I told Goldie. "And if you like Dawn so much, why plonk her on me? If she's Dawn, then give me the dark any time." Goldie tittered all the while he was lacing up his boots.

The four of us assembled on the ice, hand in hand, and commenced the three-hour session of stumbling round and round in endless circuits of the rink, which we were young enough to regard as pleasure. Along we went, four abreast, playing a painful kind of all-fall-down. Dawn, who seemed to have collapsible legs, travelled suspended between us, so that her skates only touched the ice when she fell on it. We found that this method kept us upright longer.

After an hour of getting wet through, I said to Goldie, "Let's leave the girls a little while and liven things up a bit. We'll collect some of the fellows and make a whip."

"How do you mean, Peter?"

"Well, you get a dozen chaps going along holding each

other like a train, and then the front man swings round and the others follow. The fellow on the end is like the end of a whip, and he gets swung off like a stone from a sling. Get it?"

"Good idea. You organize it, and I'll go first on the tail, Peter."

When we got the chain going, I was on the tail to show them how to do it and Goldie was just in front of me. Directly the chain reached full speed, I called out, *"Swing,"* and I don't remember any more.

I was sitting on a bench in Mendithorpe Avenue, and when I got up I keeled over. Looking down, I discovered I had skates on my feet. Then I recalled having been to the ice-rink. I took the skates off, and walked down Clerkwell Road, which led to the stadium. There was the Bentley, and sitting inside were Margaret and Dawn.

"Oh, Peter, we've searched everywhere for you. Wherever have you been?" the girls exclaimed.

"Where's Goldie?" I gasped.

"In hospital. He's broken his leg near the ankle."

"Good God."

"They took him away by ambulance, and I went to tell his parents while Dawn looked for you. It was a big house and when I knocked, his mother put her head out of the window upstairs. I told her about Goldie, and she just said that it was pretty late, so she'd go and visit him tomorrow."

I don't remember any more.

When I awoke, I was lying in bed at the hotel. It was daylight and Ivy came in. There was a small meat-pie on the bedside locker.

"Hallo, Ivy. Is it late?"

"Don't talk, Peter, but I'm jolly glad to hear you, all the same. It's nearly evening. Now go to sleep until the doctor comes again."

"Who's the pie for. Me?"

"You ought to know, Peter. You've been harping about it all day, so I brought one up." I fell asleep, despite the pie.

When Doctor Mernst came, he asked: "Feel any pain,

Peter, or a bruise on your head?''

"No, Doc, not a thing. I feel all right, except I'm so sleepy.''

He felt my head all over. "Rather unusual; obviously concussion, but no bump or bruise,'' he mused to himself.

I slept the best part of four days; lovely deep dreamless sleep. I drank it in as though I had been up since birth. On the fifth day Doctor Mernst told me I could go out for a stroll, so I sauntered upon the Downs and slumbered three more days away in the grass. I began to wonder if ever again I should be able to stay awake for two hours together.

Fork called round with a note from Mr. Putty, telling me to report to Head Office in London before I resumed work.

"What do they want me for up there?'' I questioned Fork.

"Search me, Peter. I'm only the runner with the cleft–stick.''

"Honestly, have you heard what exactly did happen at the ice rink? "

"Well, Peter, nobody seems to know what happened to you, but poor old Goldie was flung clean through the refreshment buffet.''

"Oh dear. I wonder how he is?''

"Pretty cheerful and well on the mend. He seems mainly concerned whether it will affect his bowling run–up.''

"Did he ask after me?''

"Well, sort of.''

"What did he say?''

"Well, when I told him you were recovering, he just said, 'Pity'.''

"Oh. Anything else?''

"Well, he kind of hinted that if he never saw you again, it would be O.K. by him.''

"Oh. What about the two girls?''

"Well, they said that that would be too soon, as far as they were concerned.''

"Oh.''

"But I've got some good news to cheer you up, Peter. Stanley told me some soccer talent–scouts have got wind of you in the papers, and they're going to watch you soon. I believe he said Bournemouth and Portsmouth."

I was fit and well immediately. This was good news indeed, and just what I had been waiting for. I kept a large scrap-book of all my press-cuttings, which were dog-eared from constant appraisal. Sometimes I made the headlines on the back-page of the *Echo,* with such banners as, "Gallant Pook not Enough," and "Pook Suspended Two Weeks." My favourite one was, "Pook Pinches Point." This referred to my last-minute goal which brought us our first point away from home, after a bad start in which we conceded four goals in as many minutes. This goal-rush had come about chiefly through Stanley persisting to wear his new cap, when it was obvious to everybody else that it was far too large for him.

He had shouted, "I was hunsighted," every time he picked the ball out of the net, until Kite asked him who wouldn't be unsighted, wearing a hood over their eyes.

When Doctor Mernst gave me the all-clear, I journeyed up to London and renewed my acquaintance with Miss Littlewig again. She said, "Oh, dear, Mr. Pook, I hear you've been in the wars once more. How ever do you feel now?"

"I'm fine, thanks a lot, but what do they want me for?"

"I'm sure I don't know. Mr. Renault wants to see you, that's all."

"I was wondering if they thought I was going off my rocker or something?"

"I shouldn't think so. I'll take you in now."

Mr. Renault bade me sit down, and he asked me a lot of questions about myself and Cudford.

"I'm pleased to say Inspector Groke's report on you was a good one," he smiled. "I should qualify that remark by adding that it was also, shall we say, rather an unusual one perhaps. Somewhat in the nature of a horoscope, revealing to us what you may be in the future if you can only get over the present. Anyway, Mr. Groke is a hard man to please, so you may consider yourself fortunate."

I consider myself fortunate that Mr. Groke had only two

weeks of my unnatural silence.

''Mr. Putty considers that time will mellow you, and that eventually you will settle down and make the grade. Now, Pook, tell me in your own words, are you happy at Cudford?''

Everybody seemed to be suddenly interested in the state of my happiness. ''Yes, thank you, sir, I can't complain, but do you think I could be transferred to Aston branch, to be near my aunty? I would like that very much.''

''Who wouldn't? Maybe one day, eh, Pook?

The relation at Aston was fictitious Aunty Fit, temporarily transplanted to the Aston district on my behalf, from Paris.

''Have you any further questions while you're here?''

''Only one, sir. Who pays for today's trip?''

''We do, of course, Pook. When you return to Cudford just debit your train–fare and meals to Petty Expenditure.''

Life was beginning to take a turn for the better.

''Mr. Putty tells me you have got the idea into your head of becoming a professional footballer. A dangerous notion indeed. Now let me give you a few words of advice. . . .'' I thought, this is jolly good of Mr. Renault to brief me on the best way to enter the highly competitive world of soccer, but I was soon disillusioned. His few words of advice gradually lengthened into half a volume of *Dante's Inferno,* depicting the wretched fate awaiting those who threw up the security of banking for the false gods of sport. I thought, no wonder the youth of today are always being accused of lacking the spirit of adventure so strongly commended in our forefathers. Mr. Pants was regularly threatening to kick me out, and here was Mr. Renault treating me like the Prodigal Son before he left home. I agreed to give the matter serious thought before I took the fatal step. Actually, I was giving the matter serious thought as to whether I should play for Bournemouth, if they got their offer in ahead of Portsmouth.

Mr. Renault got back to business. ''Now, Pook, tell me in your own words, do you feel up to starting work again next Monday? ''

I told him in Mr. Pants's words that it was time I got back

into harness once more.

"Well said, laddie. Good–day to you, and try to take life a little easier from now on. Let someone else have a bang at the ball now and again, if you know what I mean."

"Good–bye, sir, and thank you. I'll get along home now and have an early night."

I hurried off to the boxing at Harringay.

NINE

When I returned to work, everybody treated me as though I had produced twins the day before and got up straight away. Lily kindly lifted up my ledgers as I needed them, while to Fork I was merely an elderly visitor being shown round a factory. This touching display of tenderness lasted exactly twenty-four hours.

Even Mr. Pants regarded me in a new light.

"Ah, Peter, and what did Mr. Renault have to say to you in London?"

"He said people should mind their own business, sir. Then he hinted that I shall probably be a very young manager, because Head Office have got their eye on me for the future."

"Did he really now? But did he say what you will be a young manager of? Cudford United? Let us watch our P's and Q's, eh, Peter? Anyway, I really have got a pleasant surprise for you today, and the fresh air will do you good. I want you to go with Mr. Lovejoy in his new lorry, and deposit our old ledgers at Telby. You may take the whole day, and all I ask is that you don't go near any rivers. Can you manager that? Good. Now run along, and have a nice day, Peter."

I waved good-bye to Uncle Pants, and off we went. The position was that the bank hoarded up the old ledgers for ten years, and then it only parted with them because the vaults did not have elastic walls. Every decade the accumulation was transported to Telby, where each ledger was stored in a huge barn for ever, so that if, for example, Lord Nelson revisited the earth to know how much pay the Admiralty had credited to his account while he was away at Trafalgar, the bank had only to dispatch me to Telby and I could look up the exact amount in *"na tonib-1805."*

It always fascinated me to walk through the barn and

examine the endless rows of ledgers, rising up tier upon tier, and reflect on the Balance–Nights they had witnessed, and on the receding generations of Mr. Balls who had written them up, and on the long dead army of clerks who had chanted to get them right. There they stood, in silent, dusty ranks, irrevocably balanced for all time. It made me rather depressed.

When Mr. Lovejoy and I had safely committed our charges to their last resting–place, we returned to Cudford about four o'clock. I wandered about the town, reluctant to enter the office too early for fear of appearing ungrateful to Uncle Pants. I rang up Lily to ascertain the position there. Apparently they were fighting a losing battle, so the situation was normal.

"Don't come back for ages yet, Peter. Nearly all the ledgers are wrong, and someone's lost a cheque from the London Remittance. No. 5's till is £48 short, and Fork can't agree the check sheets. Mr. Putty won't sign the letters until he can find his glasses. Oh, I nearly forgot; Mr. Aaron is still in Lunatics' Corner with Mr. Lecher. I took him in a cup of tea, and he seemed to be crying, but ever so softly."

"Thanks, Lily. Nothing serious for me to rush back for, then? Anyway, I'll pop down the road and have some tea. See you later."

Strolling along the High Street, I met Ken Alley, a big fellow who often played back for Cudford United. Ken was a dentist just starting up in practice, and a customer of the bank.

"Hallo, Peter. Got any work for me, in the choppers' line?" he called out, breezily.

"No, thanks, Ken. The old Power–Surge keeps my teeth in shape for me, not you ivory–bashers. Tell you what though, now you mention it, I've got a sore gum right at the back."

"Pop in here a jiffy, and let me squint at it."

Before I knew where I was, he had me in the chair.

"Oh, that's nothing," he said, disappointedly. "Just a tiny skinflap over a wisdom–tooth. A wee bit of your doughnuts has got under there and made it sore. I'll fix that in two seconds. All I do is cut it, and you won't even feel it."

True to his word, I was right as rain in no time.

"Many thanks, Ken. Feels lovely," I said, gratefully.

"Pity of it is, the flap simply grows over again, and the trouble returns," he mused, more to himself than to me.

"Can't you make a permanent job of it, Ken?"

"Of course I can, but it will take five minutes at least."

"O.K., let's go. I've got hours to spare."

"That's the spirit, Peter. I'll just give you a little injection to deaden the nerve," he laughed, inserting a chromium bicycle pump in my mouth. "That useless old wisdom-tooth will probably jump out on its own."

Thus began the worst hours of my youth, as Ken pulled, and strained, and injected. One end of the mouth was cut, as though I had been wearing a bit. At six o'clock Ken got down off my lap and said, "I dare not give you any more injection, Peter, so we'd better call it a day. I'm terribly sorry about the mess you're in."

I was unable to reply because my mouth not only refused to close, but it wouldn't even relax a fraction from maximum aperture. Ken rushed me home in his car, and phoned Dr. Mernst. I caught something about the jaw was probably not broken, but come round quickly. I fell into bed hating the world, all its inhabitants, and Ken in particular.

Now I really was in trouble because the pain was unbearable, and I ran a high temperature. Dr. Mernst gave me tablets, and succeeded in getting my mouth shut.

"Nothing broken, but the jawbone is splintered," he announced. "Stay in bed, Peter, and I'll see you tomorrow. Meanwhile, if the pain gets too bad, take more tablets."

One thing was certain; there was no risk of my not stopping in bed, for I lay there as if I had been clubbed. After three days of hell, the pain subsided and Dr. Mernst let me get up. He advised me, "You must wait a long time for your jaw to heal, and then we'll get it X-rayed at the hospital. After what Alley has done with the pick and shovel to that wisdom-tooth, it will have to come out some day."

In actual fact, it gave me no more trouble, so I certainly did not intend to remind Dr. Mernst of his promise. Not until later, when I was out East, did some bone–splinters begin making their appearance, and I got our ship's dentist to investigate. He pulled the tooth as easily as a dead weed.

Consequently I returned to work four days late, and Uncle Pants wiped his crocodile tears to say, "Please, Peter, try to keep out of harm's way, if only for my nerve's sake, there's a good chap. Don't exercise, or play rough games, or cross the road. Just loll about in your bedroom at nights and do your studies."

But that is useless advice to a man who has to lead his war elephants across the Alps, so to speak, and play for Portsmouth. I considered my accidents as serious setbacks to this ambition, and I was determined to make up for lost time, as I explained in a long letter to the editor. Bruce Bold concurred fully with my opinion, and kindly sent me the latest scientific breakthroughs in the physical world.

Within a fortnight I really felt I was the old Powerhouse of former days. I went fighting back into the forward–line, scoring goals, and inspiring the team to new heights. Slowly Cudford United crept up the league–table, although to be honest it was not so much my return to form that lifted us, as the epidemic of flu which decimated some of our opponents, and the fact that Stanley now took the precaution of stuffing thick paper in his cap.

I played hardest of all when the talent–scouts were watching, and during one match there were one from Portsmouth and one from Bournemouth. I remarked to Kite, "Just look at them – practically fighting over me." After the game, one of them went over and signed our opponents' left–winger.

Every Saturday night in the *George* I bought a pint for Timothy Laing, the Echo sports–reporter, and told him how marvellous his match accounts were, and did he want a photo of me in action. He always drank the beer and then refused the photo, on the grounds that his editor would not print anything likely to scare children.

Shortly afterwards, I did receive an invitation to play in a trial match for Bournemouth, but the whole affair was such a disastrous blot on my sporting career that even today I prefer to pass it over. Suffice to say of the match that I was sent off early in the first half, mainly for teaching some great Dorset yokel how to play fair, and of the return to Cudford that Goldie, myself, and the Bentley hit a tree in the New Forest, after ricocheting off a sports–car. That is a day I want to forget, if only for Goldie's sake.

A much happier event was my receipt of a letter from Portsmouth, offering me a trial match at Fratton Park, kick–off 6 p.m. I showed the letter to Mr. Pants for the purpose of sharing my great joy with him, and getting the Wednesday afternoon off. His reaction was quite unaccountable, and I was in his box half an hour, listening to a depressing treatise on what happened to young fools who threw up the security of the bank for the perilous waters of professional football. He contrasted a short career of hazardous battle on the field, culminating at the Labour Exchange, against forty carefree years with him, culminating in the Pension and eternal gardening.

I was quite carried away by the sheer rhetoric of the description, when he concluded with, "And now, Pook, as a sensible young fellow, which path will *you* choose?"

"*Football* every time, sir," I cried enthusiastically, completely forgetting that Mr. Pants was biased on the other side.

"Be it on your own head, lad. What time does the cursed affair start, did you say?"

"Six o'clock, sir; sharp."

"Then you may leave at four, and not a minute earlier."

"Lumme, it takes two hours to get there. Have a heart."

"I will ignore the expression, Pook. I am fully aware of the travelling time. You have my decision, so go before I change my mind."

"Would you like to watch the game, sir?"

"Don't be unkind, Pook. Go while you may."

I borrowed Goldie's rebuilt Bentley and scorched down to Portsmouth, arriving at the ground with about five minutes in hand. The two teams, Probables versus Possibles, were already knocking the ball round on the pitch. I peeled off my clothes, under which was my complete soccer kit, laced on my boots, and ran on to the turf.

"Watch that fairedded fouler," roared a human loud-hailer on the terraces – addressing all Hampshire. His little party sent up a weak round of booing. So my fans are here already, I said to myself.

When we lined up for the kick-off, I saw with consternation that the opposing centre-half was none other than Ginger Jones. He was all of six feet four, but he was the shortest man in the half-back line. Ginger himself looked revoltingly fit, obviously trained down to a hard fourteen stone. I figured the loud-hailer and friends must therefore be supporters over from Sayling, the mad fools.

My team, the Possibles, kicked off, but only to lose the ball in the Probables' gargantuan wall of half-backs. They began to siphon the ball about the field as though they had been playing together on the Continent for years. During a goal-kick, our captain, a spindly-looking man named Franks, ran over to me and muttered, "We'll have to cut out their fancy-stuff. Try and get stuck into them and cripple a few. That always upsets the clever types."

"Leave it to me, chum. I know how to deal with little Stanley Matthews's customers. Push the ball down the middle, and I'll do the rest."

Next time Franks got possession, he cued the ball forward just as I wanted it – well ahead and a fraction to the left. I glimpsed Ginger Jones pounding across to meet the threat.

"Bop" went my left foot and the ball fizzed goalwards. Although this goalkeeper should clearly have been playing for his native Scotland that season, he never made a more incredible save. Being a practical man, capable of overcoming anything bar the supernatural, I reckoned that as a goal to me. But the referee awarded a corner.

As we bunched in the penalty-area, Jones growled, "You won't get no more chances like that, mate. You don't catch me twice." As the ball sailed over from our winger, I soared upwards along with the three giants, and headed it into the top of the net.

"Goal," roared the crowd.

"Free kick," said the referee.

"Free kick?" I shrieked, "Who's in goal, your brother?"

"Next time you head the ball, go up on your own steam, and don't pull up on another man," he replied, tersely. Jones said: "Watch it, Pook. That was me you used for a ladder. I've had enough of you."

The loud–hailer implored the crowd to observe what was ruining English football today. Three times Franks pushed the ball down the centre, and three times Jones stood and watched me rush through. Each time the linesman flagged for off–side.

"What's up with you, Ginger? Got the wind up? Frightened to have a go with me, on a strange ground?" I said, to relieve my feelings. Jones spat on the turf.

The next time Franks fed me a beauty, I ran on to it just as Jones and his right–half ran on to me. I got caught between them, and I felt like the nut in the crackers. Every bit of breath whistled out of my lungs.

"Foul, ref," I gasped, bending over.

"Quite right," he shouted, "and don't do it again."

"Do what again?"

"Elbow a man when he's tackling you."

Jones took the kick, with a smug grin on his freckly face. The ball carved through our pack and smashed into the net.

"That's how you want to score a goal," he said gratuitously.

From the kick–off I ran right down the field, fighting every yard to keep Jones off. We exchanged all of a dozen charges. When I could barge no longer, I fired for goal. My shot missed, but a camera flew out of a reporter's hands and landed in the crowd behind the goal.

"Bad luck, mate," cried Franks.

"Vicious, that's what that bastard is," roared the loud–hailer, emphasizing his remarks with a school–bell. I signalled to him to join me on the pitch for further discussion, or failing that, I offered to meet him halfway, and get within fisting distance.

"We don't want any of that here, Pook. You're not

playing for Dartmoor Rovers now, you know,'' commanded the referee. I thought next time I get the ball, I'll make no mistake with it.

I got it on the edge of the penalty–area and streaked for goal. Jones and his thugs limpetted onto me so that the ball got trapped in a forest of legs. I leaned low, and heaved the entire pack into net, just as Jones kneed me in the groin. ''Free–kick for pushing,'' announced the referee. *''Penalty,''* I screamed, beating the mud with my fists. ''You ever tried rugger?'' inquired the referee.

''You ever tried soccer?'' I snarled.

''Don't go too far with me, Pook, not in a friendly game.''

The free–kick was sliced, so I pounced on it and slammed the ball in the net first time.

''Penalty,'' called the referee.

''What the hell for? I put the blasted thing in the net, didn't I?''

''Jones obstructed you,'' replied the referee, with an air of sporting neutrality. ''And if you use any more language I shall be obliged to take your name, Pook.''

''My name's Pook, and don't you know it, mate.''

He took it.

The loud–hailer beseeched the referee to send me off and save the game from ruination. His cronies whirled their rattles, and voiced some primitive impulses. Franks would not let me take the penalty, on the grounds that I was too het up for such a trying task, so I signalled the trainer to attend to my groin. He healed it by wiping my neck with a wet sponge. Franks hurled his thin frame at the ball and scored a beauty.

At half–time the assistant manager called me over and said, ''I know you're keen, Peter, and you've shown us a lot of drive and energy, but take it easier, lad. You've got what it takes, but this isn't village football. If you end up in the net with three or four defenders wrapped around you, you're probably going the wrong way about things and doing it the hard way. Now, I know you're unaware of the fact, but playing alongside you are four other forwards; all nice fellows, fond of the game, keen to help you, and even have the odd smack at goal themselves once in a while. So I suggest that now and then you let them join in the fun by passing the ball to them. When they've got over their surprise, you'll find they'll pass it back to you and in this way the ball will get into the net without your shoving the entire opposition in with it."

I thought the idea over. "Yes, I reckon you're right," I agreed generously. "Of course, it's such a long time since I played in a normal forward line that I've lost touch, I suppose."

"Good. Now, just to help you show us what you can really do, I'm going to change you over with the other centre-forward for the second half, so you won't have to rough-house it with Jones. Got all that? Fine. Now let's see some real football from now on.

Having changed my shirt, I took up my position in front of Jones and gave him a brotherly smile. He grinned back at me with deep family affection written in every freckle. Every time he gave me the ball I clouted it out to the wings immediately. They raced down the field and passed it back to me directly the opportunity arose. Without hesitation I gave it to my inside forwards; received it again and passed back to them. Eventually the inside-right shouted, "For good luck's sake don't give it to me *again;* surely it's near enough now for you to shoot." I shot, and scored a lovely goal from two yards out.

I thought, this isn't a bit like playing for Cudford United in the frying-pan formation. Towards the end, I walked the ball into the net twice more, without bloodshed or injury, or even the odd defender draped over my shoulders. This must be the new scientific soccer I'd read about in the papers, I reflected soberly. Oh, well, one has to move with the times and it produced results, but I missed the old thrill of battle just the same. I wondered if rugby was undergoing the same refinement.

At the final whistle, the coach came over and said, "Nice work, Pook. You followed my advice to the letter, and what an improvement. I've never seen such an unselfish player. You'll probably be hearing from us in the near future."

"Will you be wanting me to play in the next league

game?" I inquired hopefully.

"Well now, not so fast me lad. Wait and see, but don't worry. I like the look of you and Jones; you play together like a couple of brothers. Keep it up."

The Evening News reported that a big forward named Pook had got the crowd practically rioting early in the game, and extra police moved up, but "In the second half, another player, also called Pook, came in for the other side and served up some very brainy football, in marked contrast to his bull-like namesake."

It looked very well in my scrap-book, especially with a picture of the new selfless Pook in action – feeding his team-mates with the ball as if it were a time-bomb.

TEN

I filled in the short interval while waiting to be called upon to lead Portsmouth's forward–line by working and playing hard, to keep in trim. I reassured Mr. Pants with the news that English football was about to discover the natural successor to Ted Drake, and I hinted around the office that the day was not far distant when the staff would become famous for having known me in the early days of my career. They responded apathetically to these hot tidings.

Another thing I had to do was to revise my Power–Surge drill. By this time my quest for Bruce Bold's ideal torso – the inverted triangle shape – had made my dorsal muscles so coco-nutty that it was becoming increasingly difficult to swing my arms past them when walking. Therefore I concentrated more on the legs, in order to endow them with the super human strength necessary to survive in professional football.

In the trial match, I had noticed with envy that a Probable full–back had legs so developed that at first, from a distance, I thought two little boys were standing in front of him; but when he hit the ball I knew different. I literally shut my eyes against the blast. I resolved to emulate him right away.

One day, I entered Mr. Pants's seniority box and said, "Please sir, may I see you about the word you said I wasn't to say again in your hearing?"

"You may not see me, Pook. No matter what you have to add, I have forbidden any further discussion about your low swearing habits."

'Oh, no sir, not that. I mean the thing where I don't have to come to work for two whole weeks."

"Don't tell me you're going ice–skating again?"

"No, sir, not just yet. I mean the other thing."

"Are you referring to your holiday, Pook?"

"Yes, sir. But I didn't say it. You did."

"Boy, is it absolutely impossible for you and me to have a straightforward, normal conversation, free of subterfuge?"

"I expect we could, sir, if we really tried, and I knew what 'subterfuge' meant."

"Strange; I thought the word was invented for your benefit. Now, I suppose, you don't want to go? In any case you are compelled to, because Rule 289 definitely states you must."

"Why does it, sir?"

"Because the bank, in its wisdom, realizes it is our only chance for a bit of peace," said Mr. Pants, emotionally, "and, what's more to the point, we can find out if you've been cooking the books during the year, and covering it up."

"Oh, lor'. Well, I want to go all right. I just wanted to say that I shall leave a forwarding address in the Appearance Book, and would you be kind enough to send on to me by airmail any communication from Pompey Football Club, sir?"

Mr. Pants ignored this topic as too hot for early morning discussion.

"Airmail, Pook? Are you gallivanting off to Chicago this time?"

I laughed, in case it was meant wittily.

"No, sir. I can't afford that until they revise the salary scales. Only to Paris. Where else can you go in November?"

"Paris?" exclaimed Mr. Pants, who always holidayed at Ventnor and had been brought up to regard Paris and Hell as synonyms, except that in Paris, unmentionable vice dissolved visitors in acid.

"Yes, sir, and I may come back a different man."

"I should be very much surprised if you did not; though perhaps any change in you could only be for the better."

"I mean I may return already spoken for, sir."

"What in heaven's name are you talking about now, Pook?"

"Well, sir, whatever they call it in France when you get

engaged."

"Pook, I'm extremely busy this morning and have no time for horseplay. Would you be kind enough to come back later; say about ten years later?"

I wrote to Maria and broke my long period of short notes with the following: "Dear Maria, Alec and I arrive in Paris Monday. Till Monday, Peter." Then I wrote a long letter to Bruce Bold, telling him of my compulsory vacation but making no mention of Paris. It was the first time I had ever held anything back from him, except Lily, but the very name of Paris sounded anti–Cult. I did not inform Uncle Finglebaum, because he wasn't getting any mail anyway.

Alec's financial difficulties, in the shape of two hard–up parents, pared our foreign holiday down to a bare seven days. This gave us a week in hand, so we spent the first day booking our tour with Mr. Thos. Cook, whose face had become very familiar to me in the bank on the front of travellers' cheques. I figured this vouched for the stability of the firm and the security of our fares, which were payable in advance. We spent the next five days in his office, during which time our faces became even more familiar to him.

On the sixth day, familiarity turned to loathing. He said, "You know, boys, you won't believe it but you're not the *only* persons travelling abroad this month. I'd love to attend to you all day long, but I've just got to spare a few minutes on one or two old fidgets who are going even further than you; Tokio, for example."

I thought he looked suspiciously younger, compared with his photo on the travellers' cheques, but that was probably because he had had his hair cut much shorter. One thing we could not complain about was the price. "Seven days for seven pounds" the brochure stated, below a tropical scene of beautiful girls sweating it out on the banks of the Seine. This included train and boat fares, hotel, transport between stations, services of multi–lingual couriers, and all gratuities.

"That end bit means no tipping, anywhere, at any time, to anyone," explained Alec, desperately combing the brochure to find ways of doing the holiday on ten pounds gross. "Let's go back again to Mr. Cook about the beds, and see if we can get a bit more knocked off." Mr. Cook groaned weazily at the sight of us.

"Look, lads, you just can't do the thing cheaper, unless you sleep in the gutter. We've been through it a dozen times. Listen, you're already in the cheapest *pension,* with a room in the attic, I mean in the top floor back. You're both sharing a single bed, and I've cut out the bath, early morning tea, and the midday meal. *What's left,* for Pete's sake? As it is, I wonder the hotel doesn't refuse to take you. How can they possibly afford you? Couldn't you cycle over and stay with relations?"

"Suppose we meet our friends and stay out all night. Would that entitle us to a rebate?" asked Alec, with Mimi on his mind.

"I suggest you ask the hotel proprietress," replied Mr. Cook, coldly.

"Would you phone up London again, and find out?"

"Look, fellows, there's about half-a-crown profit left in it for us on your booking, and I don't intend to eat into that with another phone-call. Tomorrow is almost your last day; *couldn't* you stay home and pack, or something?"

"Suppose we went by the short sea-route?" Mr. Cook wisely fled.

"What about your French Aunty Fifi?" Alec asked me, when we were out on the pavement. "Couldn't we stay with her?"

"Shut up, you clot; I keep telling you I only made her up for Ivy."

"Pity."

Alec and I arrived at the Gare St. Lazare covered with yellow labels, like autumn leaves. This indicated that Mr. Cook was sending over another herd of poverty-struck sightseers to help *Pension Parnasse* through a pretty bleak winter. At the station entrance a swarm of hotel touts rushed at us, but we followed Mr. Cook's multi-lingual courier through the barrier, and into his own taxi. I thought our fellow-travellers were never going to stop getting in it. On the roofrack, the luggage was piled a fluttering bush of yellow labels. I saw nothing of Paris during the taxi journey because we were travelling on the lines of the Black Hole of Calcutta, but on the way we stopped at six hotels listed in the brochure, where our fellow sufferers gradually dispersed. Soon the taxi was all ours, as the *pension* was at the bottom of the tariff. The car disappeared down some back streets behind the Madeleine, and pulled up outside a very high warehouse.

"Zis is ze *Parnasse,* please, Messieurs," announced the multilingual courier, opening the door of his mobile dungeon to let us out. Simultaneously he extended his hand, and Alec solemnly shook it. He thereupon made a speech in fluent French, until Alec flourished our inclusive tariff vouchers for his inspection.

"Everybody speaks French here, even the kids," commented Alec, as we carried our own cases inside.

Madame Parnasse greeted us unenthusiastically, and when we had filled in the police cards a maid ushered us into a tiny lift, like a service-hatch. The maid squeezed in with us, and was forced to stand with her ample bust resting on Alec's chest. He sniggered in an effort not to laugh. The lift went up, and up, and up.

"You're sure this isn't the *Eiffel Tower?"* I joked to the maid. She shrugged her shoulders and frowned, as if she had been having a word with the taxi-driver. When the lift could ascend no further, because of the big wheel which raised it, we all got out. Then we followed the maid up two flights of stairs, and eventually she opened a cupboard and signalled us to get in it.

"You go in first, while I wait here," said Alec, apparently under the impression it was a toilet. The maid pushed us both in, and handed Alec a key, on a metal tag.

"One thing's certain, we shall never lose the key," remarked Alec, showing me that the tag was the same size as his wallet. He squeezed past me and opened the tiny window for air.

"Phew, just look out of here," he exclaimed, jumping back. Far below us was a panoramic view of the city, stretching out like an aerial photograph. I noticed that our window was embedded in the hotel roof, and surrounded by chimney–pots.

In the room was a camp–bed, a jug and basin, and a foot–washer like a sawn–off lavatory pan.

"You lie on the bed while I unpack," I suggested, fed up with getting knocked over every time Alec bent down.

"Better not unpack, Peter. Where can you put it if you do – on the roof? "

"Who wants to unpack anyway? Let's push over and see the girls without wasting any more time." That solved one problem.

It was dark by the time we got down to ground level again, and we began the long trek across Paris to *Rue Flague,* where the girls lived. We were guided by the fold–map which kept dropping out of the brochure.

All the way through the centre of this pre–war Paris the ladies jumped out on the two of us and tried to drag us away to hidden delights. Alec was very concerned to find out the price of these delights, not that he had any spare money, and at one point he collected a crowd of more than a dozen girls all trying to make him understand the charges. Then he slowly converted the francs into English money with the aid of the brochure's ready–reckoner. *"Merci beaucoup, Mesdames,"* he said politely, when he had worked it out to his satisfaction. We managed to slip away while the girls were arguing heatedly among themselves about the figures.

After nearly two hours we located the girls' house in *Rue Flague.* It was protected by a massive wrought–iron gate. Alec pressed the bell–push and the gates slowly opened of their own accord. In the hall was a board with names and numbers on. Mimi's father was listed as No. 8.

"All right, so he's No. 8. What do we do now?" queried Alec.

"The only way up seems by lift. Let's try it," I suggested.

We entered a lift exactly the same as the one at the

Parnasse. I pushed a green button and we went down into the cellar. Alec tried next, and we found ourselves in the attic.

"Try button 8." Alec had had a brainwave. Button 8 worked, and we got out on Mimi's landing. From inside came the noise of a village dance in full swing. I rang the bell.

Mimi opened the door, and literally sprang on top of Alec. Another girl followed close behind, who proved to be Maria, but now blonde. "Enter in, Peter darling; I have waited faithfully for you all zis long times," she shouted, introducing me to some fifteen cadets from the Military Academy. They were all gloriously arrayed in the blue and gold uniforms of another age, reminding me of teenage Chelsea Pensioners with swords. They abandoned the revels and sprang to attention. Each cadet bowed as he shook hands with Alec and me, who had to walk along the ranks as though we had earned a guard of honour. When we were rounding the first row, Alec whispered to me, "How many more of the perishers, for gawdsake? "

When they had dismissed, the tallest one said to me, by way of small–talk, "Your wig of gold is most novel and curious to us, M'sieur."

"Zat is 'is natural 'air," screamed Maria, convulsed by the sight of it and pulling hard for proof.

"Pardonnez–moi, M'sieur," stammered the cadet, blush–ing scarlet.

"A la mode, M'sieur," I explained in perfect French.

"Alec and Peter, our good English friends, this is our welcoming party to greet you tonight," Mimi announced, point–ing along the ranks of the French Army, "and after ze supper we shall have music and dancing."

"Very kind of you, I'm sure, but won't you need some more girls then?" Alec asked her, not quite sure if the cadets were to give an exhibition of national folk–dancing.

"But of course, pretty silly boy; ze other girls come very soon."

We both breathed a sigh of relief. It was bad enough being excluded from the hilarious French repartee as though we were a couple of deaf mutes, but the attractive blue and gold uniforms killed our Burtons Specials stone dead – apart from the fact that neither of us could dance anyway.

The relieving bevy of girls arrived soon afterwards, in the shape of two plain females wearing flowered nightshirts. Even back in England, it had often occurred to me how unlucky Maria and Mimi were in their choice of girl–friends. I recall one in particular, whom we mistook at first for a little old man.

Now that everybody had appeared, except some civilian boyfriends who were to make an appearance after supper, the company sat down to the feast. Nobody looked more pleased than Alec, who was starving anyway, because he was enjoying his first experience of seeing the girls eat and not having to pay for it afterwards. Alec and I were seated next to the plain cousins, on the grounds that they had once spent a day at Folkestone and were therefore considered to be practically natives of our own land. Neither could speak the language though.

I examined the second course and analyzed, among several unidentifiable objects, peas and sliced pineapple resting on a platform of fried–bread. Alec caught my eye, and by clapping a hand to his mouth and blowing out his cheeks, registered extreme nausea. In the middle of this realistic pantomime, he found himself looking straight into the unsmiling eyes of Mimi's mother, which so shocked him that he was seized with a dreadful choking fit. So violent was the attack that the entire assembly downed tools and watched in silent sympathy. Mimi slapped his back, and said helpfully.

"Sip a little wine, you naughty swine" – whereupon poor Alec was forced to retire from the table, honking like an expectant cow. When he was sufficiently recovered to return, he gave the mother an obsequious smile before starting to eat his food with his head bowed in shame.

Without any thought of digestion, the cadets rose directly the meal ended, and began to move sufficient furniture about to allow the carpet to be rolled back for dancing. Maria turned up the radio, which was always tuned to a station that had nothing else to offer its listeners but a tinny accordion band, playing full–tilt day and night. The girls danced with four of the cadets, while the rest of the regiment beat time with their boots, in a circle.

Meantime, the father came over to Alec and I, to say, "So you are ze two young men who entertained my daughters in England," as though we were a couple of outlaws on the run. He was joined by the mother, who conducted a detailed investigation into our lives as from the natal day. When she left us for a few moments to see where Maria and the tall cadet had disappeared to, Alec whispered, "How are we doing, Pierre?"

I replied, "Difficult to say at the moment, but it looks like it's going to be a shotgun wedding. Anyhow, those swords will make a good show for the bridal arch if they don't butcher us with them beforehand."

Mother returned with the missing couple and saw them safely on to the dance-floor. Then she pinned me down with the cat, a cup of coffee, and the family photo-album, all on my lap. Having got me well and truly cornered, she continued the third degree in a mixture of French and English, so I just surrendered and said "I think so" to everything. Alec could only giggle helplessly under the strain, so she wrote him off as mentally defective and ordered her husband to take him to another room for the purpose of inspecting his collection of antique fire-arms. Alec's unbounded delight at this treat was painfully false.

When mother had to leave me to go in the kitchen for more coffee, I fled like a pickpocket and disappeared amongst the crowd which had now been swollen by the arrival of Maria's civilian admirers. Remembering the thrill of dancing with her in England, I was eager to repeat my success tonight but whichever way I moved, a wall of uniforms confronted me as though I were having a nightmare and got captured by the French at Waterloo. To make matters worse, the frantic accordion band never let up all evening, even when the announcer was speaking. Maria seemed quite content to make a marathon of it.

Suddenly I heard my voice shrieking out, "*Un moment, Messieurs, s'il vous-plait. Maintenant we must 'ave ze Excusez-moi dance. Vive la France.*" Everybody was so surprised by my fluent command of the language that they stood to attention and cried as one man, "*Vive la France, vive la France.*" While they were all swept away with patriotic enthusiasm I grabbed Maria and pushed her round the floor as though we were in a dinghy and both rowing it. Before I had done a dozen strokes, the cadets realized what had happened and they surrounded us, all saying *"Excusez-moi"* simultaneously.

Having fought so hard to get a dance I was not giving up Maria so easily but the cadets assisted me by dragging my body away from Maria and depositing it on the floor. Everybody got rather excited in the process and joined in this new game with Gallic zest, especially Maria who laughed and kicked me in the face at the same time. "Let us play ze football with Peter," she cried delightedly.

Alarmed by the friendly riot going on in her parlour, mother came rushing in and shouted, "*Cease* zis moment, Maria, you naughty one; you will ruin your lovely new shoes kicking wiz zem in such a fashion. Peter, arise from ze ground zis instant."

I arose gratefully and apologized for damaging Maria's shoes with my face.

"Enough of zis noise," she continued. "To each a coffee and zen ze party must end." Alec was allowed out of the gun room to drink his coffee, with the expression of one who has been selecting a weapon with which to shoot his guide. Despite all our manoeuvring when we said good-night, Alec and I were marched out in the centre of a squad of cadets as though we were under close-arrest. When we found ourselves outside on the pavement, the cadets put on their swords and shakos, and, with plumes waving, they escorted us all the way back to their barracks, which they insisted was on our route.

At the barrack gates they shook hands, bowed, and saluted, leaving us to tramp off into the night to follow their detailed instructions as to our course for home. These directions were so complicated that they landed us far outside the scope of our map, at a deserted race-course in, I believe, the Bois de Boulogne.

"What did they say about tomorrow, Peter?" said Alec when we rested our weary feet on a bench in the woods.

"The cadets? They invited us to come over and be taken round the barracks as guests and meet their friends."

"They must think we're crazy," Alec grunted, ungrate–fully. "I don't want to end up chained and forgotten in the Bastille."

"Oh, they're not that bad, Alec. Very polite in fact."

"All I know is that I saw precious little of Mimi. Anyone'd think I had come all this way to court her mother and father, and learn about revolvers."

"Never mind, Alec. These are early days yet. Just have patience."

"*Patience?* What we need at the moment is a compass. We're lost."

Being under an oath of economy, we were unable to take a taxi, and directly the few stragglers we met discovered we were English they sent us down a maze of side–streets which always led to a red–light district. Eventually I agreed to Alec's suggestion that we walk on and take our navigation from the stars. His faulty reading of the heavens resulted in the longest journey by night I have ever experienced, during which we crossed the Seine five times. In fact, when we were almost home we limped past a church where early Mass was just beginning.

After we had thrown ourselves exhausted into bed, Alec said, "For goodness' sake don't take up all the room, Peter. Move over a bit." Actually, I was balancing on the wooden side stretcher. Being tired enough to sleep on parallel–bars, I dropped asleep until Alec turned over. This movement thrust me clean out of the bed. Finding it impossible to get back again, I made the best of a bad job and slept on the rug. In the morning I said to Alec, "Your turn on the floor tonight, chum."

"No fear, Peter, even if we have to get some rope and lash ourselves together. Have you seen the cockroaches? Big as tortoises."

I spoke to Madame Parnasse about the sleeping arrange–ments, and after a long struggle to convince her that my complaint had nothing whatsoever to do with a desire to bring women into the hotel by night, she supplied another camp–bed on the understanding that I paid extra. This luxury was squeezed into our room folded up, and, owing to the restrictions of space, could only be erected at the exact moment of retiring to rest.

Alec grumbled all through breakfast about the lack of eggs and bacon, and porridge. We consumed the entire stock of rolls and butter provided at the communal table, in an endeavour to see our stomachs through the day without recourse to restaurants. I noticed next morning that Madame Parnasse seated us at a separate table for two, positioned near the door within her range of vision, on which reposed our iron–rations in a tiny wicker–basket.

After breakfast, Alec and I retired to the lounge, grateful to doze on the hide settee after the rigours of the night. The sad maid was sent in with a vacuum–cleaner, but as this ruse failed completely Madame Parnasse herself entered and handed us each a leaflet printed in English, advertising coach tours of the city.

Alec opened his weary eyes, and, discovering it was nothing eatable, went back to snoring. This seemed to annoy Madame Parnasse to such an extent that she shook us awake and explained how visitors were respectfully requested to vacate the hotel during the hours of daylight owing to the fact that she was expecting the decorators in any moment.

Alec and I wandered along in the rain and then sent everybody we had ever known a postcard of Napoleon's Tomb, on which we inscribed the legend, "Having wonderful time. Wish you were here." When we reached the Gare St. Lazare, we secured the best seats by the fire in the waiting–room and dozed the day away.

We had arranged to telephone the girls in the afternoon to make arrangements for the evening, and to find out if the army was confined to barracks that night. We managed this by calling in at Mr. Cook's office and using his phone.

"Gosh, seeing Paris is thirsty work," said Alec, putting on his charm smile and staring like a hypnotic at the staff's afternoon refreshment tray. The girl smiled back. I knew his mind was combing the brochure for any mention of tea at the Paris office. I explained to the girl on the switchboard that the French telephone system was beyond our capabilities. She was extremely nice about it, and put me through to Maria's flat.

A very tinny Maria answered, apparently from as far away as French Morocco, and I quickly discovered that Maria on the telephone was even worse than Maria on notepaper. The first five minutes were spent in removing from her mind the impression that Alec and I were quitting Paris for home that very evening. Every time she said *"Pah,"* I flinched away from the receiver and wondered if her father was potting at the neighbours from his armoury. Eventually I solved the problem by repeating the word "Mimi" over and over again as though I was about to burst into operatic song. Directly Mimi's voice came over the line, I thrust Alec on to the phone and retired, in the realization that there were worse ordeals by telephone than at the Zenith Bank.

Alec fared no better than I; in fact, he appeared to have mastered the art of holding a heated conversation with himself. I noticed that the entire office staff were listening with intense interest, and probably wondering when the telephone would come to Britain. At length the girl on the switchboard could stand it no longer and inquired, "Excuse me, M'sieur, but may I assist you?"

"*Please* tell the young lady we will call for them at six o'clock," I said gratefully.

"Is that all the message, M'sieur?" she asked in surprise. She accomplished the mission in quick time on our behalf and I thanked her with all my heart. Alec asked Mr. Cook, "Have you a map of Paris covering a wider area?"

"No, sir, I'm afraid we have not. We've already given you everything we can offer," he replied, and I terminated the conversation by dragging my friend out of the office as fast as possible.

Directly the two girls joined us that evening, we had to start spending money because they wanted to drink coffee at a particular restaurant on the boulevard to introduce us to the real

French atmosphere, as they put it. On the way there I took Maria's arm but she snatched it away, with a guilty look behind her.

"Only after knowing for six months may we take ze arm," she explained. "You must walk behind with Alec, please."

In this celibate formation we reached the café where I ordered four coffees on the pavement. Alec launched the sentence he had been rehearsing all day: "We were thinking of taking you two girls to the *Folies Bergère* tonight." He tried hard not to laugh at his own mad burst of generosity. This suggestion horrified both of them.

"This wicked places are for ze tourists only," explained Mimi, and no respectable French lady would be seen alive in them. My sister and I scorn such entertainments. At home our reputations is guarded with jealousy."

Alec's short list of similar resorts met the same indignant refusal. We had to take them somewhere because the evening was drizzly cold, and eventually the warm waiting-room at the Gare St. Lazare kept projecting its image into my mind.

"Are you allowed to go anywhere at all?" said Alec shortly.

"But yes, of course. Several good places. Tonight we would care to visit ze cinema. Ze programme is very proper at ze *Bijou.*"

Alec paid for the coffee and started off for the Bijou, glad of finding an inexpensive refuge for the evening, but the waiter began making a scene about something we did not comprehend.

"Service, service," he kept shouting.

"Sorry; no time for tennis tonight," jested Alec.

"He is demanding his tip, *chérie,*" whispered Mimi.

Alec went back to the waiter. "Just take a look at this, my good man," he cried, producing Mr. Cook's comprehensive vouchers from his pocket. "It covers all gratuities, so let's have a bit less of the hysterics and a bit more of the Monsewer."

This really sent the waiter up the wall, and I believe he would have struck Alec with his tray had not Mimi given him a coin with a hole in the middle, together with a blast of extremely unfeminine French. Instantaneously the man became a mass of smiles and he laid his forehead on the table in a courteous bow.

As we walked along to the cinema I remarked to Maria, "You are very quiet tonight, dear. Is anything the matter?"

If you ask silly questions, you get silly answers, and apparently there was plenty the matter.

"Oh, you Peter! We entertain you last night with grand party and you say you love me, yet only this day you are spending ze time wiz anozzer girl. 'Ow can you be so fickles?"

Apart from the fact that I didn't know what she was talking about, I had been too weary all day even to look at anyone else, and I told her so.

"*Pah!* You lie in your teeth, Peter. You are so brazen you let the wretched girl speak wiz us on ze telephone. 'Ow say you about zis one?" I spent the remainder of the walk explaining about this one.

In the cinema we sat two rows from the back, on the ground floor, and watched an endless drama of the sea, full of whales, albatrosses, and storms. I sat there in bored silence, secretly longing for the cursed whaling–vessel to sink and have done with it. At last the lights went up and a French Raymond rose slowly from the organ–mine with a fanfare of patriotic music. Alec was fast asleep with his head on Mimi's shoulder, oblivious to the perils of the deep which had raged around him.

"You like, huh?" whispered Maria.

"Madly keen," I nodded vigorously, wondering if the interval was going on for the rest of the night. When the lights went down at last, we were right back again among the giant icebergs of the Antarctic, on board the same whaler, Part 2. So the vessel had not sunk after all, but, if it was any consolation to the skipper, my heart had. The rest of the programme was concerned mainly with a conversation between the skipper and some unidentifiable woman in the cabin of the whaler. As it was all in lightning French, I could only assume the couple were brother and sister who had been separated since birth until this very evening, and making up for lost time. They jabbered away incessantly and sometimes simultaneously. The only relief was supplied by the skipper, who darted to the porthole and peered out into a black circle about every half–hour, as though expecting the arrival of a third actor at any moment to relieve the tedium of his sister. Whoever he was, he had the good sense not to turn up.

Alec's gentle snore continued with hypnotizing regularity. All round me a great deal of kissing was going on in an embarrassingly loud manner. At first I thought it must be a French habit of sucking oranges in cinemas, but when I saw the cause I drew Maria's attention to it. She flung her eyes up to the balcony and said, *"Ver' bad."* The couple immediately behind us had been at it ever since the whaler left port, enveloping me in powerful clouds of neat garlic which made me feel slightly ill and utterly unsexed.

After several days in the cabin, the screen suddenly went black and said *"Fin."* "Such a marvellous film," exclaimed Mimi as she woke Alec by standing up and letting him fall over upon her seat.

"How I love that wonderful Capitaine, Jean Routout," sighed Maria romantically.

"Would you have liked to be on that ghastly ship with him?" I asked, clearly running out of conversation.

"Ah, Paradise *indeed,"* groaned Maria, casting her large eyes upwards in ecstatic surmise.

After the show, the girls were in immediate need of more coffee, so we sat in the rain on the pavement, under the meagre protection of a striped umbrella. By this hour of night Alec was practically out on his feet, so to speak, and he sat there keeping himself awake by force, sipping coffee and blinking his blood–shot eyes. He was well past any small talk.

"You are perhaps dying, poor Alec?" jested Mimi.

"Feels like it. Anyway I hope so," he said, looking the part.

"How goes your work and studies, Peter?" Maria asked me.

'Well, I can't grumble, really, but the good news I've been waiting to surprise you with is that very soon I hope to become a professional footballer.''

Her reaction was Maria's surprise for me. ''A paid player of ze games, like ze boxer. *Pah!* Disgusting! How can we become marry–ed on such basis. Who can share ze risk of such dangerous life? What say you about zis one?''

''Well, dear, come to that, how would we be better off in the bank? In fact we'd be worse off, because Rule 7 definitely lays down in black and white that I can't take a wife till I'm twenty–five.''

''Peter! What is zis one you are telling me? Why, by zat time I shall be ze barren crone and ze joking–stock of my acquaintances. You 'ave deceived me again, you Peter.''

Weary as I felt, I argued with Maria until Alec threw the conventions to the wind and slept unashamedly with his head cushioned by his arms on the table. Mimi now looked as peeved as her sister.

''Zis strange boy, 'as 'e been drugged or something?''

''No, Mimi, it's just that he's tired. He had about two hours rest last night, but really he's had no sleep all the week because he's so excited at the prospect of seeing you again.''

''Well, now 'e *sees* me 'e don't look terribly excited. 'E seems more like Rip Van Winkle on 'is 'oliday. Better now you take 'im 'ome while 'e can still walk.''

We aroused Alec and explained we were about to escort the girls to their house. ''Thank heavens,'' mumbled the excited lover, trudging behind us with hands in his pockets. On the way back, Maria told me rather icily she would phone our hotel the following day to fix up the next date.

ELEVEN

Madame Parnasse would not accept the excuse of an urgent phone call as a valid reason for our not going out in the rain next day. Despite our fears, she was quite intelligent enough to record any message and hand it to us on our return late in the day, as she had successfully managed to do since 1898 without complaint from anyone. Therefore Alec and I passed the entire day in the Louvre, until an attendant asked us to leave, as he wanted to lock up and spend the few remaining hours of that day with his family.

When we returned to the hotel, Madame Parnasse had no message of love to give us. This was such a blow that I used her phone to ring Maria. A maid informed me that the whole family had been called suddenly to the bedside of a sick relative. Apparently in their frantic haste to reach the bed nobody had remembered to leave any message. I rang off, and Madame Parnasse reminded me that Mr. Cook's all–in tariff did not include use of phone.

"You know what; I've been thinking while we were looking at the *Mona Lisa,"* announced Alec. He so seldom thought anything, that when he did, it was usually worth hearing. "We aren't exactly a couple of balls of fire with the girls, coming here short of cash, etcetera. Likewise, *everything* about them seems different to when they were with us in England. Well, we haven't got a lot of time left over here, and I suggest we leave the girls alone until they run after us a bit. That way they might realize what they're missing. How can we compete with those fellows in the Foreign Legion or whatever it is, right here on their own hunting–ground?"

"I agree with you so far, Alec, but what shall we do meanwhile?"

"Let's go out and enjoy ourselves like we could if we didn't have any friends here at all. Besides, you're too happy a type to end it all by getting engaged. I noticed a couple of English girls staying at the *Parnasse* who might suit us later on – the ones who kept looking over at our table during breakfast, and laughing."

Having agreed upon this plan and casting the French girls out of our minds, we spent far happier days laying out our slender resources on sightseeing. We took in all the famous landmarks, too well-known to warrant description here except for the Eiffel Tower, where Alec's abortive attempt to climb it and save the lift-fare nearly led to blows with the attendant below.

We quickly discovered that by going on Vermont's Popular Cut-price Coach Tours we could not only see the sights at reduced rates, but, best of all, we were enabled to give up walking. This concession was now of paramount importance to my feet because they had degenerated into mere loose flippers over which I had no control. Every time I ambled along the hard pavements these useless appendages slapped the stones like a couple of rubber-mats, causing passers-by to turn round to ascertain the cause of such a peculiar noise. This was Alec's cue to point at me and remark: "Walk the Barratt Way," and giggle delightedly at his own wit.

By day, Vermont's economical tours gave us the opportunity to inspect and learn the full history of every tomb in the city, as though we were on the Undertakers' Annual Outing. By night, we visited the *Casino de Paris* and similar shows by contenting ourselves with seats just below the vault of the roof. These seats were constructed on the shelf principle, so that the feet of the spectators behind you continually prodded your head forward, and sloped at such an alarming angle that it seemed impossible for me not to go sailing over the people in front and hurtle down to the ant-like actors far below.

One night we decided to follow in the true tradition of tourism by attending the *Folies Bergère*. Outside was a queue of people awaiting admission and I joined this, while Alec went inside to inquire the price of sitting up among the pigeons. A tiny rat of a man was standing by my hip and he said, "I am Egyptian tourist, like you. Shake the hand." He extended a claw with a visiting card in it.

"I'll have you know I'm *British,*" I declared indignantly.

He shrugged his shoulders and continued. "Yes, I am British tourist, like you. We shall never get ze tickets 'ere; ver' full. We must buy zem in ze annex next door. Come wiz me and I show you. Also zere is ze naked swimming-pool, same girls as in zis show. Ver' excitement. Come, or you will not get ze tickets."

It appeared that the annex door was actually around the corner and across the road. "'Ere is ze annex," he said, pushing me into a large hall. A maid took my coat and he led me up a wide staircase. Apparently one could not purchase tickets wearing an overcoat. A fat elderly lady in a black gown came out on the landing and warmly welcomed me, as though I was back from Devil's Island at last.

"Come in, please, m'sieur," she crooned. I looked round but my guide must have gone through a trap-door in the stairs.

"I've come for the tickets, mam," I explained lamely.

"Oui, but of course, m'sieur. Enter if you please, this way."

I found myself in a huge luxurious room, most unlike any ticket-office I had ever seen. It was very warm and scented, and covered all over with a carpet like a red eiderdown. The walls were also red, and hung with enormous mirrors. Most confusing of all, the door was disguised by a mirror similar to those on the walls, which led me to lose its whereabouts.

The lady said, "Sit down on ze divan, *chérie,* and I will bring ze girls." She guided me to the divan and pushed me gently backwards until I fell on it. I sat there quite bewildered, and praying that Maria would never get to hear about this lot. I extended the scope of this thought, to include quite a list of people.

Through the curtains at the far end of the room emerged

seven bathing beauties, but they had forgotten to put on their costumes. Definitely Ventnor for me next year. They all cooed "Ah, m'sieur," as though they had been expecting me, and floated over to me – floated all over me, in fact. Some sat either side, two behind, one in front, and the last nymph lowered herself onto my lap. I couldn't move for a wall of pink flesh.

When my head found a way up for air, I glimpsed Madame standing in the background holding a large bottle.

"Of course m'sieur would like to treat ze young girls to a bottle of champagne first; it cost only one English pound?"

If that is first, what in hell is second? – I wondered. Thankful for any diversion, I consented to stand a round, and the girls toasted the generous English m'sieur with zest. Apparently maddened by her glass of flat ginger–ale, a tall beauty began to perform a hula dance right before me, to the accompaniment of hidden guitars. So close, in fact, that my nose was almost touching her navel. *Now* if Bruce Bold could see me he would probably clap me straight in jail.

"M'sieur is too young to look, eh?" piped the damsel on my left, putting this sound advice into practice by burying my face in her nubile bosom. I began to sweat and panic at the same time. I thought, they will have my wallet at least, and probably knife me afterwards just for the fun of it.

"I'm in an awful hurry," I wailed. "I only came in here for two tickets." The girls figured I was very witty and they giggled hilariously.

"Relax, m'sieur, and enjoy yourself, the night is yet young," they cried, forcing me to relax by pushing me flat across the divan on my back. Seven girls can be surprisingly heavy, *en masse.*

"Oo–er; help!" I moaned. Just as I was preparing myself for a fate worse than death, a brain wave hit me. I gasped, "Please let me get up a moment. I must mention something to Madame confidentially."

The nudist–camp got off me and I was able to totter across to Madame to whisper that before the party really got cracking I must wash my hands immediately.

"But certainly, m'sieur; what is worse? Follow me, if you please." She led me to a bathroom across the landing, and stood there beside a wash–basin.

"*Voila,* m'sieur; soap, towels, everyzing." She waited there, holding the towel in readiness, while I went through the pantomime of washing my hands. I thought to myself, this is a pretty kettle of fish but at least I've got out of that dreadful room.

After I had dried each of my fingers separately, the lady led the way back, while I followed behind until we reached the door. At that point she entered the room and I veered off course sharply down the stairs, past the maid and out to the street. I ran round to the theatre foyer where I saw the welcome sight of Alec searching up and down the road for me. Alec cried, "Wherever have you been, Peter? I've got two tickets but the show has already started. Let's go right in."

I stood there panting with queer feelings.

"Alec, I've just had a shocking experience and you must do me a great favour. I've left my overcoat in a cloak–room, so I want you to walk in, get it, and walk straight out again. If anybody says anything to you, tell them your friend has gone for the police. I related briefly what had happened to me, but Alec seemed to enjoy the meatier bits with morbid relish. At the conclusion he said, "You know what I think? I reckon you were lucky not to end up as a tray of meat pies." He didn't seem to mind going for my coat in the least.

I did not see Alec again for another hour, and, worried as I felt, I was not going back for him. When he finally appeared, he handed me my coat and said, "A darned pretty maid had it but she demanded a tip, so I told her about the police. Then she couldn't get rid of me fast enough."

"But it didn't take you a solid hour to do that, Alec. What else happened, to keep you so long?"

Alec would only giggle, and express the hope that I had plenty of money left.

We took up our normal positions just under the great roof of the theatre to watch the second half of the spectacle. Although

I examined some ninety bathing–belles with the aid of opera–glasses, which I forced out of the seat in front of me, I could not recognize one of the girls from the annex. It was a show to remember, especially when Josephine Baker asked all the Frenchmen in the audience to stand up. Nobody moved. Then she asked any English or American visitors to rise. The whole house stood up as one man. She said, "O.K., that settles it. From now on we'll do the show in English."

Still no message came from Maria and Mimi, so we continued to enjoy ourselves in the company of the two English girls from the hotel. Before inviting them out, we made it clear that although we had started the holiday with a vast sum of money, this had been recklessly gambled away at the casino. Our confession seemed to go down all right with them, so we invited them to join our now thrifty party on a fifty–fifty basis, or better terms if we could get them.

Alec went to see Mr. Vermont, of Cut–price Tours fame, and obtained "reduced rates for parties" tariff. Mr. Vermont's nose was an exact reproduction of a strawberry without the stalk, and he snorted through it, "Don't cut me down any lower, boys, or else it won't be worth my while sending the damned coach at all." When we went to Versailles Palace he personally escorted us, to give a thrilling account of the scene through a little microphone on the bus. He told me confidentially, "Things have got so bad since you arrived that I've had to stand the courier off. Soon I shall be driving the coach as well."

On our last night in Paris we decided to throw caution to the wind and visit the night clubs. Of course, this was impossible for us to do as ordinary guests, but by taking Mr. Vermont's "Popular Cut–price Tour of the Nite–spots – Book Now," we were able to cover four clubs at a price well below a visit to one in the normal manner. True we were herded onto a kind of minstrels' gallery right at the back whence we watched the rich people enjoying being robbed, like charity boys at the Mayor's banquet, but we enjoyed it immensely. In addition, to put us all in the party mood, the management handed each cut–pricer a bumper of cough–mixture served in an authentic champagne–

glass.

"Do you realize this?" said Alec, who had been round to the foyer to examine the tariff. "If we had come here like normal human–beings it would have cost more than our entire holiday in France." This thought gave him endless satisfaction.

The last club on the tour itinerary was the *Moulin Rouge*. Our party of Cut–Raters filed in to the special balcony reserved for merry–making paupers and we watched part of the floor show with open–mouthed rapture. At the conclusion of the cabaret the paying clients flocked on the floor for dancing, where we noticed a good many American naval officers. Shortly afterwards Alec noticed even more. He cried, "There's Maria dancing with a Yank."

"And there's Mimi doing the same thing," I replied, horror struck.

When the music stopped, Maria and Mimi returned to a large table at which was seated a fair proportion of the Mediterranean Fleet. Our two girls seemed quite capable of handling the lot and I got the impression that if there had been one officer less, Maria and Mimi would have felt lonely.

"Fancy that," said Alec bitterly, "their relation has recovered, and now he's recuperating in a night club. Anyway, one thing is certain; directly I get home I'm going to learn dancing, and when I'm an old man, people will call me the dancing bachelor."

"Time is up, ladies and gentlemen; we must tear ourselves away from the gay carnival scene, please. Come again for the evening of your lives tomorrow. Take your seats in the coach for the exciting night–drive back through mysterious Montmartre and the pulsating heart of Paris ablaze with her inviting illuminations," Mr. Vermont yelled out, yawning his head off.

Probably the Gare St. Lazare seldom witnessed a stranger parting of lovers as it did when Alec and I left it. We were safely in the train with the two English girls, all waving promiscuously to Maria and Mimi who stood on the platform in front of the escort of cadets from the Military Academy. The French girls waved their wet handkerchiefs and the cadets brandished their shakos.

I leaned out of the window and said, "We had all better stop waving things because we don't leave for another ten minutes."

"Ah, Peter, what a wonderfully short holiday it has been," sighed Maria, "but I observe you will not be lonely on ze journey home wiz your new friends. But wiz me, all I can do is to be left 'ere alone and zink of you enjoying yourselves. Never mind, we 'ave ze consolation of ze letters. I so anticipate your little messages of love."

Alec was kissing Mimi and drawing her up through the carriage window in the performance of it. He lowered her back to earth just as the train began to inch out of the station. His smiling face looked as though it had been tattooed. The cadets cheered lustily as Mimi extended her arms towards the receding lover in the traditional gestures of parting, and Alec responded by putting a leg out of the window and pretending to jump off the train into the empty arms of his sweetheart.

Maria ran along the platform holding my hand so tightly that she was in some danger of accompanying us to Dieppe without a ticket. As a last minute message for me she panted, "You will be 'appy to know our sick relative is better now, Peter."

I smiled down at her and gave her a bumpy kiss, saying, "Yes, I know, darling, and I hope he's fit enough now to go back and join his ship."

She wrinkled her nose and flashed me a lovely pouting smile. "Hooray," cheered the French Army enthusiastically as we steamed away.

TWELVE

Back at Cudford, life seemed very dull after the erotic new world we had tasted and it left indelible marks on our characters. For example, Alec converted his bedroom into a Bohemian studio, with the worn map of Paris pasted on the wall as a motif. Here the local demi–monde were able to laze in comfort instead of mine–watching with Alec and me on the promenade, at the mercy of the elements.

As for myself, I ogled and leered at everybody under fifty, until Lily put her finger on the spot with feminine exactitude. "You've changed, Peter, that's what it is. You've gone all foreign." I proved my new cosmopolitan tendencies by taking her twice to see *Drowned in the Paris Sewers,* at the *Troxy,* where, in common with the other five hundred linguists, we read out the English sub–titles in a slow sibilant chorus. Lily loved this communal exercise and she usually finished when the rest of us were silently awaiting the next line. Consequently her hissing monologue made me giggle, especially when she was trying to speed up her solo in order to be ready for the following sentence. From our front–seats the sub–titles flashed on just like the huge letters on shop facia–boards, and Lily said to me during the interval while we were steeling ourselves against the upsurge of Raymond and his thunderer, "Intit lovely, Peter? Pity though they don't have the little bouncy dot jumping along the words like they do when Raymond wants us to sing what's written on the screen." This referred to the embarrassing agony of the weekly interval song, when Raymond played as softly as he could on his Mighty Wurlitzer without injuring it, as H.M.S. *Rodney* might have endeavoured to fire a very quiet salvo of fifteen inch. Raymond's acrobatic feat of turning round and smiling at us while still controlling the monster was our cue to break into wavering and undisciplined song of incredible weakness, coming as it did from the bloodthirsty mob of sewer-lovers. Most of the volume proceeded from the female members of the audience, comprised of nervous trebles led by Lily. Her head nodded in time with the little black dot but her voice never quite kept up with it. Consequently Raymond received the song in three waves; the men's, the women's, and Lily's, which played hell with his own sense of rhythm to such an extent that halfway through he would stop playing and just beat time with his hands in a vain effort to coordinate the barnyard chorus. When everybody had wound down separately to conclusion, Raymond stood up and clapped us sheepishly until we called out "Press the button, Cecil; they want the lift in the basement," and similar cinema wit.

Secretly I felt sorry for Lily's being English because it seemed a severe handicap to any girl, and her charms shrank in my estimation. This sudden shrinkage was increased by Lily's unhealthy interest in Cashier No. 4, whose ribald jests about the silver-bags now appealed to her as Oscar Wilde *bons mots.*

Nevertheless I regarded myself as a seasoned traveller and every time Mr. Pants and I were together in his box I thought to myself he little knows he is addressing a libertine who has visited the Annex, and I often amused myself by imagining what he would have done if he had been there instead of me. It was extremely difficult to prevent myself asking him.

The biggest surprise awaiting me back at Cudford was to learn that I had been promoted. My job as junior had been taken over by a dwarf slave of tender years by the name of Ronald, so I moved up to Fork's position. Fork moved up one, and so on, to Mr. Balls, where a bulge appeared and the staff piled up like railway-trucks

Owing to the distance from home, Ronald came to work on a motor-bike and in those days the possession of such a luxury immediately put him in the Goldberg bracket. In order to withstand the Siberian blizzards which went under the euphemistic name of weather around Cudford, Ronald scared us all by arriving at the office dressed as a diver without his air–line. When he had left a trail of water right through to the cloak–room he leaned against the wall helpless, until Fork and I undid him and forced the rubber suit off, followed by his diving–boots, helmet, gauntlets, and goggles. Then we put him in the decompression chamber, so to speak, by standing him over the hot–air grid to thaw out and regain the use of his limbs.

"How deep down did you go this morning, Ron?" I laughed, as we removed the underlayers of protective clothing.

"Coo, you should have seen it, Peter. The bottom of Lukers Hill was one big lake and I had to go through it pretty fast to get up the other side," grinned Ronald proudly.

"Wouldn't it be easier to come by train, especially as they say you're delicate?"

"Well, for one thing we don't live anywhere near a station, and also the fresh air is supposed to be good for me," he explained.

Fork smirked at this. "*Good* for you? I should think it was killing you by the look of things," he observed.

Little Ronald struggled up bravely with the ledgers, two at a time, until Mr. Pants had compassion on him by ordering him to bring up only the gubbins trays and vouchers from the strongroom.

"Ronnie is delicate, lads, so rally round and bring up the big stuff for him," Mr. Pants told Fork and me.

"O.K. sir, I don't mind," I replied generously. "It's all part of my Power–Surge drill to me." Fork gave me his Maria blood–feud face.

"Thank you, Peter. That's the spirit I like to see in my office. What about you, Fork?" Fork battled with his features but could only manage a mirthless smile.

"Well, sir, really and truly I'm off *books up* now, but of course I will help Ronald until he gets stronger, if you say so."

"Good show, Fork. Nothing to equal a willing volunteer, and it won't go amiss on your report. But mind, Peter, no more of the nine ledgers – be satisfied with half–a–dozen to go on with."

When Fork got me alone he said, "You crawling great

toad; do you think I want to be lugging up ledgers all my life? What's so special about that little hospital case that makes Pants excuse him his work? He wouldn't do it for anyone else."

I had lost all interest in Ronald for the moment, to give my full attention to the crawling toad bit.

"What did you call me, Fork?" I inquired superfluously.

"You heard. A crawling great toad."

"I'll tell you what I'll do with you, Fork. You say that again and I'll hit you so hard that you won't be any use to Beryl in the marriage line."

"As obnoxious as you are, you haven't got the guts to do it. not in the office, Pook."

"Oh yeah; try me."

"Oh yeah, you crawling great toad."

"Bop."

Fork's head had the misfortune to strike Mr. Pants's porthole when it was shut, and the glass flew inside and the chief clerk flew outside.

"What in heaven's name is happening now?" shrieked Mr. Pants.

"Oo–er," moaned Fork, collecting his wits. "I fell off my stool, I think, sir."

"Fell off your stool? Good God, man, you sit up the other end of the office. How could you have fallen off your stool and landed down here?"

"I don't know, sir. All I know is I'm here now."

"Where is Pook? He must be in it somehow."

Pook was in the Midland Bank establishing an alibi with their junior.

Mr. Pants snorted. "Well, Fork, let us put this inexplicable accident down to a fit of giddiness, but you will personally pay for the damage. You understand?"

"Yes, sir. Thank you, sir."

I returned to the office and asked Mr. Balls in a loud voice what all the excitement was about. He replied in an equally loud voice that the office bully had hit Fork into Mr. Pants's box.

"Shut up, you fool," I hissed. Surely I wasn't going to be compelled to do Balls at his age.

Ronald tittered in the background, helpless with mirth.

"It's all your fault, you undersized runt," I snarled at him. "If you could have worked like a normal person this wouldn't have happened."

"Don't you dare touch me, Pook," he jeered. "I won't take the can back like Fork did. Lay a finger on me and see what happens. You've been warned I'm delicate. Even worry makes me faint, so just you try it on." I could see he meant it so I put him down again and got on with my work.

When we met for lunch in Stanley's café, I thanked Fork for his loyalty and offered to pay for the window. He accepted the offer coldly but swiftly. "And I'll thank you, Pook, not to read my *Telegraph* over my shoulder from now on," he concluded, mentally withdrawing his ambassador and declaring war.

When things had cooled off I held my customary conference with Mr. Pants on the subject of my promotion.

"Well, sir, I told you Mr. Groke gave me a good report, and now I see they've promoted me on the strength of it," I began.

Mr. Pants pursed his lips.

"As usual, Pook, you are labouring under a slight misapprehension. Mr. Pills has nearly reached the end of his tether, er, I mean his bank career, so Ronald has joined us to fill the gap. With your customary blind luck you have benefited by the arrangement, and consequently I hope to see you in your new post as a more responsible bank officer than you were in the last."

"Well, sir, one thing is certain; the ledgers sure can stand a change of management. I've been having a check on my account since I came back and it looks as though Mr. Pills has been playing noughts and crosses on it."

"That will be enough, Pook. Those who can barely write their own name should learn not to criticize their seniors."

"Oh, Fork has never criticized, sir."

"Tell me off the record, Pook, why did you hit Fork the other day? Was it on account of young Ronald?"

"Oh, sir! Me hit a senior man, or anyone for that matter?"

"Don't come the old soldier with me, Pook; but if you'd rather not discuss the subject we will drop it. Let us turn to a more cheerful topic. Now, the Zenith Bank is about to announce its bicentenary."

"Does that mean it's gone bust, sir?"

"No, Pook it has not, despite your efforts to help it. The bank has now been solvent for two hundred years and the directors have generously decided to make a monetary grant to the staff."

"So I suppose they want to know what we'd like for a present, sir?"

"They already know we would like cash, and they are acting accordingly. In your case they have decided to give you ten pounds; not because you have earned it, but because you come under sub-section B. of the salary scales."

"Very welcome, I'm sure, but how much do you get, sir?"

"Mind your own business, Pook; not that I don't know you will look it up in my account tomorrow. Personally, I would not award you a penny."

"Why not, sir? Think of the profit they make, lending money they've created out of thin air by book-entries, and calling it fiduciary credit."

"They do nothing of the kind, as you will learn when you take the Institute's examinations in banking, and I've warned you before about reading the *Daily Worker.*"

"I only read it once, sir, and then only because your paste sandwiches were wrapped in it."

"It so happened that the café proprietor unfortunately used that unspeakable material on one occasion. Stanley, I believe his name is, and a sporting friend of yours. No, Pook, when I think of a lifetime spent in the service of the bank it seems hard that a newcomer like yourself should share in the bicentenary gratuity."

"Never mind, sir, there's one consolation."

"Such as? Are you being transferred without my knowledge?"

"No, sir, no such luck. I mean neither of us will ever see another one."

"True, lad, very true. A solemn thought." Mr. Pants turned his eyes to our sooty ceiling and pondered on the problem of how the office would function without him during the bank's tercentenary. Dragging himself away from such a chaotic vision, he said, "Tell me, now you are back from Paris, are you come amongst us spoken for, as you put it?"

"No, sir, not officially. I've got a lot of deep thinking to do. In fact, I've got to re-orientate myself."

"Have you though? So my advice is sinking in at last. Have you also given up the ridiculous idea of becoming a professional footballer?"

"Oh, goodness no, sir. I'm just waiting for the call."

"Portsmouth seem a long time sounding the bugle, lad."

"Not really, sir. You don't understand these things, and I can afford to wait – I'm maturing, like good wine."

Mr. Pills was to give his farewell party in the *George* after we had finished work one Saturday. Mr. Putty emerged from his office and laid down his niblick to help Ronald by listing the postal-orders on a long bandage of a form. He accomplished this by filling it up very slowly and getting the wrong total in twice the time it took me to do the same thing. I don't think they had postal-orders when Mr. Putty was a junior, way back when the Zenith was just getting over its centenary. He always forgot to add in the stamps. On Saturdays the postal-orders poured in as though we were part of the Littlewood's organization, and the manager gradually became embedded in such a mass of them that Ronald was put on to assist him.

Mr. Pills had already visited the *George* several times during the morning to bid good-bye to some of our older customers who had known him since the days when he used to make his own quill-pens. They had decided to forget a lifetime spent in Lunatics' Corner by celebrating the hopeful news of his retirement.

Fork's sterling aid on the ledgers cut down our choir work, and by leaving everything possible over to Monday we were able to assemble in the *George* in record time. Ronald stood by the bar, chained to the hat–box which contained the High Value Package, and clasping half a shandy in his free hand.

The H.V.P. contained those banknotes which the cashiers sorted out from their tills as being too worn and filthy even for our clients, and these tattered bacteria–carriers were sent up to Head Office every week to be condemned. Rumour had it that they supplied our Lombard Street premises with fuel for the heating–system all through the winter; hence the expression, "Money to burn." Today, Ronald was chained to £4,000's worth, which was a king's ransom in those days, whereas now it would barely keep one off the National Assistance.

Lily was giggling over an unaccustomed gin–and–orange, and openly flirting with sensual Cashier No. 4, presumably in retaliation for my going all foreign lately. I reflected what a pity it would be to have a fight and get the sack just when Mr. Balls was on his way out to the breakers. However, I had a date with her that night, and we could talk it over then. Under the convivial atmosphere of the *George,* Cashier No. 4 became less and less the suave customer–contact of the office, and more and more Cashier No. 4, period. My unwholesome thoughts were interrupted by Mr. Pants.

"Ladies and gentlemen; although this is the sad occasion which must come to all of us, when a good and faithful servant must retire to his well–earned rest, it gives me great pleasure to present our little farewell gift and unworthy token of our esteem, and love, and affection for our colleague, who has for so many years guided the financial vessel of the Zenith Bank through the turbulent waters of the ocean of Accountancy – with special reference to those great log–books of the voyage, the Ledgers A to Z, without which the stout ship could never navigate the vast sea of commercial and private transactions, and whose pages are filled with the records of Mr. Pills's valuable inscriptions – I do not say perfect inscriptions because none of us is immune from error – in themselves a monument to his loyalty and industry which we have all observed with wonder in the past and shall strive to emulate in the future during our brief sojourn as members of the crew, and which ... er ... er."

Mr. Pants was rapidly drowning in his own rhetoric, and he searched desperately around for a lifebelt. Lily handed him one, in the shape of the conventional pension–kit of spade, fork, and hoe, so essential to enable the superannuated to survive on their monthly hand–out. We always purchased the spud–tackle from Messrs. Chipit and Bleed Ltd., on discount.

"I present you with our little gift on behalf of the staff, and they join with me in wishing you many years of happy toil and abundant produce with them," concluded Mr. Pants, now floating safely and forgetting the ship he had abandoned to its fate just before.

Bowing with old–world courtesy, Mr. Balls took his "back to the land" bundle and tried to appear surprised and pleased. After he had made a suitable reply about exchanging the quill for the plough–share, and never using the survivors' kit to dig up his allotment without thinking of us with every shovelful, he stood there in his new role of agricultural labourer while Mr. Pants proposed the toast.

This time Mr. Pants started to navigate the ship back to port, but halfway through it ran aground near Mr. Balls's allotment, where it was pounded to pieces on the Zenith's rocky ledgers. Just as all hands were dozing off in the lifeboats he said, "Ladies and gentlemen, I give you Mr. Pills and his charming shipmate, Mrs. Pills.

"You can keep the old baggage," mumbled the staff, draining their halves of bitter. Beryl self–consciously handed the female sailor a cauliflower of lilies, also obtained on discount, to start off the allotment.

Mr. Balls, now farm yokel, walked unsteadily out of the *George* and hesitated, as if uncertain whether to get the potatoes up for Sunday or run away to sea. Mrs. Pills led him towards the allotment.

Mr. Pants returned to dry land and remarked to Ronald,

"I see the post-bag is still strapped to your wrist, Ronnie, but I take it the mail is already safely away?"

"I'm afraid not, sir; we're just going to the G.P.O. now."

"Goodness gracious, that will *never* do; Pook, how can you set Ronnie such a bad example? You know the post must come before pleasure. Be off at once, and don't let it happen again."

Ronnie and I left Lily and Cashier No. 4 still at it, but I was glad to get away because I had a match that afternoon at Gallston, about ten miles north of Cudford. I escorted Ronald to the door of the G.P.O. and then fled to catch my train. Running along the platform, I secured a corner seat by throwing my gear on it in the first carriage, while I went along the corridor to wash my hands. On my return I found that a man had taken the corner seat and moved my gear along, but I did not say anything because my station was the next one. At Gallston I trotted all the way to the ground, where I sat in the dressing-room next to Kite, our skipper.

"You've cut things a bit fine, Peter," he chivied me.

"Couldn't help it. Farewell party and all that rot," I replied undoing my case of football armour, which had now been augmented by knee-bandages and six copies of the *Institute of Bankers' Gazette* to reinforce my shin-guards. These auxiliaries had become essential owing to the pitifully crude attempts by certain centre-halves to rob me of success and reduce Cudford United to ten men at the same time. In fact, the editor of the journal little suspected that towards the end of the season his bulky compilation was practically the only thing that stood between our team and Division 2.

I threw back the lid of the case and nearly fainted with horror, for I was staring at a brown-paper parcel bearing a red label. The label read *"H.V.P. Registered and Insured."* Its solid block shape told me there was nothing in there remotely connected with football as an amateur sport. My thoughts refused to keep still but simply went in and out of focus. Of my soccer kit there was no sign. I was incapable of saying anything to Kite except, "Start without me and I'll be back as soon as possible."

Without another word I bolted to the station, caught a train to Cudford, and stood in the corridor clasping the case to my chest. I had heart–hammering thoughts of the previous journey, when the H.V.P. had lain unguarded on the seat while I was in the toilet. At Cudford I leapt out of the train and ran down the hill from the station.

I had not gone fifty yards when I espied Ronald wander–ing towards me as though he had lost his memory. He was walking along still chained to the post–bag, with his mouth open and fright written all over his face. All he could say was "Oo–er, oo–er, oo–er," and point to the bag. I thought he was going to cry.

"Don't break down, Ronnie; I've got the money here safe as houses," I said as calmly as I could. "Let's put it in the bag quickly and beat it over to the G.P.O."

"Oo–er, oo–er," moaned Ronald, obviously suffering from shock, and still pointing to the post–bag. I unstrapped the bag and fastened it to my own wrist, and then opened it. Inside was my football gear. No wonder Ronald had been overcome.

"How in hell did we mix up the stuff like this?" I demanded. Ronald could only shake his head and roll his eyeballs. I took his arm and led him into the G.P.O.

I put the precious parcel on the counter and breathed a sigh of relief. "All's well that ends well," I gasped.

"Oh, ho, what have we here?" said the lugubrious counter irritant who knew me well, "An H.V.P. on a *Saturday?* You'll be lucky, mate. It's time you pen–pushers learned that we don't accept the responsibility of H.V.P.'s over the week–end. Friday, yes; Monday, yes; Saturday, no. Take it out of my sight; those blessed things give me the shingles."

"But you must accept it. What else can I do with it? " I stormed.

"It ought to be safe enough in the bank, ha, ha. Any road, it's not coming in here, mate." After ten minutes arguing I gave up.

"Can't we deposit it in the left–luggage office at the station?" suggested Ronald, who had now regained the use of his faculties. I gave him one of those looks Mr. Pants usually bestowed on me.

"There's nothing for it, Ron, but to try our office," I replied, knowing full well how useless this idea was, but unable to think of anything better. To open the safe would entail locating Mr. Putty, Mr. Pants, Mr. Lecher, and Mr. Gruver, and I was positive that Mr. Gruver had gone to London to comb Tottenham Court Road for more of the violent pornography he was always reading.

I rang the side-door bell and gorgeous Miss Putty answered it. "Is your father in, please, Miss Putty?" I inquired as casually as possible.

"Dear me, Peter, how pale you look. Is anything the matter?"

"Oh, no, Miss Putty, just a social call really."

"Well, I'm afraid you're out of luck today, Peter. He's gone to Linnington with Lady Erge for the mixed foursomes. Golf, of course. Oh, no, that was last week; but anyhow he's playing away somewhere. May I give him a message when he gets back?"

"No, thanks a lot, Miss Putty. Perhaps it would be just as well if you didn't mention I called. Bye-bye, dear."

"Whatever can we do?" groaned Ronald, now capable of short hopeless sentences.

I kept biting my fingers to steady my thinking apparatus. I said, "It's no go, Ron; we're in the cart. We need all the senior men to open the safe, and then we'd get rid of the H.V.P. and the bank would probably get rid of us. Now Ron, will you take a solemn oath of secrecy if I take the money home, hide it, guard it with my life, and post it first thing Monday morning? Or would you rather be killed now?"

"It seems all wrong to me, Peter, but I'm past caring. Besides I'm in the clear because I'm only the new boy and you're in charge. Moreover, I'm supposed to be delicate and worry makes me ill."

"Then faint when you're safely home, but don't explain why to a living soul. Tell your father the work's too hard or you got sloshed at the *George* – anything."

"All right, Peter, if you say so, but remember it's on your own head. If I had known it was going to be like this at Cudford, I'd have gone to some other branch."

Ronald escorted me back to the hotel and left me to my fate. Once in my room, I hid the H.V.P. under the mattress of my bed at the pillow end and arranged the pillows neatly. All I had to do now was to stay in the room till Monday, which would not be difficult to do if I pleaded a cold. The only major snag was the female Scotland Yard in the shape of Ivy. The very thought of Ivy made me undress and jump into bed in a panic. She was quite capable of smelling out the notes as if I had a pot of Irish stew secreted under the clothes.

I did not have long to wait before she knocked and walked in.

"Coo, you in *bed,* Peter?" she exclaimed.

"Oh doe, I'm riding my bike," I jested nasally.

"You caught a cold?"

"Yed, a dasty code in de dose. Better push off dow before you ged dit too."

"Oh, dearie me; not like you, is it Peter? You sound dreadful. I'll bring you up some hot gruel. Shan't be long."

Gruel was Ivy's panacea for all ills, from sprains to nose–bleeds, and the medical profession have never found a more effective one. Half an hour later she reappeared with a cauldron of cold decorators' paste and a roll of wallpaper.

"You can't do der room dow, Ivy," I protested.

"Sickness don't make you any less cheeky, do it, Peter? This is your gruel and this is an extra blanket to keep you warm. Get it all down, and it'll cure you in no time." Ivy nursed one on the kill or cure principle.

"How on earth do you make this stuff Ivy; boil down a few hoofs or something?" I inquired ungratefully, when I had managed to swallow a mouthful and force my jaws apart.

"Aren't you awful, Peter? Always pulling my leg. Any–way, you sound better already." She was right because I had forgotten the catarrh voice.

"Please, Ivy, if Lily or anyone calls this evening, tell her

I'm a bit off colour and apologize for me. Don't let her come up here because we don't want the money, er, I mean, the cold spreading all round the office.''

''All right, love, if you don't feel up to it. Now, let me put the blanket on for you, My, aren't your pillows high, Peter? You'll never doze off like that, so let me take one away.''

''No, thanks, Ivy dear, *please* leave well alone. I've got a headache and being high helps a bit.'' But Ivy wasn't going to be done out of her nursing. She lifted me forwards and removed a pillow. Then she started to beat up the remaining one very professionally.

''My, Peter, *what ever* has happened to your mattress? It's gone all lumpy. Just let me look a sec.''

I panicked badly and cried, ''Ivy, please leave the room *quickly.* I think I must get out of bed in a hurry. Be a good girl and go.''

''All right, Peter; I understand. Do you think you should have a bed-pan? Anyhow, I'll bring you up some more gruel soon, and three aspirins.'' She modestly left the room, calling out, ''You've got it bad, I'm afraid, Peter. Your face has all broken out in a sweat. Do you think I should call Dr. Mernst? O.K., I'm going.''

Directly she closed the door I leapt out of bed and locked it. Then I hid the H.V.P. under some clothes at the bottom of the wardrobe and returned to bed. My racing heart made me wonder if I really was ill. I gazed across at the wardrobe and £4,000 came up on the mirror in red neon. I hastily shut my eyes to keep out the mirage and prayed for Monday, but the interval between Saturdays and Mondays was now apparently measured in decades.

I warded Ivy off until Sunday, when I had a procession of visitors to inquire after my sudden absence. There was Kite, to tell me that my desertion of Cudford United had led to an unbelievable 8–0 defeat, in direct contradiction to the easy victory we had expected. There was Lily, to inform me delight-edly about her fight for virtue struggles with Cashier No. 4 after the farewell party. Her expression led me to believe she had emerged the loser. There was Ronald, who sought worriedly for secret signs from me that would end his black–outs. I barely sided my eyes towards the wardrobe and nodded significantly. He understood the gesture and expelled breath through his lips with relief. Apart from that, he seemed rather surprised to find me still in the country. With admirable cunning, he placed a quarter of a pound of grapes on my bedside–locker, and winked me a wan smile.

Even Fork turned up, to say that sickness was more important than petty differences and so we should bury the hatchet by shaking hands.

I thought, all we need now are Mr. Pants and Constable Barrington. Who should walk in but Cashier No. 4, accompanied by Mr. Balls, who had forsaken the harvest on grounds of rainy weather.

"How did you gentlemen know Peter was sick?" queried Ivy, the Agatha Christie of her day.

"Lily mentioned it and the word soon got around," explained Cashier No 4, smiling suggestively to our typist.

"Well, now you big strong men are here, perhaps you will help me give Peter a little surprise," she continued. People seemed to dedicate their lives to make mine a continuous series of them. "This room has no window, so it's no place to be sick in," went on Ivy ambiguously, "and as we've had the front bedroom redecorated, Peter can go in there while he's poorly. Won't that be *nice,* Peter, being in a room where you can look out of the window?"

I thought it would be hell, and said so.

"Please don't move me, Ivy dear, I love it in here, and anyway I'm too sick to be moved at present."

"Nonsense, Peter. Come along, boys, lift the furniture out, please. The wardrobe goes first, and then the dressing–table. You get back in bed *this instant,* Peter. Mother is just making up the double–bed and then you can go in, not before. I'll just get you your dressing–gown out of the wardrobe to keep you warm."

I could only lie back and gargle helplessly while the wardrobe disappeared through the door and Ivy pulled the dressing gown on me. The moment Mrs. Ruck gave me the all-clear I streaked into the front bedroom and Ivy pushed me into bed, dressing-gown and all. My eyes searched frantically for my wardrobe, but in vain. Instead, the room had built-in cupboards.

"Where's my wardrobe?" I shrieked at the top of my voice.

"Don't be so hysterical, Peter; you sound like you're delirious. You don't need a wardrobe in here, with lovely big built-in cupboards, now do you? I'm just going to fetch your things and put them neatly in there."

"Bring me my *wardrobe.* I want my *wardrobe.* It's the most valuable thing I've got. Ronnie, for heaven's sake find the wardrobe."

I was now shouting as though I was leading Cudford United towards goal. Everybody pinned me to the bed, and Fork held my flailing arms.

"He's delirious, Ivy. Better bring in the wardrobe and appease him, then send for Dr. Mernst," whispered Mrs. Ruck, worriedly. "My late husband used to be worse than this when the malaria came back every year."

Mr. Balls and Cashier No. 4 carried in the surplus wardrobe, and at the sight of it I slumped back exhausted on the pillows.

"He probably thinks it's his father," whispered Mrs. Ruck, who told fortunes during the evenings and knew about these things.

"Don't worry any more, Peter. Your father is here and he won't leave you till you're better," said Ivy, sympathetically. I caught Ronald's eye and nodded imperceptibly towards my wooden parent. Ronald gave me the barest glance of silent understanding.

I was hardly prepared to see Cashier No. 2, 3 and 5 appear at the door, but they did, with the explanation that the sight of Cashier No. 4's Morris Minor outside had aroused their interest. Then Cashier No. 1 arrived. It seemed that he had only come in out of the rain.

"Looks like when King Charles the Second snuffed it, all

over again,'' he quipped, surveying the mourners round my bed.

''All we need now is Mr. Pants and we could open up our own bank,'' laughed Farmer Balls. I did not consider that remark at all funny.

Ivy, now Florence Nightingale in earnest, pushed two hot water bottles down the bed and put on the second bar of the electric–fire.

''Go easy, dear; I'm sweating already,'' I informed her.

''Just what I expected,'' she replied, remembering her father, ''but you're only beginning to sweat it out, Peter. Soon the fever will send you into icy shivers and that's why I'm going to light the coal–fire now. Here's an eiderdown and an extra rug for you.'' She proceeded to tuck in an enormous motoring–rug, and added my overcoat on top until I was satisfactorily embalmed.

''I'm not kidding, Ivy, *I'm roasting alive.* My pyjamas are wet through already.'' I had read about self–combustion in Dickens.

''Good sign, Peter. Stick it till everybody's gone, then we'll change them, like I used to do for my poor old dad.''

''Ivy, please help me. I'm *suffocating.* Open the window quick.''

''Don't be ridiculous; do you want to kill yourself?''

''Yes, and you're doing it with kindness, Ivy. For mercy's sake at least give me a glass of water, *please.*''

Ivy returned with a scalding glass of steaming lemonade and three more aspirins, which the cashiers forced down my unwilling throat. ''Please, *please,* let me get some air,'' I begged them. Fork entered with another eiderdown while Ivy placed a bath towel over my fevered brow and face, so that I disappeared completely.

''He's dreadfully hot,'' I heard Mrs. Ruck say as though I should be freezing under the circumstances. ''Better take his temperature immediately and then phone Dr. Mernst.''

Ivy opened the oven–door an inch and thrust a thermometer into my dry mouth. ''Tell me when a minute is up,'' she asked somebody. Surely I could feel my life–blood draining into my soggy pyjamas? I heard footsteps and recognized the sweet voice of Miss Putty. "Would it be safe if I spoke to Peter?" she said. Then I heard her sobbing as though the sight of my entombed form and the periscope thermometer had overcome her. She rushed out of the room together with several of the mourners, and I could hear them quietly weeping on the landing. Were they keeping back some dread disease from me, like vicious anaemia or something lethal? I thought of this and the touching concern of the staff for my well-being until the tears came into my eyes. I believe they evaporated as steam.

At last Ivy removed the periscope, and gave a cry of dismay. "Everybody had better leave, please. The poor boy is 104," she announced dramatically. 104 – ye gods, I felt I was on the boil.

"Put some more rugs on him, Ivy, and then we'll try the quinine," advised Mrs. Ruck, determined to get rid of the malaria.

Hearing this threat, I sat bolt upright in bed and everybody gasped at my lobster condition. "Please, Miss Putty, what have you come for?" I panted, gulping in air. The men promptly forced me back again and buried me alive. Miss Putty bent over the approximate locality of my face, and said, with tears in her lovely eyes, "I didn't know you were so ill, Peter, truly. Daddy sent me round to inquire about your unusual call yesterday, and to say he's in now if you wanted to see him. But under the circumstances I think he had better come round and see *you,* don't you agree, Peter?"

A muffled explosion under the bed-clothes indicated the undesirability of such a suggestion, however well meant.

"No, don't let him come round here and see me in this state, please Miss Putty," I mumbled through the eiderdowns; "because I only wanted to warn him that I might not be coming to work on Monday. Thank him just the same for me."

"Naturally, Peter. Just you lie still and get well as soon as you can. If you get cold, ask Ivy for more blankets and bottles. . . ."

Miss Putty's voice failed her and I could hear her sobbing

with emotion. It seemed everyone in the room was bravely stifling tears.

"Everybody must leave Peter in peace now, if you please, ladies and gentlemen. The company has over–excited him," commanded Mrs. Ruck, ushering out my kind visitors. I heard Lily whisper, "I'll bring him round some flowers tomorrow, and see if there's more hope." Cashier No. 4 gave a peculiar snort in reply.

Directly the room was empty I shot out of bed, only to find Ivy standing by the door. I re–buried myself like a bird–shy worm.

"Please let me cool off, Ivy love," I croaked, "and don't send for Dr. Mernst. I'll be fine tomorrow, you'll see."

She gave me a long thoughtful frown. "You don't seem to realize how bad you are, Peter."

"The trouble is, you don't realize how bad I am," I retorted sadly.

"All right then, Peter; but if you're not improved by tomorrow we'll have to call the doctor."

"Thanks a million, dear; you're a real sport."

With that weight off my mind I fell asleep to troubled dreams, most of which concerned my being boiled alive in the *Troxy,* and when I awoke it was morning. Monday morning to boot. My watch recorded seven o'clock; only two hours to opening time at the G.P.O.

I put my hand in the wardrobe and felt about for the H.V.P. Nothing met my hand except balls of socks and soiled underwear. I threw open the doors and tore all my clothes out till the wardrobe stood empty. Gone! My brain whirled round and round in a futile whirligig of implications and fears. I ran down the stairs screaming for Ivy. She came out of the kitchen but started back at my wild appearance.

"It's gone, *it's gone.* Where is it, Ivy, it's gone?" I babbled.

"What's gone, Peter?" gasped Ivy, obviously fearing to mention it was my reason.

"The wardrobe. In the wardrobe. *It's gone.*"

"Oh, you still on about your precious old wardrobe," said Ivy, relieved. "He can't have gone, Peter. He's still up there if you put the light on. Your dad promised he wouldn't leave you while you were queer; I heard him say so."

"Shut up, and don't start that all over again. Do you want to drive me off my nut? The parcel he had inside him has vanished. Where is it? Search the hotel. Send for the police."

The raving brought the entire population of boarders out of their rooms in pyjamas and they began a fruitless search of the premises, which was made more difficult because no one knew what they were looking for, and cared less. The male inmates were being urged to force me back to bed before anybody got injured.

"When my late husband had his malaria it was just like this," Mrs. Ruck reminisced," and we had to sit on him until the fever passed. One year he even tried to throw himself out of the window. Try and restrain Peter if you can, lads."

I calmed down considerably on hearing this and retired to my room. I shut the window, just to be on the safe side. Still pretty dopey with aspirins, I looked in the mirror to examine my face for heat bumps or worse, but apart from a very beetrooty hue it appeared fairly normal. At the same time I was surprised to find that my hair had not turned white over the week–end. Then I searched the room and furniture for the parcel without success.

While dressing I made up my mind to make a full confession to Mr. Putty and throw myself on his mercy for such a terrible loss. Ivy soon knocked the door, and there she stood with fresh gruel and a bottle of aspirins. This settled the matter beyond doubt.

"Did you find your dad all right, Peter...

She suddenly found herself addressing an empty room.

At the office the strains of the 1812 *Overture* being gaily hummed by Mr. Pants as he sorted out the morning mail seemed incongruously suited to such an ordeal as lay before him. I wondered what his reaction would be when he heard the hot news that I had lost the H.V.P. Would he follow his customary policy of consulting H.O. Instructions? If so, I could imagine the entry, thus: "H.V.P., loss of. (a) Wardrobes, disappearance from. In the case of loss by staff from articles of household furniture, the following action is to be taken immediately. (i) Fill in a full report of the circumstances on Form 7538/H.V.P./9 (f), (do not fold)," and so on. On the way to work I had already worked out that if the bank decided to reimburse themselves from my gross salary it would take sixty–seven years to collect, which would make me nearly eighty–seven, always supposing I were capable of living to such a ripe old age without food, or even a roof over my head.

Mr. Pants welcomed me into his box, little suspecting this was the last day he would ever sit in it. In my despair I unconsciously called him Mr. Todders, and wondered if the bank would make him serve under Ronald. While I poured out the whole sordid story he sat there in stunned silence. At the conclusion, he asked me if I had been skating over the week–end.

"No, sir; I've been bedridden the whole time," I replied truthfully.

"Well, Pook, I don't know everything that is behind this fantastic story, except that you must have overdone it at the farewell party and had a week–end of ghastly nightmare. If it will help you recover, you should be told that the H.V.P. is safely locked up in the vaults."

"I expect you are trying to soften the blow, sir, but I've not been dreaming. In fact, ask Ronald there; he'll tell you."

Ronald appeared with a serious face, and shook his head as though he had never known about anything, anywhere, ever.

"All right, Ronnie, the game's up," I ordered. "You can tell Mr. Pants the lot now. Your oath is cancelled."

"But what is there to tell? I don't even know what you are talking about," said our child–saint.

"Well, Pook, that is that. Besides, you must know by now that the G.P.O. won't accept H.V.P.'s on Saturdays, therefore it goes off tonight."

"Sir, Ronnie is too terrified to let on and he thinks he's

helping me by keeping his mouth shut, but if you will only look in the safe you will *have* to believe me.''

''Very well, Pook, if you insist. Ask Mr. Putty if he will kindly assist us. Mr. Lecher, Mr. Gruver, please bring your keys. We must open the safe and relieve Pook's warped mind.''

The four senior men unlocked while Ronald and I watched. Mr. Putty threw open the door of the fridge and there was the H.V.P. Mr. Pants allowed me to examine it closely.

''Yes, sir, *this* is it,'' I declared triumphantly.

''We are all well aware it is, Pook, so let's sober up and stop harping on the obvious,'' said the chief clerk acidly. He turned to the manager. ''I must apologize for all this fuss, sir, but it seems Mr. Pook has had another thick week-end.'' They all laughed. What could I say?

''Now get on with your work, Pook, and no more nonsense till the New Year,'' commanded Mr. Pants, getting in his parting barb. ''Even if it had been All Fools' Day I would consider your behaviour in extremely bad taste.''

The whole thing had got beyond me, so I resigned myself to working it off. When I opened my desk to get out my writing materials I had an hallucination of the H.V.P. inside it. I slammed the desk shut and closed my eyes, like an alcoholic the morning after. I needed time to think. Eventually I opened the desk one inch and peered in. To my surprise the H.V.P. was still there. I lowered the lid in a daze, and stifled an impulse to fetch Mr. Pants. The rest of the staff were deeply engaged in their work so I broke the seals, removed the string, and tore off some of the wrappings, all under cover of the desk-lid. Then I put my eye to the crack and examined the contents. The £4,000 had turned into rough-paper.

In a frenzy of rage I ripped the parcel wide open. Toilet-paper. On top reposed a note addressed to me. It read: ''Dear Peter, Trust you had a memorable week-end. I've been in the bank forty-odd years, so I ought to know by this time how to deal with cheeky young whipper-snappers. And when you feel like coming round, my wife will be glad to see you, but I shall probably be out on the allotment. Thanks for the pension-kit.''

The note was unsigned.

This discovery, which I kept to myself, took me all day to work out, but whichever way I figured it Ronald was always part of the result. Apart from the fact that he didn't write the note, Ronald was the common factor all through; at the pub; the station; the bedroom; and the office today. Gradually I became very worked up, and when the insidious *grapes* flashed into my mind I fairly exploded. Alone in my room that night, I made a list of suspects by the Whodunnit technique, and the result looked like a page from our office Appearance Book. So I made a list of those whom I could safely eliminate. "Pook" was the sole entry.

By midnight, only the exhaustion of my Power–Surging feats enabled me to get any sleep at all.

THIRTEEN

Apart from being known for the rest of my career at Cudford as "H.V.P. Pook," I was eventually allowed to live it down, and for a whole three weeks I was the paragon banker. This entailed being nice to everybody, kind to customers' dogs, mad about the kiddies, delighted at working late, playing son to Mr. Pants's father, assisting Ronnie up the stairs, becoming brother to the typists, and a hundred other unnatural handicaps. It was murder.

Mr. Pants, now honoured parent, called me into his box early one morning for a family conference.

"Ah, Peter, my boy, good tidings await you."

"Portsmouth sounded the bugle, sir?" I inquired with my new filial voice.

"Not exactly, Peter. I have one of my little surprises for you today as a reward for your exemplary behaviour lately."

"Do you think I can stand another one, sir?"

"I'm sure you can, laddie. Now, Mr. Gruver has got his annual attack of the sinus trouble, so I want you to go out and run the sub-branch at Foxem until he returns." This wasn't bad at all.

"Thank you, sir; it will be good experience for me," I replied dutifully.

"Do your best, son, and no man can do more."

Our sub-branch at Lower Foxem, out in the valleys and forests of the Wessex countryside, was a dolls' house office situated in the front-room of Mrs. Parsons's cottage. If you were a customer you had to be pretty sharp to get in, because we opened on Tuesdays and Fridays, and then only for a few hours.

The Agency, as it was often called, was the bank's equivalent of the Chiltern Hundreds in some respects, where aged failures were got rid of until the time came for them to join the other villagers and take up soil toil.

Mr. Gruver had demonstrated in the first year of his service that he would never ascend to the dizzy heights which Todders did with the aid of Uncle Friendly and his qualified mountaineers. He had declared openly that his sole ambition in the Zenith was to stay the course, instead of following Todders to top–excutive power and ulcers. Consequently he had been running Lower Foxem Agency so long that he ranked second only to the Vicar and the Off–licensee as the big fish in a small but beautiful pond.

As the population was ninety–eight souls, including children, Mr. Gruver was not exactly rushed off his feet, and the main product of his labours there seemed to be an endless stream of highly lascivious but remarkably unsuccessful murder stories. He was such a nice mild old widower that I never really recovered from reading one of his novels which might well have served as a basis for the film, *The Dying Teller,* at the *Troxy,* except that the film version had been cleaned up considerably.

It appeared that out in the peaceful solitude of Lower Foxem Mr. Gruver lived in a brutal world of knives, guns, poisons, acids, bombs and bedroom cobras. Even his workaday sewing baskets were full of poisoned needles and cottons steeped in the essences of bottled homicide. His customary formula was to collect together the dregs of Soho, from sex–queens to flagellants, put them all in a Lower Foxem environment, and then close Chapter One. In Chapter Two until the penultimate chapter Mr. Gruver made them massacre each other in such a variety of unlikely and nauseating ways that he might have been compiling an encyclopedia of international extermination through the ages.

In the last chapter Mr. Gruver informed us that the whole thing had been a mistake, and finally he emerged from the knackers' yard which he had made of Lower Foxem to point the moral, on the very last page, that crime does not pay.

If his crimes did not pay, at least they succeeded in shocking the delighted inhabitants of Lower Foxem, who, with remarkable powers of re–integration, offered themselves for dismemberment about every three months. Mr. Gruver made no secret of the fact that he drew his characters neat, straight from the ninety–eight enthusiasts of the village, and then added a few touches of sex and vice to ginger them up. The villagers themselves appeared to revel in their vicarious notoriety, of which real life had so unjustly robbed them. In short, Mr. Gruver accomplished the remarkable feat of blowing up Lower Foxem into a kind of Babylon with pubs.

On Tuesday morning I took the big Gladstone–bag containing one hundred pounds in cash, six new cheque–books, the official rubber–stamp, and two of Mr. Grover's manuscripts, to the depot where I caught the bus for Lower Foxem. This bus, sole means of communication with the sleepy Babylonians, ran every two hours, and stopped on the way at minor hamlets consisting of one barn guarded by a milk–churn. If anybody ever got off at these stops they went through the hedge and struck out for the distant horizon, as though tackling the Great Karroo desert and well provided for the expedition with groceries from Messrs. Hardcake & Tile, (1922) Ltd., of Cudford.

At Lower Foxem I was met and escorted to the office by the guard, caretaker, messenger, and cleaner, in the form of Mr. Parsons, late of the Southern Railway, whose arduous duties of porter had left him extraordinarily frail and thin. I had not the heart to let him carry the bag, so he walked by my side with the regulation whistle at the ready, and very little breath to blow it with. I often thought that he was all right as the bank guard so long as we were attacked only by children, and then only one at a time.

Outside the cottage was a queue of three old ladies waiting patiently for 10–30 a.m., Tuesday, to come round. Mr. Parsons laid down his heavy whistle and opened up the front parlour for business. Then he retired to his endless perusal of the *Daily Herald,* by starting at the issue number and working steadfastly through to the bottom of the back page where he checked the name and address of the printers. Sometimes I wondered if he were one of those cranks who seek errors of spelling and then write to the editor about it. He seldom spoke, except to announce that Mr. Chamberlain was Nero reincarnated, and that Mosely was also Nero reincarnated. Nero, too, was over in Germany masquerading under the name of Hitler, and even in Lower Foxem where he was thinly disguised as Joe Tarrant, landlord of the *Crown.* When I grew to know Mr. Parsons better, I learned that he had had the misfortune to marry Nero's sister.

The sole result of Mr. Parsons's monumental reading was a phone call to a friend which went through the bank's telephone every day at 2 p.m. precisely. The substance of the message was always the same; "That you, Billy? This is Albert. Shillun each way *Drapers' Guild,* three o'clock. Don't mention it to Joe Tarrant. Bye, Billy," monotoned in a voice of utter dejection. Billy must have gone through life biting his tongue every time he met Joe.

The queue shuffled in before I could get the bag open, and Miss Kniper, the tallest of the three, was unable to stem her flood of conversation which had been held back since Friday last.

"Where is our dear Mr. Gruver, young man?" she demanded primly, and peering in my bag for signs of him.

"I'm sorry, ma'am, but he's got his usual touch of the old sinus."

"Oh dear, how distressing for him. What is your name?"

"Pook, ma'am; Peter Pook. I shall be attending to you until Mr. Gruver returns to work."

"Ah, well, Peter, you will find the books in the stationery cupboard under the counter, so perhaps you will be kind enough to put them on the counter before you empty the bag of riches, eh?"

I looked in the cupboard and fetched out rows of brightly jacketed novels which I deposited on the counter. Each of the three ladies added two books to the pile and then began a systematic search of the rest. I watched in astonishment.

"There's the sixpence, Peter," said Miss Kniper, handing over a coin and showing me she had selected two novels and no more. "It goes in Mr. G's little tin by the scales." I dropped the money in a tin labelled *"Digger Shag."*

Miss Kniper leaned over the counter and said archly, "I expect you know all about me, Peter; I'm Carole Dupree in *The Girl in the Suitcase.* Wasn't it thrilling? Such a dreadful death, but I didn't mind really, not after living such a life of it with all those *heavenly* men." Miss Kniper's recollections of the insatiable men caused her to titter happily. "I don't know if you remember, but when Mr. G. put me in the suitcase and left me at Victoria Station I was in an ... er ... interesting condition."

"I bet you were, ma'am. Probably been through the mincer with two of bread, just to be on the safe side," I replied, entering into the spirit of the thing.

"Oh, you dear revolting boy, how could you? Actually, Mr. G. with his usual inventive genius, had sprayed the interior of the case with an oriental chemical which turned the remains to a different blood-group and fossilized them within ten days."

"So the police opened the case, and there you were – concrete. Why, they could have used you for your own headstone, ma'am."

"Really, Peter, you are worse than dear Mr. G. I think we shall get along together famously. It is beyond me why his genius is not more widely acclaimed, especially when one reads some of the rubbish they print nowadays. How he thinks up all those *frightful* things to do to us I can't imagine. Now I must fly, so see you Friday, dear boy."

Miss Kniper hurried off to her reading, and the two other ladies followed her, leaving two sixpences for the tin. Mr. Grover's library did quite well during the morning, with a total subscription of four shillings. The Vicar borrowed *The Arrival of the Toad People* and *Walled Up in the Crypt.*

On the other hand, the Zenith wasn't having much of a day, apart from cashing two small cheques drawn on the Cooperative Bank, Manchester, under a Bankers' Arrangement. The

Verger came in for a three–halfpenny stamp, and Mr. Parsons took a credit–slip to use as a taper to light his pipe. While I had been attending to the customers I noticed that two men had walked through the office with empty buckets and, without a word, had departed with full buckets.

"Quiet 'ere, ain't it?" remarked Mr. Parsons between puffs.

"Quiet? I'll say it is; it's sound–waves in reverse. Has the water supply failed, Mr. Parsons?"

"Oh, them buckets? No, they came in for our well–water."

"Can't they go round the back–way then?"

"Afraid not. This is a kind of right of way, you see, and the well is under the stairs."

"What's wrong with their own water?"

"That's tap–water, no good for brewing. Our well–water is better than they got at Burton–on–Trent; makes a *luvlee* drop o' ale."

My youngest visitor was Elsie, who plonked down a pile of paper on the counter, and said, "Please tell Mr. G. I only had time to type Chapter Eight. He can have nine by Friday." It appeared to me that the Zenith ran its country branches on a *"Culture and Aid"* basis.

At half past twelve Mr. Parsons went to the door, drew a deep breath, and fairly shook the village with a mighty call of *"Her ... bert!"* When I had recovered from this unexpected peal of thunder, Herbert ran in with my dinner covered by his apron.

"I'm Herbert from the Crown pudding to follow what will you take with it two bob please," gabbled the newcomer.

"What's he on about, Mr. Parsons?" I inquired of the bank sentry.

"Your dinner come. Give 'im a florin from the till. Don't you want no beer?"

"No, thanks, Mr. Parsons; I'm in training."

"No beer with your dinner?" he gasped, as though I had refused air to breathe. "Cor, you should see Mr. G; he never 'as less than four pints with 'is dinner." So this accounted for the brewery atmosphere he brought back from Lower Foxem every Tuesday and Friday.

"'Afore that, 'e 'as three pints sent over at opening–time. Reckons 'e can't write blood–chillers when 'e's stone cold sober. Can't work enough 'ate into 'em, 'e says. You know our well? 'E measured it carefully one day and threw every Chink in the Tong down there, 'atchets an' all. The Tong Boss, Tye Foo Tee, was the last Chink to be killed, and Mr. G. couldn't get 'im in the well, it was so full, and 'e 'ad to chuck 'im on top of the pile and burn 'im with parry–fin. Cor, just imagine the smell."

I looked at my steak–and–kidney with precious little enthusiasm. Herbert returned with the pudding, and two pints for Mr. Parsons.

"I ain't allowed to leave the bank," he explained, eyeing me through the bottom of the first tankard, telescope fashion.

During the afternoon I had two customers. One was Miss Kniper, to change a book she had read before, and to pay in to her Home–Safe account.

"Mr. G. keeps the key on a hook where the towel hangs," she explained, handing me a tiny safe made to represent a prayerbook.

I opened it and five sixpences fell out.

"Ah, thank you, dear boy. just pop them in my purse," she laughed.

"Aren't you going to pay them in, ma'am?" I cried, desperate for trade.

"Oh, no, I never pay anything in. They are my reserves for the silly old electric–light meter."

At 2.30 the big account came in, for which the Zenith must have depended upon for its existence – Lower Foxem off–licence – and swamped me with over two hundred pounds in cash and a pile of cheques. I worked frantically to cope with this landslide because the bus left at three on the nail, and the next one was not till five. Apparently Mr. G's lurid tales were not entirely fictitious.

"Lot of money from such a small area, surely?" I re–marked to my guard.

"Well, I wouldn't say that. After all, it's luvlee 'ere in the summer, but the other eleven months is pretty so–so. In fact, what with me missus and no trains to look at, its only the beer every night wot stops me goin' off me rocker!"

Mr. Parsons said this so vehemently that I thought it wise to drop the subject in case he ran beserk there and then.

The Cudford bus pulled up at a minute to three, just as the Vicar called with a handful of parochial paying–in books.

"Sorry, Vicar, you just missed the boat; there's the bus," exclaimed our would–be suicide, faithfully guarding the door against further business. The bus–driver hooted impatiently, as though frightened by the solitude and eager to be back in the gay metropolis of Cudford.

"Apologies, Vicar. Have to see you Friday," I shouted.

"Good show, these can wait," he cried, waving the parochial accounts.

On the bus I sat next to Goldberg, who was running the only other Agency in the village, for Westminster Bank. I asked him, "You seem to have a lot of till–fodder in the bag, Goldie; does that mean you're pretty busy out here?"

"Yes, Peter, we keep going all right. You see, we've got the book–maker's account, the library account, the midwife's account, and the chemist's account, besides the doctor and the old hag who tells fortunes. Then of course, there's the big off licence and the *Crown* itself."

"Surely there's not *another* off–licence, Goldie?

"Oh, yes. Over the top of the Undertakers'; very steady trade. Most days the doctor comes in for the odd game of chess, but if he is busy he phones his moves through. Actually, I'm out here to widen my experience before they send for me. I shouldn't say this, but I'm a marked man, you know."

Marked men in the bank were those whose outstanding capabilities foreshadowed early managerships, Area Controllers' posts, and even Todderships in extreme cases. Todderships went only to those able to combine financial genius with the qualities of a successful Master of Ceremonies. This latter art was fully covered by Uncle Friendly's Course 31, *"The*

Complete Salesman," and his follow–up course, *"You, too, can have Friends."* I had sent away for the free specimen lesson offered, but the heading, *"Why does Everybody shun You?"* put me off from the start.

At Lower Foxem, Goldie gained his experience in a flimsy structure built on the lines of a stall at the village féte. It was completely burglar–proof inasmuch as thieves saw that it did not even keep the rain out, and they assumed therefore that it was beneath their skill to crack it. This arrangement saved both parties a lot of trouble, because there was nothing inside once Goldie had departed with the Gladstone–bag, unless they wanted to use the phone.

The bus arrived back at Cudford at 3.30, and I entered the office feeling like the remittance man just returned from the Colonies.

"How did you fare on your first day in charge, Peter?" asked Mr. Pants apprehensively.

"Fine, sir. Busy as sin all day, what with one thing and another, but I managed to cope."

"But what happened really? Break the suspense, please, Peter. Where are the police? Who has been injured? What accounts have we lost? Surely you managed something? I know; you lost the bag down the well."

"Oh, sir, of course not. Here it is, safe and sound as usual. I'm the new, mature Pook, responsible and trustworthy, sir. I'm a walking fidelity bond."

"Open the bag, Peter, because I know it's empty. You've come back by car, which a dealer sold you for the till money."

Looking hurt, I opened the bag and revealed the proceeds of Lower Foxem's alcoholic indulgences. Mr. Pants seemed almost disappointed. He checked the contents and they balanced to a penny.

"Strange indeed," he murmured, "but what about the bus season–ticket? Perhaps you took it into the depot and got a refund on it?" I produced the ticket, safe in its celluloid frame. Mr. Pants made a funny face, and I gave him the faithful retainer look.

"All right, Peter, I give up. What happened?" he grinned placing an *agent provocateur* arm round my shoulder.

"Banking is an exact science, sir, and that's all there is to it. You either do it right, or you do it wrong. As for me, I guess I'm Mr. Right."

"I don't know where you dig up all these slogans, Peter, but you say people have been in and out all day, yet you've returned with only one decent transaction. Now, I've often wondered what Mr. Gruver does out there all day, so how do you explain that?"

Perhaps Mr. Gruver could, but he was snug in bed, typing.

"It's a case of potential consumer interest, sir," I stalled. "Just people inquiring about our banking facilities, and all that."

"Was this potential consumer interest a *nice* girl, Peter?"

"Don't be like that, sir; you know I've overcome it. Actually, today has given me several new ideas for Mr. Putty's suggestion box."

"You know very well I have already forbidden you to put any more frivolous suggestions in the box, Pook, ever since the last one of yours which upset Mr. Putty for a week – 'Fit a fire-guard over the chandelier in the manager's office,' indeed."

"No, sir, the genuine article to draw trade, I mean."

"In the Zenith Bank we do not draw trade; we increase the number of our accounts, Pook."

"Well, have it your own way, sir, but you want to make a bigger killing, don't you?"

"We may desire to expand the bank's economic resources, yes."

"Therefore you want the ordinary man in the street to plonk in the odd quid or two."

"Ouch."

"Well, to nail him you've got to have a call-bird, like the barkers do. They throw coloured combs at passers-by to attract their attention."

"I was not aware your father was ever a coster, Pook, but are you proposing that Mr. Putty should stand outside the Zenith

Bank, distributing free combs and crying, 'Luvverly fivers today; get your luvverly fivers 'ere'."

"Well, no, sir, not exactly. But the time will come when the banks will have to advertise to attract the emerging artisan class, as the *Mirror* calls the strikers. Little cultural draws, like ... er ... well, like a small select library in the banking-hall, and a cup of tea with a free fag like the *Troxy* does in the afternoon. Perhaps a bit of soft background music thrown in. Even the Cathedral does that, and look how it packs 'em in."

"Very ingenious, Pook, but do you realize what would happen if we did? We'd be full up with your fellow layabouts from morning to night, spending a pleasant day in the Zenith Amusement Arcade and nothing else."

"Oh, sir, be fair. You can't really call Lady Erge a layabout."

"Hm, hm, sometimes I wonder if you can help it, Pook, so let us change the subject to a more sober one. You will be sorry to learn that you will soon be losing me."

So, they had caught up with old Pants at last. Chief clerks seemed to be ten-a-penny at the Old Bailey of late, where they explained to cynical judges how they had allowed their stamp collecting hobbies to grow so large that they eventually included the Bearer Bonds. I gave him my condolences.

"This is terrible news, sir. You should have been more careful."

"I have been careful all my life, Pook, and now I reap the reward."

"Perhaps we can visit you, sir. Once a month, I believe it is."

"You will be welcome any time, Peter. It is not far; only over to Aston. I am to be manager there in place of Mr. Ronuk, who has retired prematurely."

"Congratulations, sir," I cried with enthusiasm and relief. So he was not bound for the hulks after all.

"Thank you, Peter, I'm sure. I've given you a good grounding in your work, but naturally this transfer will come as a blow to you."

I tried my compressed–rubber face, but failed to squeeze out the timely tear.

"My place will be taken by Mr. Disher, so watch your step, laddie, for he is a Marked Man."

"Oh lor'."

I talked the matter over with Fork during the lunch–hour. Fork was still retaining his ambassador at home, but he had consented to let me have a formal chargé d'affaires. He said, "Well, when all's said and done, I'm glad the poor old devil has got a branch before they put him out to grass; he's tried hard enough. Not that I regard Aston as much of a branch, but at least it's a twig. They little know what they're in for, up there."

I thought, Tilly was safe, anyhow.

I felt so sorry for Aston that I rang them up in the afternoon, to put them in the picture in case they were still cheerful. A frightfully cultured voice answered the phone.

"This is Aston Branch speaking."

"Oh crumbs. Can I talk to Fred."

"Fred who?"

"No, Fred Rutter."

"Sorry, he's away. I'm here on relief. But this is Mr. Brompton Mainwaring–Flit."

"Which one are you?"

"I'm all of them."

"Oh, sorry; I thought it was a motto. Where's Fred?"

"Mr. Rutter is unfortunately in hospital."

"In dock? What's up with him?"

"I believe it is a slipped–disc or a burst blood–vessel. Something revolting anyway."

"How did he come by that, Mr. Brompton and so on?"

"Mr. Hut tells me that for some wager or certificate he was endeavouring to lift about half–a–ton of ironmongery off the ground, and he collapsed in our strong room. The weights went clean through the floor and fractured the drains. Only yesterday Mr. Hut had to send for the brewers' men to remove the equipment on their dray."

"How *dreadful* for him. I'll write to him this very

evening."

"You wouldn't be the Peter Pook who was here on relief, by any chance?"

"Yes, that's me. I know all about Fred because I'm a fellow Brute."

"Well, Mr. Rutter says you will soon be a dead Brute, so under the circumstances perhaps a letter might retard his recovery. He mentioned something about visiting Cudford as soon as he could walk again, in order to ram something down your throat. A badge, I believe he said it was."

"Oh lor'. Thanks all the same for the tip, Mr. What's-it."

I rang off despondently. Reading *How to Win Friends, and Influence People* hadn't done me much good, by the sound of things. All I seemed to do was to lose friends and injure people.

Whilst I was engrossed in Fred's inexplicable disloyalty to our Cult, Mr. Putty came storming out of his office waving a large advertising-poster as though he was the matador in a bull-fight. He did not waste words, but pointed a trembling finger to the yellow cloak. I read the inscription proudly. It said, *"Peter Pook v Bandsman Bangle."*

"This. Is this *you,* boy?" he spluttered, making the poster rustle with his emotion.

"Yes, sir. Wednesday evening at the Town Hall, in aid of the *Peace in our Time* campaign. Everybody will be there but I can get you tickets if you like, sir."

"Tickets, bah. Do you realize this is a common prize-fight, and you are a clerk in this bank? Haven't you any brains, boy? What would our customers say if I were on an all-in wrestling bill as *Panther Putty versus The Masked Terror?"*

"Well, with all respect, sir, they'd say you hadn't got a chance. Not a bookmaker in Cudford would touch you, sir."

"Grrr. Don't make me ill, Pook. Have you indulged in these dreadful exhibitions before?"

"Yes, sir, quite often. Last time, I fought Fireman Tucker in Southampton."

"Oh, my godfathers. What happened?"

"I did for him in the third, sir. Clean through the ropes."

"Was the unfortunate man injured?"

"Only hurt his hand, sir. He hit me in the dressing-room after."

"Why, Pook; as if I couldn't guess?"

"Well, sir, he reckoned I clouted him when we were shaking hands."

"This was pure fabrication, of course?"

"Well, sir, it all depends on how long a man takes to shake hands, I suppose. No good being a slow shaker in that game."

"Be that as it may, I positively forbid your appearing on this programme. Understand? To add weight to my decision, it is prohibited in H.O. Instructions."

"With great respect, sir, it doesn't seem to be. I've checked. Everything else is forbidden except boxing as as amateur."

That did it. Mr. Putty and Mr. Pants combed the great tome to find this unprecedented omission, and Mr. Pants quoted long chunks off by heart. He did all he could to squeeze me into the vetoes included under *"Processions, public, walking in."* Unless one was actually following the coffin, processions were orgies of corruption to bank-clerks, but even Mr. Putty had to admit that my contest hardly constituted "a slow-moving assembly of persons engaged in public demonstration in the open air."

The "open air" clause saved me. Mr. Pants pinned his faith first in *"Lotteries, tickets for,"* and then *"Sporting Activities, Money inducements."* I explained that when I entered the ring, there was no luck or lottery about the result, and as for financial reward, I even had to pay my own expenses in the interests of the *"Peace in our Time"* fund.

They finally got me under, *"Duels, principals, seconds, patrons, or participants' widows."*

"But that's not fair, sir; that Rule got left in from the old days, like in the Stationery Order where you can have pounce-boxes if you can't get used to this new-fangled blotting-paper."

"Don't come the barrack-room lawyer with me, my lad.

I know I'm only the pathetic bald-headed old fuddy-duddy around here, because I've heard you mention it to your precious pals, but your contest is out. It's only this antiquated Rule that prevents me from impaling you on my paper-spike, so be thankful it is still in the book.''

''Would it be in order, sir, for me to box under an assumed plum-name, as they call it?''

''If you venture to do so, Pook, you will find that your plum thing will cut very little ice at the Labour Exchange afterwards.''

''Oh, lor. Did you ever fight a duel, sir?'' Carrot time.

''No, Pook, and what's more the thought never entered my head until I met you. That ancient Rule was required when young gentlemen entered the service of the bank, but the compilers never envisaged the day when the intake would include members of Casey's Gym.''

''Then I take it, sir, that you wish me to withdraw my support for the peace of Europe?''

''Yes, that is what I have been hinting at, in my rough old-fashioned way. And I might observe that if Europe was not full of young Pooks eager to knock Bandsman Bangle's head off, the fund would not be needed.''

''But I always thought you liked sport, Mr. Putty, and you. . . .''

The manager threw the poster at me.

Thus did the notorious Bandsman Bangle keep his unbeaten record, as the M.C. announced to the blood-thirsty peace-lovers in the Town Hall that Bout No. 7 had been unavoidably cancelled.

He was pelted with beer bottles.

FOURTEEN

Mr. Pants held his last meeting with the sorrowful staff in the *George,* with halves of bitter all round. His appointment to the twig at Aston was so important an occasion that even Mr. Putty was present, ready to provide the farewell speech and hand over the traditional promotion–kit of Conway Stewart Pen and Pencil in Case, obtained at ten per cent discount at Messrs. Chipit and Bleed, Cudford.

Our revered chief clerk spared a few words for every member of the staff, who were looking surprisingly cheerful under such a separation. When he came to me he put his arm round my shoulder and said, "Ah, Peter, far be it from me to introduce office matters into the jovial atmosphere of the inn, but I hear weird and disturbing tales about poor little Ronald's accident yesterday." He looked down at the midget banker by my side. Hearing his name mentioned, the casualty gave us a wan smile. The end of Ronald's thin nose was wrapped around with sticking plaster, and his pale face was entirely devoid of eyebrows or lashes.

"If I were not answering the call to promotion, Pook, I should feel compelled to hold an inquiry into the unfortunate accident," Mr. Pants continued gravely, "because it seems a remarkable coincidence that the gas water–heater in our cloak–room has been lighted safely for many years until you offered to clean the pilot–jet yesterday, immediately prior to Ronald's entry with the office matches."

"I expect it has got old and worn out," I replied, automatic–ally wondering how Mr. Balls was faring in all this wet weather. Probably planting rice.

"That's as may be, Pook, but there are rumours circulating among certain members of the female staff that this dangerous occurrence is connected with Ronald's refusing to pay protection money to cover up some boyish practical joke of which you were the victim. In short, blackmail."

"Oh, sir, what a horrid idea. Ronnie, Mr. Pants thinks we've quarrelled or something. Tell him we're the best of pals."

Ronald smiled bravely. "We're the best of pals, sir," he muttered, in a mechanical voice lacking any conviction.

"Well, well, I'm very pleased to hear it. Little Ronnie, here, needs our best treatment and assistance, for, besides being delicate, he's a very special junior, aren't you, Ronald?" beamed Mr. Pants. Ronald certainly looked a very special junior at the moment. Mr. Pants turned to me and whispered, "If his father learns about the gas-heater we're all for the high-jump, especially you, Pook."

"How do you mean, sir; what's so special about him, apart from juvenile shrinkage? Lots of bank-clerks are delicate, or else they'd be working somewhere they enjoyed."

"Please lower your voice, Pook. Mr. Putty gave strict instructions that Ronald's indentity was not to be made known among the staff, for obvious reasons, but I may as well mention it to you, as I am leaving the branch. Hasn't his surname struck a chord in your mind – Renault?"

"Well, to be quite honest, sir, what with the motor-bike and whatnot, I did wonder if he was related to the French car manufacturers. He must be rolling in it, sir."

"No, Pook; more important than that. His father is none other than Mr. Renault, our Staff Controller at Head Office," whispered Mr. Pants in an awed voice and bowing slightly at the name.

"Oh godfathers," I gasped, spilling some beer. "Excuse me a moment, sir." I turned to Ronald and said, "The party's on me, Ron, so come over to the bar and have another shandy."

"That's the spirit, Peter, go and drink with your chum. I know how you young rascals like to get together," called out Uncle Pants benevolently.

At the bar, Ronald said, "All right, Peter, but no rough stuff, mind. I'm not feeling too hot after yesterday."

I laughed with an effort. "Here's your double shandy, Ron, and here's to your good health. Just forget all about that protection lark; it was only a joke to see what kind of a man you are, and now I know! I'd like you to muck in with me, and I'll teach you Power–Surge so that you can be big and strong like me."

Ronald's face lit up. "Would you really, Peter. That's mighty generous of you and it might do me good, at that. Mind though, I don't want to get like you, but half–way wouldn't hurt. I tell my dad everything, but this will tickle him pink. That reminds me; he wants to meet you next time he's down this way."

I hastily thrust a ten–shilling note into Ronald's pen–pocket, and tried to get the grapes out of my mind.

Mr. Putty in speech mood, and pressing forward regard–less of the roistering spectators of Mr. Pants's exit.

"... And so, ladies and gentlemen, let us try to bear up with the thought that we are losing a friend, but gaining a manager." The staff bore up bravely and ordered more rounds. "Mr. Pants has long been my doughty first–lieutenant, through the long and perilous voyage across the oceans of. . . ." Here he filled in charts and soundings from Commercial Geography, followed by the log–books, principles of marine navigation, observations on nautical fish–life passed *en route,* and then ended up near port but slightly off course owing to the gathering blanket of International Fog and the extinguishing of lighthouses around the coast of Germany.

At all events, assuming Lieutenant Pants ever reached harbour under the hair–raising navigation of Captain Putty, he could look forward to a safe berth at inland Aston, proud in the knowledge that, having dragged his ship up the Cud Valley, his name was high on the *Mentioned in Dispatches* roll held by the Board of Admiralty, now transferred to Lombard Street.

"I give you, ladies and gentlemen, *Captain* Pants," barked our manager, handing over the telescope case by Messrs.

Conway Stewart. Captain Pants saluted his mutinous crew and put out to sea again for a short farewell voyage of thanks. As usual, he lost his ship just over the horizon, but today his new rank enabled him to sail merrily on without one, until he got hopelessly engaged with the Germans, at Jutland of all places. Facing the Kaiser's broadsides was too much for any admiral who tried it by leading the line without visible means of floating. Consequently Mr. Pants followed his ship to the bottom, with the stirring cry of, "Splice the main-brace, me hearties." This popular signal was already well under way to such an extent that we did not even look for survivors.

"Anyone'd think we were all in the blasted Navy," said sexy Cashier No. 4 over his grog-tot. "We start out with Drake and his cockle-shells and end up being blown out of the water by the German Grand Fleet before we can drop a ball in our twenty-five pounder. You're the Mister Know-all round here, Pook, so how do you account for it?"

"Because we're not all crumpet-chasing pacifists like you, chum, and Putty and Pants were both in the Navy in the last war while you were shivering in the air-raid shelter with your hands up," I replied, always willing to enlighten the ignorant.

Cashier No. 4 gave me the sophisticated sneer and said, "One day you'll get *such* a tanning, Pook, and then you'll learn that brawn isn't everything. This is where you want it, up here." He pointed to his temple, and I thought he might as well have it on there as on his jaw. Just as I was measuring the distance the cry went up, *"He's off,* three cheers for Mr. Pants."

I rushed to the door with cabin-boy Ronnie and the rest of the staff, to give three huzzas at the gangway for our departing chief. Mr. Pants and I shook a vigorous good-bye with both hands as though we were Double-Surging, and he cried out good humouredly "Maximum Endurance Reached, Peter. Ha, ha, I hope I shall be able to write by Monday, after that. God bless you all."

"God help Aston," roared the matelots.

"Best of luck, sir," I called out sadly.

Cashier No. 4 shook his head. "So the poor old blighter's

finally made it,'' he reflected.

At this time, Mr. Pants was barely fifty.

Our chief clerk went off in a blaze of glory because his departure coincided with the march past of the band of the Royal Wessex Regiment in full blast. In the near-side file I noticed sadistic Bandsman Bangle, whose solid chest was engaged in pumping wind into a small clarinet. Attached to the end of the instrument was a visiting-card of musical notation, conveniently held up by a silver clothes-peg, on which was recorded twelve notes of the *Teddy Bears' Picnic* in order to assist Bandsman Bangle's limited memory.

''When does the snake come up from the basket, Bangle?'' I shouted wittily. Under the circumstances, it was impossible for him to turn his head but I saw his eyeballs leave the music to slew round and look at me. When he had got the picture his eyes went to slits before they returned to the *''You're sure of a big surprise''* bit. Even his military discipline could not hide the fact that Bout No. 7 might well take place in Cudford High Street, right outside the Zenith Bank and Mr. Putty's front window.

Nothing was sacred to Mr. Disher, the Marked Man who succeeded Mr. Pants. On his very first day he had Mr. Lovejoy tear down the Box which Mr. Pants had cherished for so long. Mr. Disher took one look at the box and said, *''BUMPH.''* Down it came.

He was a short-well-built young man who toddled briskly round the office with his hands in his pockets and his shoulders hunched, like a rugby player on a cold day. In fact he played rugger for the Zenith's 1st XV in London, and for the county. To me, he was a new banking phenomenon.

While the box was being demolished he trotted up to the notice-board and stared at it for one minute, reading Mr. Pants's long, typed prohibitions copied from H.O. Instructions. One of these epistles gave me the impression that as long as one went through life without folding any form in two, one was certain of a Toddership.

''Bumph,'' grunted Mr. Disher, ripping off the notices wholesale and hurling them into a waste-paper basket. Then he stared at the green baize and rubbed it with his knuckles. Surely he did not intend clawing that off as well? He left it on.

Half the stuff I carried round for Mr. Disher's inspection was apparently *bumph,* and went straight from my hands into the basket. Consequently he sat for long periods at his empty desk, gazing out at the cathedral spire and drumming his knuckles on the wood. At his feet stood two bulging waste–paper baskets of this new bumph.

Even Mr. Putty was not safe. He emerged from his office with piles of papers he had been working on by the midnight oil and passed them to Mr. Disher. Without rising from his stool, Mr. Disher threw them straight into the basket. "Bumph," he declared, smiling happily at Mr. Putty.

I remarked to Ronald, "It would save time if we all chucked our work into the incinerator the moment we finished it."

"Well, it beats me, Peter, but isn't he *quick?* just think what it was like with Pants," said Ronald, admiringly.

Mr. Pants had operated on the Great Wall of China system, where time and labour were of no account. Apart from his own vast toil, he tried to check every item the whole staff handled. Consequently his desk disappeared during the day under mountains of journals, files, letters, vouchers, and pass–books. In fact, Mr. Balls used to pile up the big ledgers inside the box as though he were on piece–work during the building of the Great Pyramid of Cheops. As a result of this gravitation of everything to the box, half the staff were always trying to get in there to find the journals they wanted in a hurry.

One of my duties every Friday was to compile the weekly Cash Account for Lombard Street, and have it checked by Mr. Pants. I would carry the Cash Book very high in the air in order to place it on the summit of the Pyramid, and Mr. Pants always greeted its arrival with, "That will have to wait for the cool of the evening," as he struggled to get through the labours of the tropical day.

Today, I prepared the Cash Account at my desk and just as I blotted the last entry an arm reached over my shoulder and signed it. "Right," grinned Mr. Disher. Glory be, the man wouldn't even let you get to his desk now. I looked at Mr. Disher's signature, contrasting it with Mr. Pants's copperplate engrossing. All I saw was a straight line with a curl at the end, like a fish–hook lying on its back.

"Let's get out," was a phrase ever on his lips, and, indeed, from the moment he rushed into the office of a morning that was all he seemed to think about. He would stand for ages by Mr. Lecher's desk, hands in pockets and feet tapping, gazing up at the office clock, waiting to sign Mr. Lecher's overdraft applications.

"He's only been married six months," Lily explained to me, shyly. Lily used to enter Mr. Pants's box in the afternoon for the daily dictation of those monumental banking expositions which our clients received in place of letters, and which Mr. Putty signed long after he had eaten his high–tea upstairs. Nowadays, Lily hardly knew what to do with herself because Mr. Disher answered some of the letters by phone, some by one sentence, and the rest he ignored as bumph. None of the senior men dared write a letter after lunch, and all correspondence had to be signed by Mr. Putty immediately after his midday meal.

Mr. Disher kept his desk clinically clean, so that only the regulation whistle lay on it. On his first day he found the lid would not shut, even after Mr. Pants had taken away loads of his personal papers. Mr. Disher went red in the face and hurled the contents on the floor. Then he slammed the lid and never opened it again. "Ronald," he shouted, "bumph." Ronald went round and filled a sack with it.

When the customers came in for their weekly social call on the chief clerk, so dear to Mr. Pants, Mr. Disher refused to see them. He spotted them as he gazed out of the windows, and promptly got under the counter where he sat on a waste–paper basket. Viewed from the back of the office, this pantomime sent Ronald and me into sobbing hysterics, particularly when Lady Erge came in. She would lean over the counter, right above Mr. Disher's head, and croon to Cashier No. 1, "Where is your fascinating young sub–manager, Mr. Fossil? I simply must see him about my late husbands' wills.''

''Out,'' exclaimed Mr. Disher, grinning all over his red face, and making no secret of the fact that he appeared to be sitting on a privy.

''What did you say, Mr. Fossil?'' ejaculated Lady Erge, with a jerk.

Mr. Fossil couldn't say anything at the moment, because he was spluttering into his handkerchief. When he recovered, he said, ''I'm frightfully sorry, Lady Erge, but Mr. Disher has been called away on urgent business.''

''Oh, how tiresome. I could swear I caught a glimpse of him through the bank window just now. Never mind, I'll call tomorrow.''

''Would you care to see Mr. Putty, ma'am?

''Er, no; the matter requires Mr. Disher's personal attention, thank you, Mr. Fossil,'' replied the lady. Mr. Putty had lost some of his glamour since the new arrival. Off she stalked.

Mr. Disher came out of the basket looking none the worse for having been crouching at Lady Erge's very knees, and muttered, ''Bumpher type.'' Then he resumed his inspection of the spire's weathercock.

One glorious day I received a short note from Portsmouth Football Club, telling me that they had not forgotten me, and I could expect further news shortly. Getting hold of Mr. Disher, I told him the full story of my impending departure for the glamour of public adulation.

As he listened he gazed longingly at the office clock, and when I had broken the shattering news to him he said, ''Good for you,'' and threw the precious letter down into the basket. Then he stared out of the window. Not knowing whether he had even heard me, I bent down and retrieved the document for my scrapbook. I didn't know what to make of him, but Head Office did, because he was to become the youngest area manager in the service.

When Mr. Disher went downstairs to tear out the coupons from the bonds, I thought I had him.

''I've got to come down with you, sir,'' I explained.

"Bumph," he grinned, showing me four sets of keys, and hurrying off alone. But he was back in two minutes so I waited to accompany him downstairs again for the cutting routine, and the oily pin dialogue. He shook his head violently.

"Done," he snapped, throwing the four sets of keys on my desk and trotting off to see if the weathercock was still working.

When Mr. Disher received the morning mail he really went into rugby action. The big Head Office Letter came sailing across the office like a mortar-bomb, right into my arms. Then he flicked through the letters and ran round the office, passing sections of them to the relevant clerks. The last heap he gave to Lily, and returned to a Buddhist-like contemplation of the police-whistle.

On Tuesdays, our quietest day, Mr. Lecher announced, "Mr. Disher wants everybody away by 3.30, so look lively."

"3.30?" I gasped, "why, we're often later than that on *Saturdays.*"

This was true, and the latest I remember getting away on my half-day was just after midnight.

"I can't help that," continued Mr. Lecher. "The chief says he does not want any night-watchmen on the staff, and anybody who is not off the premises by 3.30 will get kicked in the cobblers."

Here was a man after my own heart. The staff worked like fiends to preserve their vital organs, while Mr. Disher stood over Mr. Lecher and hypnotized the office clock, as though his first child was due on the hour. At 3.20 I yelled out, "Country Clearing £9 short." Mr. Disher was on me like a flash.

"Bumph inversion," he snorted, "Probably 78 for 87."

He threw the lists in all directions and stabbed his forefinger into the National Provincial column. Then he toddled off without another word. As usual he was right.

At 3.25 Mr. Gruver staggered in with the fodder-bag from Lower Foxem and Mr. Disher pushed him straight through the office into the safe; pushed him out again minus the bag, and locked the grills. Mr. Gruver never looked so startled in all his life.

"Go home," commanded Mr. Disher, and walked out of the office.

"He hasn't signed the Head Office Letter," I screamed, rushing after him with it. I caught our chief clerk over by the Cathedral, where he put his fish–hook on the document without pausing in his stride.

"Thank you, sir," I gasped, "and good afternoon."

"Bumph," he grinned, pointing back at the Head Office Letter.

When the Cathedral clock was still echoing to the half–hour bell the staff gathered round the bank entrance like a flock of lost sheep, not knowing what to do with themselves. The pubs were shut and it was too early for tea, so I said to Lily, "What about you and me going to the *Troxy* and seeing *Eaten Alive by the Octopus Women,* first house?"

Lily giggled. "Well, Peter, that's very kind of you, but after all, I'm only an *English* girl, and anyway, Boo–boos here is taking me already."

"Boo–boos? Who in hell is Boo–boos?" I demanded. Lily pointed to a very scarlet Cashier No. 4.

"When we go to the pictures, he buys me a quarter of assorted boos–boos and feeties, so he's Boo–boos and I'm his Feeties," Lily explained, radiant with *Mackintosh's* assorted romance.

"The office will be interested to learn your new code–name, Boo–boos," I chaffed him. At the moment he was a very scowling Boo–boos, more like a peppermint–humbug. So this was the language of love that Lily was always hinting at with her Peterkins and Pookie–wookie nonsense. I must remember to ask Mr. Putty what his secret love–name was. Putty–fingers, perhaps?

Lily marched off to be devoured by the terrible Octopus Women, and probably by Boo–boos later. I decided to write a letter to Bruce Bold and get his massive views on the subject, and meanwhile I returned to the hotel to profit by the early finish with an extra hour's Power–Surge.

Life at Cudford under the dynamic Mr. Disher and free from that notorious choir–master, Mr. Balls, made me see banking in an entirely new light. The tonic effect ran through the whole staff, and even Mr. Putty seemed to leave more and more of his responsibilities to the chief clerk. In this way he actually got so much practice with the clubs in his office that he made the Cudford team within a few months.

By now everybody was frightened to give any work to Mr. Disher in case it got hurled into the waste–paper basket, and even the manager dare not place so much as a postal–order on the bare desk. Mr. Disher checked everybody's work on the guardian angel principle, by standing behind them and signing the forms the instant they were completed.

While he was waiting, he threw open all desks and drawers and tipped the contents on the floor. After a week of this treatment, we couldn't find a scrap of rough–paper to figure on anywhere in the office. I kept a sheet in my pocket because my unmathematical mind refused to work without my doing small sums with the pencil, until Mr. Disher snatched it from me one morning as he was speeding past my desk.

"Bumph," he laughed, tossing it out of the window. Not that he was one–sided in this manner, because I saw him eating his sandwiches one day, prior to a rugby match, and after the first bite he flung the lot in the basket. "Stale bumph," he snarled.

Ronald turned to me and tittered, "If his wife has a baby, I don't fancy its chances."

I defy any person, even Mr. Pants, not to laugh if they could have seen Mr. Disher sorting out the office documents. No matter how high the pile, he tore through it with his characteristic speed, classing the contents either as *bumph* or *tripe.* The bumph went on the floor for Ronald and the sack, and the little pile of tripe returned to the vaults. His only other sub–division of matter was bank–notes, which he referred to as "good bumph." Consequently, when he checked the cashiers' tills he counted one hundred–pound bundle of notes and then weighed the rest against it, as though it were rush–hour in the *Home and Colonial.*

The big brass scales went *clang, clang, clang, clang,*

clang, in the process, and Mr. Disher, talking to himself, said, "Good bumph, good bumph, good bumph, good bumph, short bumph, in time with the scales. This was a lightning operation in contrast to Mr. Pants's weekly hour of counting everything within sight, right down to the twopenny receipt stamps, and forgetting the amount when half-way through.

However, even I was a little surprised when Lady Erge came in one day and called me over to the counter. I happened to glance down by my legs and there was Mr. Disher smiling up at me from under the counter. "Out," he snapped. I had to fly for my handkerchief and cough into the till.

"Please, Peter, I am in rather a hurry and I don't see dear Mr. Disher about," she crooned. Ye gods, the man was biting my knee.

"Would you be a dear and give me my pass-book. Please make sure all the income-tax bumph inside it is in order. Particularly all those bumphy vouchers for the War Loan interest. Really, I can't seem to spot Mr. Disher anywhere, Peter."

"Posted abroad," from under the counter.

"What did you say, Peter?" Lady Erge inquired.

"I said, it's such a fraud. You know, such high tax for you."

"I quite agree, Peter. Absolutely disgraceful, but you don't have to laugh so heartily about it. You wouldn't if you were in my shoes."

"Bumph boots," from under the counter.

I retired to Mr. Lecher, unable to cope any more. I said, "Please, Mr. Lecher, go and attend to Lady Erge. She's leaning right over Mr. Disher and he won't keep quiet. If I go round there again I'll get the sack."

"Better send her into Lunatic's Corner, and I'll deal with her there," volunteered our genial bank psychiatrist. "When our Lady Erge starts talking about her bumphy vouchers it's time I gave her the treatment."

As Mr. Lecher entered the Asylum, I heard Lady Erge say to him, "Ah, dear man, have you found all my tripe...?"

Mr. Disher disappointed me inasmuch as he refused to

hold any family conferences with me or anyone else. All he wanted to do was to go home. The old ruses which had worked so well on his predecessor failed dismally, mainly because he discouraged my conversations by examining his shoes during the opening gambit, and walking away directly I had got to the second sentence. Not being one to give up easily, I tried following him round the office but he evaded me by locking himself in the toilet and singing "Leave me alone, let me wander; Don't tie my hands, just let me roam."

Frustrated, I consulted Mr. Lecher on the problem.

"Have you ever managed to speak to Mr. Disher?" I asked him.

"Oh, yes. I had to take him to task for throwing all Mr. Putty's letters to Messrs. Cod, Lumpit & Sofa about the mortgage in the waste-paper basket. Mr. Putty was quite upset because he had done eight pages on it. Mr. Disher just grinned, took my own papers on the matter and tore them up. I got a bit hot under the collar so he said, 'All office-work eighty per cent bumph, fifteen per cent tripe, five per cent good bumph. Mortgage cancelled by phone. Let's get out.' Then he left me flat, walked out to the street, and grinned at me through the window. What can you do with a man like that?"

After hearing this, I set a very cunning trap for our chief clerk. I showed him the poster advertising my contest with Bandsman Bangle, but keeping it out of his reach in case it followed the rest of my work into the shute. I said, "Would you mind if I fought Bandsman Bangle in the Town Hall, sir?"

"No," he replied, jumping off his stool.

"But Mr. Putty says I mustn't, sir."

"Good for him."

"So I definitely have your permission, sir?"

"Yes."

"What will Mr. Putty say when he finds out, sir?"

"Old poster; more bumph."

"Oh, crikey." I threw it in the shute myself.

Nobody suffered from Mr. Disher's "Keep Britain Tidy" campaign more than poor old Gruver when he returned from

Lower Foxem. I heard him pulling open his drawers and screaming with shock as he put his head right inside in frantic search for his manuscripts.

"They're gone, *they're gone.* Who's swiped my blasted papers? he raved, near to tears. "Months of sweat, and someone's bagged the lot." He threw all the drawers on the floor, and peered into the recesses. "Not left so much as a flamin' paper-clip. Who's responsible for it, because, mark my word, when I find him I'll garrotte him while the parryfeen's catching light."

"Responsible for what, Mr. Gruver?" inquired Mr. Putty., who happened to be attracted by the spectacle of Mr. G. climbing bodily into the drawer spaces.

"If it's you, you idiot, your liver's coming out on the end of a harpoon," shouted Mr. G., unaware of Mr. Putty's presence. The manager went beetrooty.

"Control yourself, man, and come out of there this instant," he roared. "Now, what is it you've lost which is depriving you of your reason and causing you to insult your own manager?"

"Oh, godfathers," moaned Mr. Gruver, standing up. "Only some bank papers, and, er ... er ... some personal documents, sir."

"Very well. When you have calmed down, come into my office. I, also, have cause to complain, seeing that my desk drawers are suddenly bare." Mr. Putty strode off to take out his own drawers and tip up his knee-hole desk.

I stood there watching gleefully, interested to see how it looked when somebody else was on the carpet for a change.

"Bumph," Mr. Disher yelled, from his desk at the other end. The magic word galvanized Mr. Gruver into action, and he streaked down into the cellars. When the staff left the office he was still down there, working away like a rag-picker's outing.

As I left, I shouted down the stairs, "Mr. Gruver, I don't want to bother you when you're so busy, but Mr. Disher says he is going to inspect the sub-branch on Tuesday. Thought I'd just tip you off."

Mr. Gruver collapsed over the sacks.

The fatal day which was to end my sojourn at Cudford arrived out of the blue, and introduced itself by a ring on Mr. Putty's desk–bell. Ronald answered the summons and came out looking for me. "He wants you in the temple, Peter. Trouble, I should think."

Inside, Mr. Putty had a letter in his hand and he appeared extremely grave.

"Ah, Peter, I'm afraid I've received an urgent summons for you which will probably come as a bit of a shock. Sit down, lad, while I read it."

"It's quite all right, sir," I replied confidently, "I've been expecting it for some time. The club told me I should hear from them soon."

"I regret to say it's not from Portsmouth, Peter. A bigger and more important team is after your services."

"Then surely it's not *Arsenal,* sir? They never saw me play, as far as I can remember. No, it can't be the *Gunners."*

"No, Peter, not the Gunners, but you are getting warmer. It is His Majesty's Government, and they are calling you up for military service, along with others of your age–group and certain reservists. You are required to do six months' training, in view of the world situation at present."

"But why, sir? Mr. Chamberlain says it's to be peace in our time, and all that. Why pick on me when it could ruin my career at a vital moment? Six months just about covers the whole football season. What about that famous piece of paper Mr. Chamberlain got from Hitler, which he waved about at the airport?"

"More bumph," said Mr. Disher, who had joined us to hear the news. Mr. Putty continued.

"I'm sorry, Peter, but the matter is completely out of my hands. Let us hope that 1939 will see the international situation gradually improving in Europe. After all, it will be only for six months, and the *Daily Express* predicts no war this year, next year, or ever."

"Bumph," snorted Mr. Disher, "Fleet Street bumph."

Unfortunately, Hitler didn't care whether I played for Portsmouth or Pekin, and Mr. Putty's optimistic prediction of six months was almost seven years short.

Mr. Putty handed me some forms and said, "Here is the railway voucher to take you up to London for the interview and medical examination. I don't think you will be exempted on medical grounds, eh Peter? They might want you for carrying tanks across rivers, ha, ha."

"Very unlikely to fail me, sir," I replied, remembering my visit to Dr. Crippen in Harley Street.

For a few minutes Mr. Putty was on the high seas again, in the Great War, where he gained the D.S.O., and he gave me many useful tips concerning life in uniform. For once, I listened to him with genuine interest.

I was the only person to be called up in our office during the 1938 crisis, except Mr. Lecher who was an officer in the Territorials. Everybody seemed sorry to lose me, especially Fork who had to take over my duties temporarily and move down the scale.

Lily treated me as though I were already lying fly–blown on the battlefield, by piping her eye every time she spoke to me. She said, "Peter, Mr. Putty has told me to have a whip round the office staff to buy you a ... a ... a farewell present, and as you probably won't need the usual *spade* and...." For some unaccountable reason, she burst into tears.

"Lily dear, don't cry for me. Nothing is going to harm me. I hope. You shouldn't have bothered about the present, but as I shall soon be playing for the Forces I really would like a pair of those new–style boots they've got in *Freeman, Hardy and Willis.*"

Jealous Cashier No. 4 allowed Lily to take me to the *Troxy* for the last time, on the strict understanding that I played no tricks with Feeties, and that I shot myself immediately they issued me with a rifle. "After all," added Boo–boos, spitefully, "One of us has got to do it." Lily and I sat crouched in the trenches all evening watching *All Quiet on the Western Front* and when the artillery barrage opened up facing us, I was compelled to seek refuge in the Gents with shell–shock.

I really went to town with my embarkation party in the *George* with halves of mild all round, and half of Cudford in there to swig them. All Cudford United turned up, together with everybody else I had tormented over the years. Bandsman Bangle put in an appearance to inform me that, under the circumstances, he would not regard my departure as running away from the inevitable, and he was prepared to wait six months, or, if needs be, to eternity. The nicest gesture of all was dear old Mr. Pants coming over from Aston especially for the occasion, and bearing an ambiguous message of sympathy from Fred Rutter.

Stanley arose to lead the assembly in a new song entitled, *"Hor 'e's a holly hood hellow,"* with great success. Fork whispered in my ear, "It's bad enough whenever you sing, but it's not considered good form for the subject of this song to join in it."

Swept away by the triumph of his first song, Stanley introduced *"We hon't want to hoos you, but we hink you ought to hoe,"* and this old sender–off was taken up by the entire *George* with almost unnatural enthusiasm, particularly by Boo–boos who shouted it right in my ear, in case I didn't know the words.

Mr. Pants weighed anchor and put out to sea for a short cruise of oratory, but he ran aground well off course, right in the centre of Berlin. All hands stepped ashore, and Mr. Pants escorted them into the Reichstag to listen to a belligerent address which he delivered to Hitler and the gang.

"We must have squeezed up the Rhine," Cashier No. 4 remarked to me. "Anyway, it's better than being seasick at Jutland."

But Mr. Pants was just coming to Jutland.

"Here we go again, Peter," Cashier No. 4 remarked. "Load the for'ard crossbow and light the arrow – the Grand Fleet's in sight."

Lily wiped her eyes as Mr. Pants's comrades fell all around him during the action, which terminated in the unex–

pected tableau of Mr. Pants supporting the wounded Nelson in his arms. He barely concealed the fact that I was Nelson, and Lily fairly howled.

"Where the hell's that fellow Drake got to, then?" complained Cashier No. 4. "We left Plymouth under his command, surely?"

Mr. Pants handed me over to Hardy, and presented me with the new football boots, and, most touching of all, a letter signed by all the staff, declaring how they, etc.

"*Good-bye* bumph," grinned Mr. Disher, looking around for a basket.

This unsuspected gesture on the part of my colleagues filled me with an equally unsuspected love for them, and I said in reply, "Thank you one and all. What can I say on this sad occasion... ?"

"Nothing. Try it for a change," advised the staff.

"Just this, then. Try not to take my going too much to heart, and remember, bear up with the thought that it's only six short months and then you will all have me back again."

Groans from the staff. "I'll be waiting for you," cried Bandsman Bangle loyally.

I little thought how long it was to be before I did see them again, or that some of them I should never see again.

Gallant little Ronald, shot down as a fighter-pilot during the Battle of Britain. Mr. Lecher, lost at sea, presumed drowned. Fork, separated from Beryl for the duration, in a prisoner-of-war camp. Cashier No. 4, thrilling his wife, Lily, with a D.S.O., for leading a destroyer against the German Navy, ironically enough.

Bandsman Bangle, relentlessly attacking his way to a V.C. Knowing him so well, I should have thought he would have got one or two more. And so on, down the list.

As for myself, modesty forbids me to mention my war record, except to say that perhaps few men ever engaged in battle with so many enemies. Apart from the Germans, the Italians, and the Japanese, I had to contend with the Americans, the Australians, the Welsh, and, sad to relate, the English. And to show I am not a biased person, I must confess that in 1942 I declared war on the Russians.

This localized outbreak of hostilities led the embarrassed authorities to award me a bar to my D.C.M., or to quote the official citation more fully, *Detained for Court–Martial.* But that is another story.

FIFTEEN

Directly I was seated in the train for London I became my old self again, full of excited anticipation for the new scene I was about to enter, and without a regret in the world at leaving the bank behind. In fact, the way I felt, banking might have been something I only dreamed about as a toddler.

The express rushed through Aston so fast that the tiny station seemed to rock back with shock. I caught sight of the Zenith Bank in the High Street, and towards the church who should I see but Mr. Hut, being dragged round the village as the wolves took him for the daily struggle he called his constitutional. I remembered how more than once Mr. Hut had returned alone to the office, exhausted and dirty, to exclaim, "Let them find their own way back. We were heading out of the county, and if I hadn't managed to leave go the leads the perishers would have had me across the marshes on me belly."

The train was non–stop for Waterloo, where I got out and headed for the *Mecca of Muscle,* Clapton Common, E.5. Despite Bruce Bold's printed veto on personal callers, I was determined to meet him in the flesh and thank him for giving me a body which my country was about to be proud of, and feed and clothe into the bargain. Admittedly not such a vast structure of bas–relief muscle as the Master had himself, but a pretty fair reproduction. In any case, Bruce Bold's physique would be a handicap in the forces, for those bulbous shoulders alone would ruin the drill formation of any regiment.

I grew extremely excited as I approached the district of the Cult and thought of all the long letters I had penned to this very street. Although a second–hand clothes dealer directed me with elaborate and detailed accuracy, I could see no sign of the marble Parthenon I had studied so often on the notepaper-heading. In fact, such an edifice would have looked most out of place, among the shabby warehouses and general-shops where I stood.

I located the precise address, and found myself outside a store crammed with small bundles of fire-wood and cans of paraffin. The facia-board overhead announced that the owner traded under the interesting name of, *"Penny a Bundle."* I rattled a can, and out walked the original Beatnik. In his hand was a chopper.

"Oojer want?" he inquired, discovering I was a dead loss in the kindling line.

"Berruce Bowl-ole? Oh, 'im. If 'e ain't art, 'e's up the effin stairs, mate." I mounted the rickety staircase to 269a, to see if Mr. Bold was in or art. Pinned on the door was a race-card, with "Back in ten minutes," scribbled on it. A second note was sticking out of a milk-bottle. It said, "Seven pints today." What was that, to support such a body? Hanging from the door-knob was a sack, at the bottom of which was another note inscribed, "Usual. Pay Monday." I deduced from the bread-crumbs that Bruce Bold ordered his loaves by the hundredweight. Already delivered by the doorstep reposed a crate of beer, a sack of potatoes, and a great carton of oatmeal.

I assumed that these items were to keep the editor going, until the main evening meal. I was surprised to find no carcass of a bull among the groceries, because Bruce Bold exhorted his readers to live on red meat to the exclusion of everything else, and if possible, raw. At first, raw meat had made me jib, but gradually I got to like it until my family feared I had got the blood-lust or something. Eventually my father rationed me to one ounce a day, as though he were weaning an alcoholic. Weaker members of the Cult suffered considerably from the editor's drastic diet, as the Letter Page testified. One ungrateful Brute even wrote in to say that he had developed scurvy through it, and that the hospital dietician was forcibly feeding him with lime-juice and spinach. They had forbidden him so much as a cup of Oxo.

As I sat there on the beer crate, waiting for the Editor, it suddenly struck me that I was waiting in vain. Of course, I saw it all now. This lowly address was a cunning subterfuge to sidetrack personal callers who violated the privacy of the great body architect. I had to smile to myself at the thought of Bruce Bold controlling his vast muscle empire from some lofty Parthe–non in the West End, safely protected from the incursions of intruders like me. If possible, my admiration for him increased twofold as I pondered on the business sagacity of the man. I decided to write him an account of this delicious anecdote, and let him see I was man enough to appreciate a joke against myself.

"Ain't no goodjoo 'angin' abart up there if 'e's art," called the original beatnik, from the store. " 'E allus puts that card on the door when 'e goes art, even when 'e goes on 'is summer 'olidees. Fink'e's gawn up West to die."

"Gone up West to die?" I cried in horror.

"Yus, mate. 'E went up there yesterdie, an' I finks 'e 'ad to go again to–die." Glory be, what with the farmers at Aston and the inhabitants of E.5., no wonder they were pressing for *Esperanto.*

"Do you know where it is, exactly?" I inquired.

"No, mate, but by the wye 'e was gettin' 'isself up, I fought it must be Buckinim Paliss." Could be, at that. He deserved it, considering what he had done for the citizens of tomorrow throughout the land and the farflung outposts of the Empire. Many of the more unreadable letters in *Brute Strength* were signed *"Mbula" or "Mustapha Coco,"* and this breath of foreign atmosphere helped to colour the vivid pages of the magazine beyond description. A large proportion of these dusky Surgers seemed to find that the Cult increased their reproductive powers to bursting point, and they wrote in to ask Bruce Bold if he would kindly put them in touch with lonely Lady Brutes throughout the world.

Despite his ban on anything remotely connected with sex, our editor passed on these embarrassingly frank appeals to other interested parties, but he endeavoured to discourage such activities by levying a handling fee of five shillings (foreign currencies accepted) on each letter. The consequences of this penpal column were reflected on page I2, wherein Aunty Brute conducted a catch 'em young feature, entitled, *"Baby Brutes Corner."*

The lady obviously worked on the survival of the fittest principle, judging by the tiny tots in nappies, who were photographed in the conventional poses of weight–lifters – celluloid barbells and all.

Only the intrusion of an enormous hand at the rear indicated that the sturdy little mites were not yet quite capable of going it alone.

Yes indeed, the odd M.B.E. had often been doled out to many a less worthy man than Bruce Bold.

Being rather short of time, and a full programme ahead of me, I hurried away to Lombard Street where I had to report to Mr. Renault, who wished to give me the banker's farewell. As usual, Miss Littlewig greeted me in the outer office.

"My word, Mr. Pook, you seem to get bigger every time we meet," she cried, turning her head as she surveyed the shoulder–span. "Soon you'll have to come in the door sideways, at this rate. Goodness only knows what army life will do to you."

To show her I wasn't just a show–piece I lifted her up and sat her on top of a filing–cabinet. "My word, aren't you *strong,* Mr. Pook. Put me down this minute, for heavens' sake."

Whereupon I caught hold of her and, with a quick two–handed snatch, heaved her right up on top of the stationery cupboard. The typists giggled, and squealed, "Ask him for a date *quickly,* Miss Littlewig."

"Oooooo ... er!" she screamed, kicking her legs, "what–ever will Mr. Renault think... ?"

"I think the time has come for the army to deal with our friend," said Mr. Renault, appearing at the door. "The poor old Zenith has lost control of him." He was actually laughing. "Before you join up, Pook, be so kind as to bring Miss Littlewig back to earth."

In the sanctum, Mr. Renault bade me sit down, and offered me a cigar. I shrank back from the box as though he had a viper coiled up inside. "Remarkable," he mused. "Still the same old Pook. How long can you keep it up, lad? My son Ronnie tells me you have initiated him into your Cult, with a view to improving his general health. Very kind of you, Pook, as long as the thing doesn't get out of hand like it has with you. Or, come to that, poor Mr. Rutter down at Aston."

Was this man omniscient? I defended myself immediately.

"Fred was in too much of a hurry, sir. He wanted to be a manager before he was strong enough to bear the burden, so to speak." I found it helped with senior men to explain things in their own language. "Never run while you can walk, sir." Mr. Renault agreed to follow this wise maxim of mine, and said, "Tell me in your own words, Pook, what really happened to Ronnie down at Cudford? Is it true that you had nothing to do with his accident?"

"His accident, sir? Me, sir?" I stalled for time. Mr. Renault had an unfair habit of sniping at you from the most unexpected angles.

"Yes, Pook, you of all people. He tells me some yarn about his motor-bike back-firing and blowing his eyebrows off. How on earth could he have had his face anywhere near the exhaust pipe?"

"Didn't he tell you, sir?"

"No; that's why I'm asking you. Ronnie couldn't think of a reason at the time." Ronnie wasn't the only one.

"Was I there, sir?" I inquired, guardedly.

"All right, Pook, that's all I need to know." Mr. Renault shook his head and smiled. I couldn't follow him at all.

"Now to business, Pook. Are you going to choose the Army?"

"Well, sir, if I get any choice in the matter it will be the Navy. I've already got a good nautical background because Mr. Putty and Mr. Pants have always run Cudford branch like a man-o'-war, and I feel the changeover wouldn't be difficult."

Mr. Renault grinned. "You won't go far wrong if you strive to emulate those worthy men, my lad. I was in the Navy myself, in the Great War." Who wasn't? "Actually, I was in the finest body of men in the world – the Royal Marines, raised and paid by the Admiralty, *per mare, per terram,* if I remember rightly."

Mr. Renault's eyes took on a faraway look, and he began to sing, A *Life on the Ocean Wave.* When he finished, he gazed out of the window and murmured, "Ah, wonderful days, wonderful days."

Pulling himself together, he said, "Well, Pook, if you join the Navy please be very careful with it; more so than you have with the Zenith. Remember, it's the only one we've got and it's very old, so treat it gently."

"I promise you I will, sir, so set your mind at rest. But after hearing you, sir, it's the Royal Marines for me, every time. Great men, and a wonderful uniform. Nothing else will do."

"Good for you, Pook, and I hope you will make it. Whichever service you join, the Zenith will make up your salary so you won't lose deal in the matter. How much do you earn now?"

"Nearly two pounds a week, sir. I believe I shall get fourteen shillings a week in the Forces." Everybody wanted me, but they seemed to employ me on the basis that I wasn't worth much.

"Splendid, Pook. The bank will make up the difference, so you will still be drawing two pounds a week, with nothing to worry about."

Whichever way one looked at it, I appeared to be in a financial rut. "Supposing I get a commission, sir? Will I have to pay back the extra money to you?"

"Good grief, no, lad. Anything over your bank salary is your own.

"Then my best bet is to work for a commission, sir." I didn't want to be a burden on the bank.

After further pleasantries Mr. Renault shook hands with me, saying, "Treasure your time in the Forces for they may be the happiest days of your life, although you may not realize it now. Keep out of trouble, do your duty, and forget the bank for a whole six months. If you want a commission, just salute everything in sight. Good-bye, lad, and *good luck.*"

I sprang to attention, saluted, and marched out of his life for ever, because he retired in 1944.

At the centre where the medical examinations were held, my next port of call, I was greeted by several of my old chums, all awaiting their turns for the quacks. There were, among others, Francis, Goldie and my old rival, Ginger Jones. They looked strangely unfamiliar, sitting around in their birth-day-suits. Goldie said, "We've made a pact, so that whichever shower *you* join, *we* don't. It's bad enough working in the same town with you, without *living* together, and we reckon we deserve six months off."

Ginger Jones laughed. "All except me, Pook. I'd like to come in with your mob. I feel I ought to protect you from all those rough soldiers in the Regulars." I gave Jones the icy sneer.

"I know how to look after myself, Ginger boy, without you hanging on. In any case, you lot aren't fit enough for my mob. We don't cater for the walking wounded."

"Hark at it," jeered Jones, "God's gift to the nation. Once you've been through the quacks here, you'll find yourself drafted to the *Queen Alexandra's Nurses.* What's your choice, anyway?"

"The Royal Marines," I said witheringly. Jones was not crushed. "*You* in the Royal Marines! Not likely, mate. When that lady doctor in there sees your wedding-tackle, Pook, it won't be the Royal Marines for you. Ho no, it'll be the *Royal Hospital,* first in the queue for the vet."

I thought what a pity it would be to demolish Jones just as he was waiting to be examined, so I said, "I realize you can't help being offensive, Jones, seeing that you only came to England for the potato-picking season, but I am prepared to bury the hatchet, in any part of you you care to name. Bandsman Bangle was lucky, so don't you press your luck."

Things were really warming up, when a bald, emaciated little man wearing spectacles touched my arm. "Don't fight, lad; life's too short for anger," he gasped.

I glared down at him. "And you can belt up, for a start," I snarled.

"Now, now, my boy, that's not the spirit to start your service with," he admonished. "Conserve your energy for all those doctors. What a pantomime it is, to be sure. Anyway, I'm all right, because I've failed first time. Weak heart and poor eyesight, you know. Of course, they don't realize I *drink.*" He smiled at his good fortune, and coughed all over me.

"Oh, by the way, my name is Bernie Morris. I'm a sort of inbetweener, so to speak. Not old enough for the last war, and not fit enough for the one that's coming. Years ago, H. G. Wells predicted this one for January, 1940, you know. Wise old bird that."

"Oh, lor'," I exclaimed. Even Mr. Wells seemed to be intent on ruining my football career.

"The doctors seemed quite annoyed I was sent here at all," continued the talkative little man. "Reckoned I should be in a nursing–home, of all places. Me, with a thriving business to run. I told 'em it is overwork; doesn't do to mention the drink in this kind of place. Never mind, rejecting me is a blessing in disguise really, considering I've got a wife and eight kids to provide for, not to mention the one in the oven."

"Are you in the clerical line?" I asked, feeling it was time I said something to the sick and needy.

"Oh, bless you, no boy. There's precious little money in that lark. Actually, although I shouldn't boast, I'm sort of a national figure in the world of journalism. I expect you've heard of me, the famous health consultant." I had to plead ignorance.

"There's money in it, boy, but don't it carve up a poor devil? No wonder I'm seedy, with all the tripe the readers send in. Only wish I had some of it here for you to read. F'rinstance, there's a great overgrown peasant down Cudford way who'll be the death of me before's he's done, and he's only one of 'em. Yards and yards of it he sends me, full of the revolting details of his adolescence, the flaming lot. And then people wonder why I was driven to the bottle." I tried to speak, but nothing would come out only "Bab, bab, bab......

"He's merciless, that's what he is. He spares me *nothing,* right down to the last gory detail, and the next thing you know, he'll be coming up to see me. Mind you, I've sent him exercises which would kill a perishing ox, but he seems to thrive on 'em. But I've just got hold of one from a friend of mine in the circus that should finish him off for good. It's a beaut. I can't divulge what it is, of course, except to say that no one in the circus has ever done it twice, but he's got it coming to him. I'm only waiting for his next letter, and then off it goes to him. Funny thing, now I come to mention it, he hasn't written this week. Unusual."

I looked down at the little wreck with the big spectacles, and managed to stutter, "What did you say your name was... ?"

"Bernie Morris, lad. But probably you would know me better under my professional name, Bruce Bold. What's yours, sonny... ?"

He was addressing an empty chair. "Where's he. . .? Well, this modern generation's an unsociable lot, I must say. Still, that's the way it goes. I'd better toddle off and think up something new and sensational for the next issue. . . . ."

"Peter Pook. Your turn now," yelled the orderly.

I passed through the medical board, and on to the Royal Marines in a kind of open–mouthed trance.

THE END